HIDDEN MEMORY

A HIDDEN SERIES NOVEL OF ELARIA

BY TIFFANY SHEARN

Hidden Memory by Tiffany Shearn

Published by Tiffany Shearn

Auburn, Washington, U.S.A.

www.tiffanyshearn.com

Copyright © 2021 Tiffany Shearn

This is a work of fiction. All names, characters, and events are the product of the author's imagination. Places are either the work of the author's imagination or are used fictitiously. Any resemblance to actual people, living or dead, or historic events is coincidental.

Cover design by Jonathan Lebel.

Edited by Maxine Meyer

ISBN: 978-1-7377111-2-4 (paperback)

For my sister, who has been with me and the Hidden Series since it was first a rough draft in my mind.

PROLOGUE

It was a feast such as Nikai had never seen. The aroma of succulent meats roasted to perfection swirled around his head, but that was not the course upon which his eyes feasted. There were vegetables and fruit here! Fresh produce was so rare in the Kalachi Desert. Oh, and the wine. Nikai had not tasted wine in…well, far too long by his reckoning. How could Lord Kahnlair bring such a banquet to the middle of this desolate wasteland? No... He would not question his Lord in any way. His power was beyond anything another could claim, and nothing was beyond the reach of his desire.

It was finally Nikai's turn to reap the rewards of long devotion, to be selected for a mission of great importance as so many others before him. Nikai knew he was not the greatest fighter nor the subtlest of spies. Those were the people sent many years ago to infiltrate and destroy the people choosing the wrong side and setting themselves against his Lord. He had heard of their countless successes over the years, as he suffered through the desert heat year-round and longed for the opportunity to join them.

He knew people were still chosen periodically to replenish the forces outside of the desert. Just last week that rat, Andre, had been honored. And he was one of the lazy ones! Always shirking his responsibilities. *Okay, so I might do a little of that, too. And trying to skim from provisions for the gilar? I would never attempt that.* It was never a good idea, and not simply because the gilar were the Great Lord's favorites. Remembering the frequent screams from their district sent a shiver down his spine, becoming a cold knot in his stomach as the door opened.

There were only three entering, but it was the Lord's Commander and right hand flanked by two gilar. Gilar did not have human skin, but were covered in scales like a snake. The slit-pupil, yellow eyes peering out of their heads were unblinking. That venomous yellow color was echoed in the lethal spines running two lines down their bodies. They began at the base of the skull and wrapped up and around to come over the head like horns. Smaller spines continued down the shoulder blades and arms until the elbow joints, where they again grew in size. The last few on the forearms were almost as large as the rounded head spines, but flattened and sharp as a newly-honed blade. Spines and strength enough to rip a man in two meant the sabers at their sides were there out of preference more than need.

"Is the feast not to your liking? The kitchen was told to set out a variety to please every possible palate, but if there is something else you desire, I am sure we can find ways to accommodate you."

Her melodious voice, at once sweet and seductive, seemed to fill his mind. It drove away the fear and all thoughts of the two gilar. Nikai's breath caught as he drank in the sight of her. Commander Tiria was beautiful. The swell of her hips and breasts provocatively concealed, and just enough dark crème skin revealed as she moved toward him to drive a man's thoughts to dangerous places. Seeing his mind follow the common pattern was enough to put a smirk on her full lips. As there was no joy in her eyes, no one would call it a smile. Still, it did not take anything away from her beauty. Men found that hint of danger alluring, or they refused to believe its truth.

Is she to be part of the feast set out for me? The thought came unbidden as he failed to stop his eyes from roaming.

Nikai could see, all too vividly, the uses for keeping her around. His Lord deserved the pleasures 'Commander' Tiria was sure to provide, but a woman as his right hand? Maybe if she had demonstrated power of her own.

"It is wonderful... I... I did not think it was for me." He finally managed a breathless response.

"Please," she poured him a cup of wine, "eat your fill. You will need your strength to be of use to Lord Kahnlair. He has asked that I ensure you will suit his needs before you are taken to him later this evening." Tiria poured a second cup for herself and moved to sit at the other end of the table as Nikai filled his plate.

"I have waited for this for so long, Commander," he began rambling in eagerness at her welcoming gesture. "You do not know how much I have wanted to serve the Great Lord in the other lands. I'm not so good a fighter as all those others, but I always thought I could be good at getting information. See," Nikai shook a food-filled hand in her direction, getting into it now. "I look like regular folk, so they would trust me. Probably take me into their confidence if I told them I escaped and could give them information. Instead, I would be taking information to give back here. Making sure that the Great Lord could easily defeat those filthy races."

Tiria's eyes flared, and her mere presence felt

suddenly threatening. "You think Lord Kahnlair needs you to be victorious? You doubt his power?"

Nikai stopped mid-bite, his eyes widened and darted about in sudden fear. "No! No, I ju—I just thought..."

Tiria sighed and a smile returned to her lips. "Never mind. I must apologize. You see, I tend to become rather protective. It is my job to look for the traitors, and that can make me a suspicious person. However, I know in this case you are simply eager to do your part for Lord Kahnlair's campaign."

"Yes. That is exactly what I meant. I never meant it to be taken any other way, and I would never betray the Great Lord, Kahnlair. Never."

"I am certain you will never betray him. Please, continue your meal. We have time before you are called." Tiria's smile shifted, but Nikai could not pinpoint the difference.

A couple of hours of feasting and endless talking passed easily for the enthralled man, and Nikai was feeling a slight tug of sleep from the relaxation, food, and wine.

Tiria stood gracefully. "It is time for you to learn why you are here. Please, follow me."

With intoxicated excitement on his face, Nikai rose a little unsteadily to his feet and followed Commander Tiria into the hallway. Much to his discomfort, the two gilar he forgot during his meal fell in close behind him.

Emboldened by the wine, he asked, "I'm entering formal service for the Great Lord, do we really need guards?"

"Yes."

The next question died in his throat when she glared at him, her eyes sharp. Without speaking, she clearly told him this was not the time to ask questions. There was a new gleam in her eye making him uneasy.

Empty corridors rang with their footsteps as they moved deeper into the palace, and echoes played off the walls for a moment after they stopped to stand before a locked door. It opened to a narrow stairway leading down, and his escort swept him forward. A chill prickled Nikai's skin as he descended, which did nothing for his nerves. His alcohol haze faded with every step. Desert nights were cold, more so in winter, but this cold was different; unnatural.

Finally, they arrived at the end of the stairs. Only then did the smell reach him.

Great Lord, what is that stench?

It was of rot and excrement and blood as if something died violently and was left to decay, and Nikai found it terrifyingly alluring. His heart pounded in his ears. Death and blood. Destruction and decay. He had never known those smells before, not like this, but he knew them now. Nikai turned to flee, but the gilar easily held him in place.

"This is why the guards remain," came whispered words from Tiria's lips brushing his ear. "Do you see now? We knew you would try to run. They always do."

"Please let me go. Please, I will do anything, just let me go. I don't deserve this. I've served faithfully, always worshiping the Great Lord. Please." Nikai's pleas fell on deaf ears and he began to struggle against the hold on him.

Tiria opened the door and led the gilar—carrying the protesting form of a desperate man scratching futilely against their scales—through the door. They tied him to the stone table and left without a word. As those three departed, the door closed. Nikai whimpered as he froze. Only his eyes moved, darting around the room. Warm liquid trickled and spread from between his legs, and his heart stuttered a beat. For days he would wish it stopped at that moment, he would wish he entered a room of simple death, he would wish he

had never lived, but for now, he simply gave voice to his fear
and screamed.

CHAPTER ONE

She was going to be late again. It was almost 8 o'clock, and traffic was not moving. Another weather-related accident; she could see the emergency lights flashing ahead on the flat stretch of road. You would think people would know how to drive in the rain, considering it never stopped here.

Oh well, meeting isn't until 9, she thought to herself.

Alexis Craymore learned years ago to deal with uncertainty. It was the earliest emotion she could recall from just about sixteen years ago. She still woke up some nights reliving those first terrifying moments, where every detail rushed in to fill the void of her mind.

There had been no memory of anything, as though she did not exist before that moment. Looking back, she knew she...emerged...in a side street within the city. Gigantic structures reached toward the dark sky in a solid, lifeless pattern. Some light came from within those structures, but most came from the poles spaced along the sides of the path leading in opposite directions. Below those lights sat objects large enough to be dangerous beasts, but they did not move, and—at a second look—she could see they were idle mechanical objects. Strange sounds and smells floated to her in the cold autumn air. Metal creaked and clicked. Odd honks and growls sounded in the distance. Chemical and burning scents flooded her nose. None of it anything she could name.

To the few she told of the first memories before her senses overwhelmed her, it sounded peaceful, possibly even wonderfully exciting. In truth, it was terrifying. To not know who you are or where you are. Desolation is the word that comes to her mind, looking back.

At the time, however, her panic and all other senses were quickly drowned out by the pain radiating through her body. Her head and back were on fire, feeling as though someone tried to rip off her skin and drive knives in deep at the same time. It was enough to make her curl up and lay down in the freezing street crying for the pain to stop. Too afraid the pain would increase if she moved at all, that is how she was found, nearly run over by the first vehicle to pass.

Her physical arrival was as naked as her memory. No clothing, no identification. The woman in that car, Mrs. Jenesee, spoke softly, wrapped her in a blanket, and called the police. A skinny nine or ten-year-old (their best guess) girl found naked and bleeding on a city street in the middle of the night crying made all the worst possible scenarios race through their minds. They found no signs of molestation when they examined her at the nearest hospital, but there was other damage indicating physical abuse. Her head and back boasted injuries no one could explain by anything other than cutting open her skin. No weapon was ever matched to the wounds.

Missing persons reports were searched along with fingerprint databases and birth records. No one came for her. It was a sad case, as the little girl, without memory or name, was sent into the system and slowly became just another orphan as the outrage at her condition died down. The old adage, that few wanted to adopt an older child, or risk adopting an emotionally damaged one, held true for her. She was given the name Alexis, a birthday, and records of identification for when she would need them. Memories were slower to come by, but over the years, they did.

Now Alexis, twenty-five according to her paperwork, had put herself through community college to earn a two-year degree and managed to find a good job she could enjoy and live off of. She was proud of everything she accomplished, for the most part on her own. It was only her second year with the small manufacturing company, and she was working hard to show management all she had to offer.

Today she was to give a presentation to the district manager about some improvements she suggested on their shop floor. They had been successful at her own tiny plant, and the company wanted to see if they could be adapted to the different manufacturing configurations around the company. While the work was most definitely hers, she was more than grateful to have a plant manager who not only ran with her idea on the floor, but was now giving her the chance to be the person to share it.

Finally, she made it past the accident! Going much too fast the rest of the way, Alexis made it to the company building in no time. She still had over half an hour to get in there and go over the presentation one more time, just to be sure all the angles were covered. It was a business casual office, so she didn't need to worry about heels with her slacks and blouse, but she did wear a jacket for this meeting. One she had removed the shoulder pads from to minimize her brawn.

No one would call her a model, but she could pass as the attractive girl-next-door if you discounted some of the muscle. She had fair skin over a body well-toned from the martial arts training she kept up with to keep her from getting restless and feeling trapped in her own skin. Her hair was lighter blonde in the summer, edging toward mousey most of the year, but it worked with her bright blue eyes. Alexis thought her eyes were her best feature. The color was a striking shade, almost magical, and people were drawn in when she smiled. It served her well when she stumbled through social encounters.

The third-floor conference room was more than large enough to hold everyone they were expecting. A few minutes to finish setting up before everyone started filing into the conference room and then she would start in on her well-rehearsed—her laundromat buddy might say obsessively rehearsed—speech. Naturally, she greeted everyone with a smile as they came in. It never hurts to do a little networking. Though the company might be small, she could start to make a name for herself with important people in a growing industry.

Time to go, so why did a headache have to start now? Alexis stretched her neck out and grimaced toward the wall before turning around.

Everyone settled in, and she smiled as she began speaking. Unfortunately, the headache grew steadily worse with every breath she took. It pounded at her. The ache radiating down her spine with each beat of her pulse. Her smile fell flat, and she felt sweat beading at her hairline against the strain.

Just a few more points to cover, then some questions, and you can take a strong painkiller. Please, not the back, too, she thought as her mind flashed back to that childhood trauma. *I don't want to go through that again.*

Her vision blurred with pain and panic. She closed

her eyes, pinching the bridge of her nose as she tried to take a deep breath.

"Are you all right, Alexis?" Was that her boss asking? He was always so nice to everyone.

"Fine, just... Aahh!" Screaming in agony, Alexis dropped to the floor at the front of the room. "No! Please...not...again!" She managed between ragged breaths as people jumped to their feet. In the background, someone was told to call Emergency Services, but her world narrowed to pain shooting through her head and back as she writhed on the floor trying to make it stop. Unlike all those years before, this time the pain was not ebbing, but growing more intense as the seconds passed until something happened no one in that room could fully describe or comprehend.

The air around Alexis began to shimmer and glow as her skin tore apart. Another scream ripped from her throat. She was on her hands and knees, arching her back trying to distance herself from the torture. Blood dripped in a steady stream down the sides of her face and soaked her blouse as bulges emerged from the torn skin on her back. None of the witnesses in the room staring slack-jawed in horror saw the wings erupt with a spray of blood. The woman was gone. Only her bloody, torn clothing remained on the floor to say she had ever been.

Alexis was no more. Those memories ripped from her mind until, once again, nothing remained. Her thoughts were only of pain unending and a sense of falling. It was darkness all around her. Darkness and pain became her world until she crashed through branches, spinning wildly as she fell. Scraped, bruised, torn, broken, and bloody, she hit the ground with near crushing force and heard another damaging pop with the thud of impact. With no idea who or where she was, the woman curled up, cold and in pain, on the ground with tears streaming from her eyes.

CHAPTER TWO

The pain lingered. If she did not move, it remained at the level of a throbbing ache. Unfortunately, as the pain slowly lessened, it gave way to panic. Her life, her mind, was a void her strongest feelings rushed to fill. Something whimpered. She shook in terror. Her eyes darted about seeing nothing as her breathing sped up and her vision narrowed to a pinpoint before blackness took her.

When she returned to consciousness, the panic remained, but started out more remote than before. Questions assailed her mind. *Where am I? Why did this happen to me? What else is out here?* Her imagination provided ever darker things she might face. She recognized she needed to calm down. She needed to look at the situation rationally and make an assessment. Instinct—or was it training? —seemed to finally take over. Her breathing and heartbeat slowed, and hopelessness gave way to practical thinking.

She could only guess how long she had lain there on the forest floor. Her memories were clouded and scrambled without any clear indication of when or how she first gained consciousness. Anything she knew before was gone or never existed. But, as far as the current situation necessitated, it did not matter.

Tall trees and dense foliage surrounded her in every direction. Everything looked parched, ready to flare up at the slightest spark. The sun was moving toward the horizon, so it was mid to late evening, but little light reached her as the canopy blocked the sun's rays before they made it down. What she *could* see, from her position on the ground, the forest floor was clustered with shriveled vegetation.

"You wasted too much time cringing, crying, and panicking," she berated herself out loud.

There was no telling what manner of dangerous animals lived in this forest. With all the blood coating her, she was practically calling out to scavengers in the area. In unknown terrain, it would be best to move in daylight; so little time remained this day to make progress.

Shifting to stand gave her a fair enough assessment of her injuries as she grit her teeth against the spiking pain. Her left side had taken the worst of it. A dislocated shoulder, at least one bruised or cracked rib, and a sprained ankle. On the right it was only a sprained wrist and tender knee. Well, tender in relation to the rest of her bruised body. From what she could examine, it would be difficult to find a spot of skin not covered in black, blue, or red. No way to know for certain, but she did not think she had any serious head injuries other than general scrapes, bruises, and whatever happened to her ears. She could feel dried blood around the tips, and they stung like they were cut up as well. Other scrapes lined her body including a longer cut across her right thigh. Fortunately, none appeared to be so deep or serious she was in danger of dying from blood loss.

Her back was her greatest concern, and the most difficult to inspect. The wings were coated in drying blood as though she bathed them in it, and the joints where they connected to her back were a mess of tender exposed flesh and still-oozing blood. The hours of delirious inactivity allowed insects to come and use these, and other, wounds as a feeding and breeding ground. By stretching her neck to look over her shoulder, she could glimpse the white larvae wriggling slowly as well as some ants and beetles. Her stomach lurched, and her head spun. She looked away before she was sick or passed out again.

First step, resetting the shoulder. It would be safer with someone trained to fix it, but she would make it work. All it took was a tree and a swift, carefully angled maneuver to have her groaning in pain and falling to her knees as darkness swept over her vision momentarily.

At least my arm will be of some limited use now, she thought to herself, breathing hard from the strain.

Determinedly pushing herself back to her feet, she carefully brushed as many of the insects from her body as she could and inspected her surroundings again. There was no significant difference from her assessment from the ground. The canopy was thick enough to shroud the forest in constant shadow, likely even at mid-day. The ground cover grew surprisingly thick in the shadows. Its density was oppressive enough to send a shiver down her spine. The humidity pressing in on her conflicted with the picture presented by the dry foliage and served to make the forest feel additionally smothering.

Panic churned in her gut again for the briefest moment before she breathed deep to regain control and dampen it, wincing at the pain in her chest. Panicking would help nothing. She needed to get away from the blood, then find shelter, water, and food. That was easy enough to decide, but difficult to implement. Walking was an effort. Every injury screamed with each step, each breath.

Either this or become a feast for the first scavenging, carnivorous beast to reach me.

The thought crossed her mind, and for a moment, she considered whether that would be a better fate. It was dismissed as quickly. She knew she could handle this pain. Now she simply needed to choose a direction. She looked around, and her gaze fell on a sliver of light winning through the thick branches from the lowering sun.

West, I think. I may not be able to pace the sun, but it will give me the illusion of a few extra moments of light.

Setting off, she forced her damaged body to keep a steady pace while walking as carefully as possible. Her injuries still sent constant reminders, and threatened to throw her into pain-induced unconsciousness. She also gained new scrapes with every step. Her feet were slowly shredded by the forest floor, but there was nothing she could do about it without a scrap of cloth.

What was unexpectedly frustrating was the jarring pain radiating through her back, shoulder, and chest every time one of her wings brushed a branch, bush, or tree along the way. After yet another low branch impacted both wings at once, and she fought back to consciousness against the blackness, she considered ripping them off herself.

She closed her eyes, head drooping, and took time regaining her feet. Her head was bent with her chin against her chest when she finally opened her eyes. This brought to her attention her nakedness, and made her consider a potential solution to both issues.

"Maybe," she said aloud as she considered how to maneuver her wings to cover herself, "that might just work."

As her wings still felt…new to her, it required a bit of concentration to get them to move the way she wanted. The raw, swollen flesh of the wing joints screamed in protest as she forced her wings to curl down and around. With her arms raised outward, they folded to wrap around her body. They were large enough that when the movement was complete, they covered her chest, torso, and even a hand past her crotch. Her wings were translucent like a cloudy emerald, and it was the dried blood still coating them providing the most concealment. Now, however, they would not continue to slow her down.

Darkness fell. She was exhausted from her injuries, the traveling, and the lack of food. Lack of water would be an issue had she not found a small stream soon after her wing wrapping experiment. She heard it before anything else; a light trickle at the edge of hearing calling out to her. Apparently, her hearing was better than she thought, because the edge of hearing turned out to be far away, and the stream was lucky to be called a stream at all.

It was a stingy flow about a hand wide weaving between the trees at the center of a much wider bank, but still a welcome sight. She drank her fill—slowly to not make herself sick—then set to cleaning her injuries. The blood still worried her the most. She thought it was a beacon for anything with half a nose, but the water offered a chance to dim that beacon. Rinsing her back was a struggle. It was painful to reach and beyond her line of sight. She knew even then a few bugs still nestled in there despite her efforts.

Eventually, limited time and lack of progress won out over cleanliness. A source of water was not the safest place to remain, and she wanted to find a defensible position to rest. Before leaving, she drank again and took advantage of a nearby fallen tree. A branch was already half broken away from the trunk, likely from its fall. She pulled, twisted, and bent the branch until it snapped the rest of the way from the dead tree.

It earned her several additional bruises, more pain, and a new film of dirt, but she also gained a crude weapon. The walking staff was nearly as tall as she. Breaking off the few smaller twigs coming from it as she resumed her trek, it became relatively smooth to handle. The best part though, was that it appeared to be strong enough to take her weight. With this, maybe she could fight, or at least posture, long enough to scare off any attacking animals.

After those two fortunate discoveries in quick succession, it was a long while before she found a suitable place to rest. Coming to the top of a slight rise in the forest floor, she could make out a rocky outcropping through trunks and branches in the distance, highlighted by the last, dwindling rays of the sun already set behind them. Mapping the sight in her mind, she headed for those rocks, pushing aside the pain to gain speed. Even with that effort, it was dark well before she reached her destination. She slowed her pace to maintain her footing and heading in the dark. She also pushed down the growing fear and anxiety rising with the darkness, morphing it into a wary alertness, to keep her head.

Finally, the outline of the rocks was visible through the trees, and she began gathering fallen leaves and grasses from the ground. As with the size of the stream, her senses tricked her. The rocks were smaller than she thought, and she swore they had been closer than the distance travelled to reach them. At the time, she thought she had a chance to arrive before the sun set, and the rocks looked so small because of the distance. Instead, she found a tiny hill of rock too hard and dense for the surrounding trees to take root. It was as good as she was going to get. There was a recessed spot with an overhang to serve well enough as a marginally defensible place to rest, and the rocks might retain some of the day's heat.

She threw down her pitifully small bundle against the rock and frowned at it. There was no chance she had enough to try to make some sort of bed, and she was nearly asleep on her feet. Easing herself down, she gathered the leaves up again, curled up with her staff, and used the little pile to cushion her head.

Despite her exhaustion, it was some time before sleep came. Her mind kept running over the possibilities of what could happen should she sleep. Every imagined noise from the forest startled her to semi-wakefulness. There would be no time to react, to prepare, to attempt to frighten off an animal coming upon her. At some point she realized one of the sounds she heard was an echo of her own breathing off the rock, which allowed her to relax a fraction. However, terror could not fight off the fatigue of her body forever, and it eventually took her over the edge into sleep.

A sudden, sharp pain in her back jolted her awake, and she jumped up with staff in hand without even a thought preceding the action. Scanning the rock, she found a couple of scavenger rats who thought taking a few bites out of her would make a good morning meal. These were not small, docile creatures to run away at the first sign of trouble, but rodents the size of a large, domesticated cat. People—especially bleeding people—did not immediately register as predators to them, and they would fight for their food.

Both rats ruffled their dark, scratchy fur to puff it up, and held their leathery tails stiff and ready to aid in sudden movement. They made a sound halfway between a hiss and a squeak as she swiped with the staff. One let out a pained screech as it was caught by the swing and thrown against the wall of her sleeping place and stopped moving. It was either dead or unconscious. The second rat scurried past her and away. They would fight, yes, but they became cowards against a recognized threat.

"Well, I hope that is the worst I face out here," she said to the rocks as she twisted awkwardly trying to see how much additional damage the rats did to her injured wing joints.

It could have been worse. She woke so quickly it seemed nothing more than a few nibbles of missing flesh. Infection was still her greatest concern with open wounds, but there was nothing she could do to treat them. Her 'friends' had woken her just after sunrise. The rest was not as long as she could have used, but the sleep helped her regain some lost energy despite her muscles and joints stiffening considerably. A hopeless futility still gnawed at the back of her mind, but she forced herself to ignore it.

Food might help, she thought as her glance strayed to the dead rat.

The sun was not even completely up yet, she had time to indulge a little. *Indulge in eating a rat? I doubt those words are often used in combination.*

Searching the area surrounding her sleeping place, she found some crude tools to suit her needs. Sticks and dried grass to spark a fire, though it took much longer to make enough heat to spark than a flint stone would have. A sharp chipped stone served as a knife to attempt butchering the carcass. The rat's skin was tough, and the stone difficult to hold, so she received several tiny cuts on her fingers for her troubles. With no water nearby, she had to clean the blood off her hands as best she could with grass as she waited for it to cook.

It was chewy, and tough, with little meat on its thick bones, but it was wonderful. She ate every morsel, sucking the last bits of meat off the bones. She felt better after getting something in her stomach and she could have eaten at least one more.

"I should move on," she spoke again to her empty surroundings and looked up at the rocky overhang. "There is not enough here to live on."

She climbed as high on the rocks as possible. A small and jagged portion of the jutting rock reached about the top of the trees. As her head breached the canopy, she was startled by how bright it was above in contrast to the dark below. Even with the sun up far enough it *should* reach down between the branches and into the rocky clearing, it still only cast a pale glow to the forest floor as though a veil was held over the canopy trapping most of the light. She took a moment to bask in the glow.

Looking around, the moment of ease fled as she saw no landmarks of note. Shadowy-green foliage stretched forever in all directions from her tiny rock island poking out from the sea of green. There was no sign of civilization, and the nagging sense of despair prickled forward once more. Could she survive alone with nothing? Would she starve to death out there? Tears pricked before she swallowed them down.

West again, I suppose. There is no use trying to change directions all the time. I would end up going in circles and getting nowhere. With a decision made, she climbed down and turned west.

CHAPTER THREE

Days were adding up, and there remained no sign of other people in that wilderness. The speed at which she could travel compounded the issue. While she pushed her battered body as much as possible without further damage, the injuries held her back from an easy pace and called for additional rests throughout the day. Her feet quickly became the worst impediment to her movement as other cuts and bruises slowly healed. Each day brought new cuts, scrapes, and bruises, no matter how carefully she walked, and she could not stifle the whimpers of pain with each step.

That was the tenth day walking west, and her food and water situation drained her more than all the injuries combined. After the fortunes of the first day, chance turned against her. That small stream and the rat to break her fast were the most food or water she had seen. An ache burned constantly where her stomach ate away at itself, and dehydration sapped her strength. Her lips were cracked, and her tongue felt thick in her parched mouth.

She found mostly dried stream beds provided her short, open paths through the thick, dried brush. At the same time, they taunted her with a lack of water, and she concluded she was seeing the effects of the dry season in that land. At every waking moment she was aware of the surrounding sounds, sights, and smells. A couple times, her vigilance was rewarded with the discovery of a few small edible roots or with trickles or tiny puddles of water. The roots tasted horrible, but were probably safe enough to eat.

She was not sure about the safety of the water, but her need for it always overcame the caution about how fetid it might be. She made sure to take her time and slowly drink as much as she could of the silty water she managed to dig up. At times, she was reduced to licking moisture from the stones.

Recently, that vigilance alerted her to a stalker creeping in her wake, and she found herself constantly checking her grip on the walking stick to assure herself it was still there. She saw the creature one morning at a distance between the trees. It was a large feline creature with golden fur on its back fading to white on its stomach and paws. Its movements were fluid, and she would have called it beautiful were it not for the hollow, starved look. The angles of its body were all too sharp as the bones stood out starkly against the emaciated flesh.

She thought it was unlikely to wait much longer before attacking, as it had yet to lose interest in her. From what she could hear of the creature's movements, it sounded like it usually slept during the day and caught up to her at night. She would need to be wary at night for the near future, which would only add to her exhaustion.

That afternoon, she stumbled upon a green area where the plants were a little less brittle, though no water could be seen. If she dug deep enough, there was a chance water would slowly seep into the bottom of her hole if it was around. Desperate tears threatened as she eased herself to the ground, but she was so parched that nothing fell. Her fingers dug into the hard earth, scraping on rock and roots that had to be pulled or dug around.

How deep have I gone?

The soil became moist, and she dug further still. She waited, breathing hard from her efforts, and watched for it to fill. Slowly, drop by drop, water seeped in. Swallowing convulsively, she waited for a tiny puddle before leaning her head in to slurp it directly. There was maybe a mouthful of water before she needed to wait for it to fill again.

Knowing she needed more water, and knowing she probably needed to stay awake that night, she decided to rest for a while there and fight the animal when it came. As the hours passed, she napped by her hole and woke multiple times, drinking the water as it collected. Dusk settled over the forest and, with it, her stalker woke and moved. With quiet paws, the sounds disappeared, and she sensed it was near. Rising to her feet, she took a balanced stance and peered around the gloom.

She last heard it to the east of her position, and when she focused in that direction, she eventually made out the outline of the cat creeping forward. Based on the starved look of it, the dry season made prey scarce, and hunger made it bold out of desperation. The cat knew she was awake and felt her attention on it. It puffed up and began to circle her even as she did her best to puff her own form up larger as well. Not having fur, it was somewhat less effective, but she stood tall and wide and made a lot of noise.

Her opponent was less than intimidated by her display. They circled, and the cat gave off a low growl as it charged and swiped at her with its claws. She rolled to the right but was a moment too slow and received four new gashes on her arm as a result. She ignored them and swung her branch like a quarterstaff as she rose. The move caught the cat off-guard as it was already attacking again. She made a solid connection with its head and immediately followed through with a swipe at its shoulder.

Bleeding over its eye, the cat shook its head and ran off into the deepening night. It was not quietly stalking as it ran away, and she followed the sound through the brush for some time before allowing herself to fall asleep. The following day, if she stood still and quiet, she could hear it softly padding after her to the distant rear. It was staying up wind and would attack again. She was the only food around. Fortunately, she was relying on sound, not smell, to know it was coming.

As the days wore on, her injuries either healed or she became accustomed to the pain. The back injury remained worrying. She swore it felt warm to the touch and swollen around her wings, which likely meant the joint injuries had become infected. They would heal, or they would not. There was nothing she could do about that situation, so she ignored it and moved on.

One could not maintain terror for an extended period, so the fear became common and the panic attacks less frequent. She found an easy rhythm allowing her to favor her remaining injuries as needed, and the monotony of walking through an unchanging landscape allowed her mind time to consider what she had not before. It was too quiet there. There was nothing beyond the rats and cat that attacked her to be seen nor heard. Surely a forest this size would host a greater number of animals seeking an easy meal. If not that, several types of smaller woodland creatures should be running or flying about. Even the drought she suspected could not account for their absence. It might have been a welcome absence if she thought it made her safer, but it felt...unnatural.

Her body told her it was time for another break. They were demanded more and more frequently, and she suspected the beginning of a fever resulting from the infection. She eased herself to the ground and off her cut and blistered feet, taking as much care as possible for her other bruises, breaks, and lacerations. When her rear finally touched the ground, she was breathing more heavily from the effort than from simply walking along. Once it was done though, and she lay still, her aches and pain became a pulsing numbness.

Were it not for the healing ribs, she would have heaved out a sigh of relief, but she wondered if she was actually feeling better or worse. Moving up her body, she consciously worked to relax every muscle. Calves, then thighs. Tighten. Relax. Butt. Abs. Her efforts aborted at her shoulders. Every muscle tensed suddenly and she stopped breathing to listen to a new noise coming from behind. Skin prickled as every hair stood on end. Something instinctual told her this sound was very bad. There were ticking, or clicking, noises along with what she would best describe as many scurrying legs. Her stalker hissed and growled at this new player.

Perhaps my stalker found other prey? No, she is an ambush hunter. This hissing and growling is defensive posturing. With that thought, a more disturbing question arose. *What would be attacking a natural predator?*

Whatever it was could not be good for her. Any doubt the cat was the one in trouble vanished with an eruption of yowling cries cut suddenly and sickeningly short. The cat was not well-fed and might not keep this new hunter—or hunters? —sated for long.

This is the reason the forest is so barren. The thought washed over her with uncomfortable certainty. Fear and panic, so long held at bay, surged to the fore and held her paralyzed.

The world froze with her. Nothing moved, nothing sounded in the woods as she held her breath, her eyes darting from shadow to shadow. The shuffling resumed and threw her fear up another level, but it also startled her into action. With teeth clenched against groans of pain, she pushed back to her feet and set off at a rapid pace.

Sometime between fighting down the fear of her pursuers and the pain drilling into her deeper with every step, the sun finished its course through the sky. The chill settling in was simply another minor discomfort, but she could not continue in the darkness descending. It would be hours before the moon rose enough for her to travel safely, if she was able to continue at all.

She found tears on her cheeks she had not even known she shed. Her body betrayed the agony her mind denied. It lanced through her with the effort required to lower herself into a resting position. Exhaustion, rather than relaxation, pushed her drifting into blackness.

It was still night when she woke from a troubled sleep, but the moon was up, and half-full, enough to provide light to see. A muffled cry escaped her lips when she first tried to stand. Her legs throbbed and fire ran through her ribcage and back. She suspected some of the old injuries had been aggravated in her rush, but she could not pinpoint anything specific through the pain.

Her nails, chipped and dirty, dug into the ground as she bit back a sob and contemplated giving in, just staying here and letting whatever was out there end it. Hurt, ignorant, alone… Death was all but a certainty, as it was for the cat. The choice was between allowing it to find her now or pushing herself through more torture before it caught her. A quiet scurrying, and the occasional click, mixed with the creaking of weight among tree boughs, floated to her in the night air. Idly, she picked up and toyed with a thin, sturdy stick from the ground beside her, thinking it might be useful for stabbing if it did not snap too easily.

Anger flared in her gut at the previous thought. *Coward! Giving up is easy.*

It helped to hear the accusation and truth in the thought. The effort to stand had her gasping for air and shaking, but the grim determination remained when she gained control. Gritting her teeth, she set off into the thick shadows at the increased pace of the last half day.

The rest of the night passed by in an unpleasantly slow haze, and she allowed herself only one pause when she came across another small stream of water. She drank her fill of the silt-filled water and splashed some on her inflamed back. She knew this water was only making it worse in the long run, but with those creatures closing, she simply wanted to soothe the fire for a short time and find what little relief she could.

She heard the creatures slow, with the coming of the sun. They were either nocturnal or tiring. Either way, it did not seem like they were going to give up another meal just to rest, and it still sounded like they were moving faster than she was capable. To make matters worse, there were more of them to the south now within range of her hearing. Anger, this time at fate in general, drowned out the hopelessness struggling back to the surface of her emotions, and she used the anger to crack open a rotting log in her path.

Her expectations had not been high on finding anything within, but it paid off with three weevils. Slimy, wriggling, and tasting of warm decay, they slid one-by-one down her throat and into her empty gut. *Rat was so much better.* She was grateful for the energy they might provide, but still had to force herself not to retch before continuing. West remained her direction. If...no, *when*, she corrected her thinking. *When* she managed to overcome the closer pack, she wanted as much time between the first and second waves as possible.

It was only about an hour after mid-day when she heard them closing the final distance. She told herself to find somewhere to make a stand. The most defensible place ended up being a tiny clearing without too many trees and with one side blocked by a close tangle of bushes.

Well, now I might only be attacked from three directions at once...so long as they are not capable of jumping the distance from the trees behind me, she thought grimly, but also noted with some small satisfaction there were a few larger stones, about the size of a fist or two, in the area that might be of use.

Her first sight of the creatures brought a mingled sense of awe and disgust and sent a shiver down her back. They had none of the sleek grace of her feline stalker, but the disjointed and hard lines of insects. Unfortunately, these insects were tall enough to reach her hip and longer than she was tall. Their segmented bodies were covered in bristly, black-grey hair all the way to the skin surrounding the beady, black eyes and gaping mouths. Rows of sharp teeth moved in unison and convulsively retracted inward, like their jaws were not entirely connected to their skulls.

The thought of being caught on those teeth and drawn further into the jaws sent another shiver down her spine. All the clicking she heard, that is where it came from; the tapping and scraping of all those teeth as they moved and closed against each other. There were six in this pack, and they spread out before her. Two were hooked into the trunks of a couple trees with back legs looking as sharp as talons, while they all raised similarly pointed legs at the front like weapons.

Injuries and panic melted before an enveloping state of calm. Making a few short, sudden movements, she realized the number of legs allowed them to move easily in any direction, and they reacted quickly. There was a moment of stillness, when no one and nothing moved. Then, the small clearing was a flurry of action.

The creature closest to her sprang forward with one powerful thrust, two more rushed at her, scuttling along the ground, and the others closed ranks. There was a satisfying crunch as her rudimentary staff connected with the one in the air, altering its course to the side. Taking advantage of her momentum, she spun the end of her staff around to land on the head of one creature before jumping over another using the staff as support. She had to dance out of the way of a stabbing rear leg the moment she landed behind them. Even with the awkward maneuver, she brought the staff above her head, planted her feet again, and drew it down with all her strength. Her target was evading even as it connected, and only a couple spindly legs were caught under her blow.

She had no time to savor the sound of breaking bones, or shell, and the oozing of pus-colored ichor with the second line closing in on her. Her tired mind had forgotten about them for a moment. To give herself time to reassess the situation, she backed away quickly and repositioned closer to the wall of bushes.

It bought her only a moment. Three crouched and jumped as one. She instinctively rolled beneath them, only to be hit from behind as she came up. Heavy weight pushed her stumbling forward, struggling to remain on her feet. Teeth dug into her shoulder, and she cried out as the new pain lanced through her. Through the red haze, she barely managed to raise the staff in time to block sharp legs from stabbing into her chest. All her strength went into holding them away, but this time she knew the others were turning to attack again. Sending up a wish for luck, she shifted her weight, grabbed the smaller branch from where a wing held it tight to her body, and jabbed it back toward the creature's head where she guessed its eyes were.

A sickening slurping sound came as the wood sunk into its target, and a sticky substance slopped onto her neck before the sharp teeth released their hold. With a quick spin, she knocked two more out of the air mid-leap and stood so her back was not directly facing any of them. Five were still alive and closing in, but only one was uninjured. Its unhampered movement made it the greatest threat, so she crept slowly in its direction. Judging the moment right, she raised the staff and turned to feign clubbing the injured one beside her true target.

The sudden movement had the creatures tensing for action in reaction. The one in front of her began to shift out of the way, and the other took the bait, springing in another attack from the side. Her staff paused at chest level. She turned slightly and thrust the smaller end of it out hard. Opposing forces impaled the thick wood deep in the creature's torso, and she stumbled backward a step before gaining control of the momentum. She switched her grip to use the force and weight of the dead creature to bring it down on top of another.

Trying to pry that longer branch out for the next attack would have been useless, so she let it go, dropped to her knees as she twisted and, with another wish for it to hold out one more time, plunged the little, bloody stick deep into the wound on the creature's middle section. It dropped to the ground twitching and dying with a broken shaft in its side, but there were still two alive and prowling toward her.

She backed away slowly, her breath wheezing out in short, pained gasps, and reached for the embedded staff, but the nearer one leapt before her hand found it. Rolling out of the way, she landed hard on her still tender shoulder. Stars and tears clouded her vision, and she shook her head to clear it. Limping steps approached more quickly, and she scrambled blindly away, feeling around frantically upon the ground. Her vision finally cleared at the same moment her hand found purchase on a loose rock. She clutched it and sprang to the right as a sharp leg stabbed out where she had sat. With the rock already above her head, she gained her knees and brought it down hard between the creature's eyes with an audible crack.

One left, she told herself, but it was momentarily lost to her senses.

The pounding of her own heart was the only noise in the suddenly quiet forest. She stood still, frozen in a crouched and ready position looking and listening for it. There, a snapping just at the edge of the bushes. Lunging out of the crouch, she sprinted toward her staff, still sticking out of a dead creature as the last one surged toward her.

They both jumped at the same time, and she desperately reached for the only weapon remaining to her. Her hands wound around it as she fell, knocking it down with her. Landing on her right side, she rolled to her back and braced the staff against the ground. The creature was already on the down-arch of its attack. There was no way it could avoid death. Its own attack provided the force bringing it down upon the end of the staff. It was too much weight for her to support for more than the moment of defense, and she barely moved her legs out of the way as the body toppled to the ground, still twitching.

Breathing hard, despite the scream of her ribs with every deep draw, she lay there unmoving to let her heartbeat return to normal. With the immediate threat gone, the extent of the damage from this encounter made itself known. She was lucky to be alive at all, but the creature's bite on her right shoulder was almost sure to fester like her wing joints. It was deep enough to reach the bone in her shoulder, and it did not feel like it would stop bleeding anytime soon.

Still lying on the ground, she listened for the other pack. Though it felt like an eternity, the fight had not taken long, and there was some time before dark. Her best guess was that they would not catch up to her until after sunset. Pushing away the thought, the certainty that she would not make it through another encounter, she struggled to her feet.

Moving to an area away from the fighting, she grabbed some dry moss off a tree, hoping it was the kind that might help rather than something that might kill her. Taking a handful of it, she reached back and slapped it into the bite wound to help stop the bleeding. It would not matter if she avoided an infection by bleeding to death, and there was nothing else available.

Her next task was to recover her rudimentary weapons. She had to knock over the staff and leverage with her feet to dislodge it from the two bodies. *It might not be a finely-honed blade, but it was effective enough for a time,* she thought while looking at the broken halves of her little stick. It would be of no more use, but she might find another along the way.

The other pack sounds larger. I will not be able to defend here again. It is too open. She closed her eyes and sighed. *I need to keep moving.*

"Keep moving," she ordered aloud.

Taking a slow breath, she moved west at her easy pace again rather than the rushed walk she managed earlier in the day. It was all her remaining endurance would allow. Hours passed by as the sun made its way below the tree-tops, and still the creatures came. Further into the growing darkness she went and could not stop to rest for even a moment. If she did now, she would never wake.

Full dark came without her seeing a remotely defensible position. They were close. She could almost count their number as feet moved across the forest floor or branches above. She considered turning to face them in a hopeless last stand, rather than being run down and slaughtered like a frightened rabbit. The hand she used to wipe the sweat and silent tears from her face was shaking. She did not know if it was from fear, fever, or fatigue. Her forward movement stopped, and as her hand fell away, a flicker of light caught her attention.

She strained her eyes through the darkness, holding her breath and willing herself desperately to see it again. Precious moments passed without the light returning, making her think she was losing what was left of her mind. Finally, it came again. She locked the direction in her mind and quickly headed toward it.

Help or hopeful thinking, either way, it was now her goal. Death was no longer a certainty, and she quickened her pace as much as she could, trying to stay ahead of the creatures gaining ground. It was not long before a quick glance back told her they would shortly be within springing distance. Ignoring the pain, she dropped the extra weight of her staff and ran, heedless of her injuries. The last reserves of energy she managed to drag up from somewhere unknown sent her sprinting across the ground and through the trees and bushes toward the flickering light. Toward what she could only hope was aid and not a firefly in the night.

"Help!" she tried to yell, but it was little more than a gasp.

She continued running. Hearing them just behind her, she drew in as much breath as she could. "Heeelllllp!"

The effort left her gasping and straining. She would not be able to yell out again, and she struggled to keep her footing as she ran on until her ankle finally gave out beneath her on the uneven terrain. She tucked her shoulder in as she crashed down to the ground and went into a roll. Nimbly coming up facing the distant light, she tried to scramble to her feet again.

One of the creatures was already coming down out of a jump and landed at her feet. It stabbed at her with one of its sharp front legs, pinning her calf to the ground. A pained cry came out, but she was already grabbing the small solid object her hand found. Wood, stone, whatever it was. She swung her arm and thrust her upper body back to lean back on her knees and reached for the creature's eye. It was one vulnerable spot she knew, and it was all she could think to do. She dug in, and it reared back, releasing her leg just as five other creatures lunged into the air toward her, with more still coming.

It took most of her remaining energy to roll away as they landed, practically on top of her. Once more, she attempted to scramble to her feet, pushing slowly through the last of her reserves, but her entire right leg was going numb and she stumbled again.

Vision blurred, and reflexes slowed, even as she sensed an attacker falling upon her. The loss of feeling continued crawling up her body and she was left with no strength to push the creature off. She whispered for help one more time as the blurred shadows of the insect creatures surrounded her. Hoping the numbness would last until it was over, she closed her eyes on the tears and let go.

CHAPTER FOUR

Larron and his elven messenger unit were only two days into their journey before the first attack. Trakins were dangerously persistent and clever pack hunters. The size of their groups most often ranged between five and twelve, but it was not uncommon for several groups to hunt the same area, sometimes in tandem.

While they would turn on each other if the hunt ended with not enough for the pack leaders, it usually only became that bad after they scoured an area clear of prey. Their intelligence brought them as close to reason as any beast he hunted in the realm. It was most likely two packs joining to attack them that first time, as there were eighteen to fight off. Bealaras was on watch, while the others took their rest for the night, when he heard a few clicks and shuffling movement in the underbrush all around and alerted the group.

One or two people alone would not have been able to survive, even if well-armed. Their two front legs were coated with a substance they secreted with an anesthetic effect. It left a victim numb and unconscious within minutes of injury. They could also climb trees, so Bealaras descended and joined them in a circle around the horses, protecting them.

Though, he and Thanon kept their bows out and stood slightly back.

The two of them would fire until the remaining trakins closed, then join the fight with their swords. Arrows threaded between the trees and found their mark even as the rest of the packs surged forward and began to spread out to surround them. Larron positioned himself to take on the first two and allow Bealaras time to switch weapons. His sword flashed, finding weak spots and severing limbs. He danced between the legs and teeth, cutting his attackers down one by one.

Nearly a third had gone down to arrows, but not even with five defenders did they escape unharmed. Thanon's arm was cut when he dodged a jumping trakin too slowly as he switched weapons, and two of their horses suffered lacerations. None of the injuries were serious. If it had only been Thanon, they would have continued when the sun rose. The horses could not bear the burden of two unconscious mounts, and they could not afford to leave them behind so soon. Fortunately, the sedative effect lasted no more than half a day, and they were traveling again before the sun peaked.

Since that night, they faced only one additional attack from a pack of seven. As intelligent as they were, it seemed they did not well judge the number of prey before attacking. Their intelligence is overridden by a driving instinctual need or lack of experience with armed groups.

They were somewhat scattered, but Larron had never seen such a concentration of trakins in this, or any, forest. His group would probably make it through, but the messenger scouts the Derou elves sent before would not have fared well.

They travelled alone and light, designed for speed and stealth, not combat. He doubted they would find remains along the path, and he felt a helpless anger at the senseless death. One or two were meant to be able to travel undetected past their enemies more easily, but the trakins were an impossible barrier. For months, they had sent people to their deaths. That was always a possibility, but it was more difficult knowing they never stood a chance.

A chill breeze awakened Larron to the fact that evening deepened the darkness around them, so he called a halt. It was safer to set up a defensive perimeter at night along the old path they followed, as the slightly open area allowed for better targeting at a distance.

In times of peace, that trail was used often enough by the few elves traveling between the Derou and Palonian Woodlands that it had not become overgrown as it was now. Though, in those times, the forest to the east of the Derou Woodland was not dark and lifeless either. The trakins were steadily draining the land like carnivorous locusts. Larron himself had traveled through the eastern forest by more paths than this, and he could remember the life, the light, and the sounds filling it then but eerily absent now.

Even should Kahnlair be defeated, it will take decades, if not centuries, to heal the damage he has wrought upon our realm. It was another tragic side effect of the war, and the elves had nothing and no one to spare for such concerns.

The horses were relieved of their burdens and taken care of, and food and water were passed around in the now familiar routine. All was dealt with in relative quiet. It might be there were no gilar or other enemy forces around to hear them, but the shadows pressed in on the party from the moment they stepped beyond the Woodland border. None felt comfortable beneath this canopy. Their voices seemed out of place. When they spoke, it was often with lowered voices reflecting the dire situation their people faced.

"Were it not for the sake of the horses, Commander, I would say we should ride through the nights and take turns sleeping astride to be rid of this place." Lieutenant Geelomin said to him as they moved their packs away from the horses, his dark eyes scanning the forest.

"It does make one long for the comfort of the Derou, but I will be grateful beyond measure if this is the worst threat we face in reaching the Palonian."

Palan joined them beside the small fire they started to warn off any isolated trakins. "At last reports from the war councils, the only gilar forces en masse in the north were around our Woodland. Do you think Kahnlair has shifted his focus in this direction?"

"We have not had word from our allies in over two years. It is very possible their lines have been overrun in that time, but it is also possible they found a way to shift the momentum in our favor," Larron answered.

"The gilar contingent surrounding the Derou has not increased. We would likely be facing more if they were not still occupied elsewhere."

Geelomin frowned at Thanon. "We were not facing fewer of them either, Thanon, so by your logic our allies also made no progress. And there are always the vampires that continue to increase in number."

"I will not dwell on the possible negatives."

The elder soldier snorted a laugh and shook his head at their young companion. He was a bright spot among the group, with a positive attitude pushing through all barriers and hardships they faced. "I long to share your optimism."

Thanon laughed and grinned as he took his position for the first watch. The rest of them settled in for the night. Full dark came on quickly in the thick forest, and the former hunter stood alert for sounds indicating approaching danger.

He kept his eyes away from the fire and peered into the woods, but it was like trying to pierce a thick veil.

It was more often the noise of an attacker giving away their approach. The soft clicking and shuffling of trakins was easily distinguished from the more common forest animals. Before the war, the life of the forest was something Thanon knew almost intimately, which was why the lack of those familiar sounds here was disconcerting. It was also why a soft cry brought him instantly on guard.

A bird, perhaps? He wondered.

There was something moving in the distant darkness, though what it was he could not yet tell. Thanon roused the group, and in moments, they stood quietly, straining to listen. Just as they were beginning to raise questioning eyebrows at Thanon, it reached them over the crackle of the fire from a short distance away. Branches, twigs, and underbrush snapped as something large pushed its way quickly in their direction.

"A pack, perhaps?" Larron asked.

"Most likely, you can hear the clicking now, but there was something else as well. Whatever it is, it is likely the thing crashing through the brush."

"Should we investigate, Commander?" Geelomin asked.

"We would best hold around the fire rather than allow them the opportunity to attack the horses without us to defend. We have the ad—" he stopped as a cry came from the forest. "That did not sound like an animal."

"I agree. We are not the prey this time. Someone else is being hunted."

"Palan, take to the trees to watch over the horses. The rest, with me. Geelomin, Bealaras, come around on the flanks. If they are after something else, we may be able to dispatch most from a distance before we need to engage."

Everyone moved without hesitation. Four people quickly, but cautiously, making their way toward the origin of the cry and the increasingly obvious sound of a trakin pack. Larron moved to the left side, keeping his eyes moving for any trakins on the perimeter, but he found they were all focused on their prey and did not notice him and his men approaching.

As his sightline opened, the vision presented was not promising for the victim. A body lay beneath one trakin, while at least twenty others crawled or leapt toward it. Without a word, his knocked arrow was released, striking the trakin covering the body. Other arrows flew from the forest even as he drew back another and fired again. They might be too late to save this person, but they could prevent these creatures from consuming him.

Some of the trakins continued onward, but with the sudden appearance of a threat, most turned to face their attackers. The ambush was effectively reversed, and the trakins were forced to split the pack's attention, becoming the hunted.

The speed of the archers cut their numbers significantly before they could spread out enough to herd and surround his small group. Two made it through the arrows to engage him, but he had time to stow his bow and draw his sword in preparation. He took the head of one quickly and stabbed the second even as an arrow came flying to *thunk* into the carapace joint on the opposite side. As the last one fell dead, they counted out before cautiously moving toward the body, still alert and prepared for any trakins they might have missed or overlooked.

"He came from that direction," Geelomin nodded toward the obvious trail blazed through the forest. "So close to help. You have to wonder what someone would be doing out here alone. Even we sent our people in pairs," he paused and grimaced. "Though, maybe he was not alone at the start."

"Is he alive?" Bealaras asked.

While the three stood guard, Larron knelt next to the body hidden beneath the trakin and rolled the foul carcass off. What he saw was so contrary to his expectations it left him frozen in momentary surprise. The body was female. She was covered in layers of dirt, sweat, blood, and grime and had too many injuries to count with a quick glance. Most surprising of all, she wore next to nothing. The green garment was far too small to serve any functional purpose. It was little more than another layer of skin. There was no cloak against the colder nights, no shoes or boots to protect her feet from the cutting terrain.

"Why would a woman be out here alone and in such a state of attire? The humans tend to keep their women wrapped in wool more than anyone." Geelomin's question reflected Larron's own thoughts and reminded him of their vulnerable position. He moved quickly to examine her with his field medic training.

"She is alive," he said, again surprised, "but severely wounded. I need to bring her back to the light of the fire to make a better assessment."

Larron gathered her in his arms and carried her back to camp. While Palan—though curious himself—remained on guard, the rest gathered around Larron and his charge.

"She was attacked before tonight, and more than once," Larron said as he examined her wounds more closely.

"Surely, she could not have survived an attack on her own with, quite literally, nothing on her?"

"This wound on her shoulder says otherwise. It appears to be the bite of a trakin, and it has stopped bleeding.

Is this moss?" That last was said more to himself in
confusion than the others, but he shook his head and
continued. "A bite such as this would still be bleeding if it
had come in this attack. Bring me water and the meds pack."

Geelomin frowned. "Using our water for this purpose
will mean needing to find a source in this fouled forest. This
woman is unknown to us. She could be an enemy."

"You propose we leave her?"

He sighed and shook his head. "I would dislike
leaving even an enemy in this condition. I will not leave a
stranger of unknown allegiance without aid."

Larron looked around the group and saw nods of
agreement, mirroring his own thoughts. Bealaras handed him
the pack while he continued his examination. He moved her
hair enough to reveal a pointed ear. "I believe she is an elf."

His lieutenant leaned forward and squinted as though
that would allow him to see past the dirt and blood better.
"She does not have the look of an elf."

Bealaras looked from her to Geelomin and back,
considering. "She does have some elven features, though a
bit off."

"What do you mean?"

"Elves have a ratio that is taller on average than
humans, and it holds true in most of our features. I see it in
paintings I compare as well as in the few visitors to our
Woodland. Her ratio is off a bit from true elven, but it is not
necessarily an absolute. You do not think she could be half
elven, do you? I have not met enough humans to judge on
appearance."

"Impossible," Palan snorted and scoffed at the idea
from his perch.

He silently agreed with Palan's statement from the
trees as he shifted her to gain better access to her shoulder

wound but paused as an even greater surprise had him rethinking everything he believed. Shaking his head, he breathed out. "I believe Bealaras is correct. She is likely only half-elf."

"How? Larron, that is…"

He understood the disbelief in his lieutenant's voice. "Not possible. I know. I will explain after I treat some of the more serious wounds. Perhaps she will be able to offer some answers if she recovers. Set up overlapping guard shifts, we do not know if she has escaped from some enemy that is following."

Larron started cleaning and bandaging her more significant and accessible lacerations, beginning with the still-bleeding stab in her leg. She was gaunt, and her lips cracked, indicating she had not eaten or had much to drink. But her muscles remained toned, which told him the malnutrition was relatively recent. By the time he was through cleaning and binding her open and exposed wounds, the guard was already changing and Palan joined him. Shifting her to lift her head, he held a waterskin out to Palan.

"Help me by dribbling a little water into her mouth. I want to start her on more water tonight, or I fear dehydration will finish what the trakin began."

The two of them worked at a painfully slow pace to have her reflexively swallow a tiny amount of water. After the first time, he placed some of their medicine beneath her tongue to start it working if she could swallow more. He would try to have her drink again two or three more times tonight and more into the morning until she woke.

"Geelomin, I will need you to assist me as well, please? I will not be able to access the remainder of her injuries on my own."

"What is it you need us to do?" Palan, still kneeling

opposite, said with unconcealed interest.

He hesitated before answering and pursed his lips, knowing how insane the truth sounded. "We need to unwrap the wings from her body. They were most likely damaged, since she did not fly away from the trakins. I cannot check for other injuries, nor properly wrap her ribs and shoulder, with them in the way."

"Vampire?" Geelomin had his sword out at the mention of wings, even before Larron finished speaking. It was a natural response. No other race with wings existed in the world. Not anymore, or so they all believed.

"No! I believe she is fairy. At least, based on our lore, it fits."

The two of them stared at her, mouths open, with looks of incomprehension on their faces. Geelomin recovered first and shook his head as if to clear it before sheathing his sword and regained his military composure. He probably did not believe it yet, but he had orders and could compartmentalize like the best of his soldiers.

"How do we go about unwrapping fairy wings?"

Palan's responding chuckle was a little hysterical before he muttered in disbelief. "A statement I never would have guessed I would hear."

Answering that question took some investigation. Her wings looked like a solid piece of material wrapped around her without seams or openings. Finally, they found a smooth overlap at the back near the wounds he was trying to access and gently pulled the edges away. The infected area where the wings met her back was immediately obvious to everyone. Training or not, the swollen and oozing injuries were an awful sight. He could not treat them until the wings were completely opened away from her body, though.

They grimaced at the sight and gently shifted her

weight around between the three of them until the full wingspan extended over the ground and then covered her lower half with blankets for warmth and out of respect. Her joints, where the wings connected to her back, were grotesque. They were partially healed but had become infected at some point recently and were the likely cause of the fever he felt in her skin. The medicine he gave her would slowly help fight the fever and infection both, but the area needed to be debrided. She, thankfully, remained asleep from the trakin sedative throughout his efforts scrubbing and removing the pus, dirt, and dead tissue. Palan started to look ill and had to step away as he scraped at her.

"Larron, this is not possible." Geelomin, never a squeamish soldier, whispered to him as he worked.

"I know. And yet…"

"Not only half elf, but half…legend?" he asked. "It cannot be."

"You have seen the ears, the wings. You have heard Bealaras's comments. He would best be able to identify visual traits other have missed."

"How could no one have known? She is of an age to have been born before the war began. Even if we ignore the parentage question, an elf would have brought their bonded life mate and child home, if only to visit and celebrate."

Unless they died before they could do so, he thought to himself. The two of them looked at each other, heads shaking with no good answers before they finished taking care of her injuries and settling her to rest.

***

She did not think death would be so painful, dying maybe, but being dead? Surely not. Every movement of the ground jarred her sensitive nerves and she almost groaned.

Why would the ground be moving? A more logical voice asked her foggy mind before she made a sound.

The smell of animals and the sound of soft voices started to reach her over the pain, but she did not have time to think about the implications before mercifully drifting back to sleep. The training of the cautious and alert fighter stood no chance against exhaustion and fever.

When she woke again, her mind was clearer. Her senses snapped to attention at her unfamiliar surroundings, and she took note of the bindings on her limbs. Without giving a sign to the people nearby she was awake, she took in as much as possible. The movement was already slowing, coming to a stop, and her eyes opened a crack to see the ground was steady below. She was tied to a horse, though whether it was simply to keep her from falling or as a prisoner, she could not be certain. It might be safest to find some means of defending herself.

People approached on both sides of the horse, and she forced herself to remain motionless and give the impression she was still relaxed in sleep even as her heart sped in anticipation of movement. Already at a disadvantage due to numbers and uncertain of their intentions, she needed to regain some measure of control. To assume they were friendly was not a luxury she felt she could afford.

From the corner of her eye, she saw the person on the left side of the horse—where her head hung down—carried a weapon at his waist. They untied her feet first, and she let them dangle as they moved to her hands. The moment both hands were free, she rolled from the horse and drew the sword at the man's side in one fluid motion, before spinning behind him.

Quickly looking around, she noted five men total,

three with arrows nocked and sited in her direction. The second man, who had been untying her, brandished his own sword on the opposite side of the horse.

Their reflexes are as fast as mine, she thought, and her heartbeat sped up. *This is not good.*

To cut off the angles of fire, she backed up while drawing the man with her toward a tree, the blade at his throat and her hand on his shoulder.

"Hold your positions! Not another step!"

"Do as she asks," her hostage said with surprising calm. They looked wary but followed her orders, and she realized she must have the leader in her grasp. He added, "and put away your weapons. She will not harm me."

"You do not know that," warned the one closest to her. He was the darkest among them. His skin and hair were both a rich dark chocolate color, with eyes to match. He held himself like a soldier and looked at her without blinking, seeking an opening to strike.

"This is nothing more than fear," another responded. A little too intuitive for her comfort in this case.

"Put them away, Lieutenant."

For a moment she stood in shocked silence, poised to kill him if she felt they were bluffing and positioning to attack. They slowly followed orders, easing their arrows from their bows and sheathing the sword. She still did not trust them. They were quick and could easily turn on her the moment she released her captive.

"Who are you? Why was I tied to the horse?" she called from behind his back with a voice not as steady as she would like. Her hostage answered.

"We are messengers, and you were tied to ensure you did not fall from the horse's back as we traveled. With your injuries, I would not have taken up the journey again, but our message is urgent, and these woods are not safe."

This one was calm under pressure. He spoke with authority and understanding. She was impressed despite herself, and she began to feel her reaction to them may have been extreme and perhaps a little premature. Her focus turned from the others to regard her hostage more closely. He was about a half head taller than her, with dark, raven-black hair and tan skin. The body held against hers was well toned.

For the first time since her fall, she was aware of how little she wore. They had given her pants that were too long and a blanket tied around her neck and hanging down her front. It was probably to allow her wings freedom, but she suddenly felt exposed, much more so than when she had been traipsing through the forest nude.

Well, there was no one to see me then!

She wanted to step back to distance herself from him, but at the same time, she wanted to keep him right where he was, and for more than the protection of a living shield from his men. His calm presence was comforting. She wanted to soak the comfort into her skin and hold it close. A slight movement brought her out of her reverie, but it was only the horse. Every single one of them stood frozen, waiting for her to come to a decision.

She swallowed and was pleased when her voice sounded calm. "I am free to leave if I wish? Go my own way?"

"We will not stop you, nor harm you in any way if you leave now. Though, I would advise against going off on your own. As I have mentioned, this is a dangerous area in which to travel." Caught in indecision she could not respond and stood watching them all. "You may hold my weapon for a while if you wish. If you decide to leave us, however, I am afraid I will need it along our journey."

There was a smile in his voice she found both endearing and irritatingly patronizing.

"I do not need your weapon. I am capable of taking care of myself without it."

They had submitted first by putting up their arms. Hers had to be the next show of trust. She was outnumbered, and without a means of defending herself, but this standoff was neither in her favor nor necessarily warranted.

It was a dumb move to attack, she admitted to herself.

Perhaps she would stand a chance if she were healthy, but her body was already threatening to give up on her. With a deep breath, she stepped back from him and smoothly turned the handle of the blade to return it. Her stance was stiff and defiant, but her eyes remained on her outstretched hand in submission.

He slowly reached for the handle, brushing her hand as he did, and her heart leapt. Her eyes snapped to meet his.

This is no time for foolish infatuation! You saved yourself, he only helped a little at the end. She scolded herself mentally at her extreme reaction and forced her eyes to take in the rest of the people around them. None drew their weapons, but their hands were on them. Her hostage already moved back toward the horses.

"We will not be stopping long, only enough to feed and water the horses. Would you care for something to eat? Some water?" She could not hide the longing and desperation in her eyes. It took all her restraint not to rush over and snatch the skin held out toward her, but she hesitated.

"What about your supplies? Do you have enough to share?"

He shook his head and smiled at her. "We already need to search for a water source, so a little more will do no harm. I would prefer you partake, as it will help you heal.

You should drink slowly at first, though, as you are dehydrated and too much at once could make you sick."

Based on those concerns, she concluded he was also likely their medic. "Thank you, for this and for seeing to my injuries."

She gave him a fair chance to revoke his offer, and with it still standing, she eagerly grabbed for the water skin and gingerly took a seat on the ground. He handed her a portion of food and they left her alone to go about their work.

All five of them had a similar look about them. No one was as dark as the Lieutenant, but the rest of them were varying shades of brown ranging from his deep color to the tan color shared by their leader and one other. Their hair was also in shades of brown and black, with only one of them having a reddish tint to his lighter brown.

The food was some hard bread with salted meat. She began to eat and drink carefully so she would be able to keep it down. She already knew the risks from her deprivation. After so long with nothing, the taste of real food in her mouth was blissful. The small meal was surprisingly filling, but it was nowhere near the amount her body needed. It was still the most substantial thing she had eaten since the rat.

Feeling only slightly guilty, she drank a great deal of water in that short time and did not offer the skin back. When she looked up, she noticed her benefactors getting ready to leave and felt a sudden terror at the idea of being left alone. It was something she could not handle again right now. She was searching for signs of other people, and these seemed kind and capable enough.

"May I come with you?" She blurted out, and all five turned in unison to look at her. Carefully pushing herself to her feet, she held out the water skin. "If you are worried about your rations, I will promise to not take any more."

Thinking about her behavior so far, she continued. "Or attack you."

"Again," the one called Lieutenant added rather unhelpfully.

"I will not attack any of you again," she looked at the not-helpful one, "unless in self-defense."

Two of the others snorted, but otherwise remained silent.

"You may join us and share our rations. Do you know how to ride?" the leader asked, indicating the horse she had been tied to.

The animal was placidly munching and ignoring them as they talked. It felt familiar, and she thought she knew the mechanics involved. "I think so."

"You think so? Does that mean you have only seen others ride?"

Her brow furrowed, chasing a thought at the edge of memory but just out of reach.

"Perhaps," she said approaching the horse, aware she was limping worse now from her injuries.

That day and night of running and fighting had cost her, and she was weaker than she wanted to show. Without the fear of imminent death pushing the pain aside, she was not going to be able to pull herself up there. The distance between self and saddle was immeasurable in that moment. She could feel the attention of the leader waiting behind her.

"May I offer assistance?"

"That would be appreciated. Thank you."

She expected him to offer a step, so the hands grasping her hips were a bit of a shock. His strength was deceptive with his lean frame, as he easily lifted her onto the horse's back. From the care he took to avoid putting pressure on any of her serious injuries, she was now certain he helped bandage them all, and she fought back an embarrassed blush.

She recovered from the surprise and relaxed as the throbbing subsided some to lean forward and pat the horse's neck before finding her seat. The five men quickly and efficiently completed their preparations to leave as she watched before gracefully mounting. The leader issued seemingly routine commands about positions, one took off at a faster pace, and they set into motion without another word. Following their lead, she urged her horse forward as well, and her former hostage maneuvered to ride at her side.

***

He looked over at her as he rode and saw her jaw was set and her posture stiff. With her injuries, he had no doubt this would be a painful ride, but he could not delay. Any delay would only add risk they could ill afford.

"May I ride with you?"

She shrugged and winced at the movement but pretended like it was nothing. He would have laughed at her stoicism, but those injuries were no laughing matter, and she had been shaking in terror earlier.

"Your back injuries were infected. We had to clean the area and remove some dead tissue. You will need treatment again for the next few nights to fight off the lingering fever and any of the infection we could not remove."

Her eyes roamed his face with scrutiny. He wondered what she looked for, and wondered more what she saw before she nodded subtly. "Thank you for helping me; for the medicine and for killing those things. I thought I imagined the light of your fire in the darkness and that it was over for me."

"I am pleased we were near enough to assist." He said, honestly glad they could save at least one person from the trakins. "There are some questions I would ask about your situation, if you are willing."

"Sure, but do you have a name I should use? Unless, of course, you prefer I address you as 'Commander.'" A smile played at the corner of her eyes, and he relaxed a fraction, glad whatever this ordeal was had not broken her.

"My name is Larron, and I will answer with the title or my name." He smiled in return. "Palanthuiel is scouting ahead, and he usually goes by Palan. The others with me are Lieutenant Geelomin, Bealaras, and Thanon." He went through introductions, and each of his people gave a curt nod, wave, or smile as he said their name. "And you are?"

A look of confusion replaced the smile. As she hesitated, he felt his guard rise. "You can call me Annalla."

"Hm..." *An odd way to answer,* he thought to himself.

They could return to that topic if his other questions did not flush out the answer in due course. "Alright, Annalla. I have to ask, what in all the realms were you doing in the middle of this forest alone and unequipped?"

She shrugged and winced again before rolling her eyes and sighing. The entire move conveyed irritation with her injured state, and maybe the broader situation, without her needing to speak a word.

"Things are a little weird right now."

Well, that was an inadequate answer. He said nothing, raising an inquiring eyebrow and waiting for her to go on with the patience for which his race was known.

"And you wouldn't mind hearing why things are a little weird. You won't believe me," she said finally but sighed and looked ahead.

He was not sure her eyes were focusing on the forest before them or in that blurry state of remembering. "I don't remember anything before twelve days ago or so, if I'm adding them up correctly. The first thing I *can* remember is falling…and pain. My wings ripped from my back. My head pulled in all directions. There was falling and breaking through branches or spinning off them before hitting the ground."

"You were shot down over the forest?" Larron thought back through her injuries, but did not recall any arrow wounds or any that looked like they would be from vampire claws.

Her hands tightened on the reigns as she lifted them in frustration. Moonshine, the pack horse she rode, sidestepped in response before settling down again. The recovery was automatic, so he suspected she was a trained rider. Her expression remained pinched though, even if her seat did not. "I don't think I was flying. I don't even think I *had* wings. It doesn't make sense, I know, I just… Anyway, I fell, got beat up by the trees on my way down, and have been walking and running from monsters ever since.

"This forest seems to go on forever. I was losing hope of ever finding another person out here. There is no sign of civilization anywhere."

Little of what she said made sense, and he struggled with where to dig further.

"This forest is not inhabited. You would need to exit east or west from here to find any settlements." Larron responded to her comment to give himself a moment to think. "Alright, let us focus on the last twelve days first. You mentioned monsters. How many trakins did you face in the first pack? The creature you were running from before we found you." He clarified at the confused look on her face.

"Six, a few hours before dark."

He blinked and stared. "Six? With no weapons?"

She smiled at his surprise, and he liked seeing the frustration fade. "I had a branch, a stick, and a rock. And some thick bushes at my back. I'm lucky they got me with teeth instead of one of their stabby legs. I think that's what put me under at the end."

"You are correct. It is a reason we usually try to eliminate them from range or as a group as much as possible. It is impressive you were able to escape a pack on your own. Where were you walking from before the attacks?"

"From the east mostly. Though, it was hard to track without landmarks and I was forced around some of the areas where the thorny bushes grow close. I chose west as a direction and stuck with it as much as I could based on the sun. I crashed less than a half day from a rocky outcropping that just made it above the canopy. That is the best landmark I can think of that you might recognize. The rest just looked like a forest." Her eyes met his, asking if he recognized her description.

He shook his head. "I do not know of such a place. You were likely closer to the eastern edge of the forest, but I doubt you would have found help sooner in that direction."

This meant she was either not willing or able to tell him information of what was taking place beyond the forest. He disliked that they were travelling blind to enemy movements, but as intelligence gathering was one of the reasons they were sent, it was a known issue.

"If you remember nothing from before, I suppose that means you do not recall your family or where you grew up?"

"I'm sorry, no. I really wish I did," she shook her head and paused. "Not that I don't appreciate the save, but why are the five of you travelling through this dismal place if it is not inhabited?"

The question was not unexpected, but she was still a stranger who offered them little to no information of her own.

"We are bearing messages to our kin in the east," he answered vaguely before deflecting the topic once more. "Despite the overgrown look of it, this path has long been the best route through the forest. You were fortunate to pass so close without any notion of your surroundings."

"I don't mean to pry. I think you mentioned a mission before. Since you saved me, and then did not attack after I held your own sword on you, I'm inclined to believe it is not something dastardly."

Larron felt himself smile at her clear suspicion of them in return. She might need them, but she did not yet trust them. Maybe her story would change once she found they did mean to help her.

"Having treated your injuries, I am more inclined to believe you a victim rather than the perpetrator of something 'dastardly.' You must, however, forgive my hesitation regarding your memory loss. Most suffering such a complete loss would be incapable of making it through what you faced. Incapable is not a word I would use to describe you."

This was a sticking point for him. She claimed complete memory loss prior to a specific point in time, but no apparent loss of skill or learning. He knew there were physical and emotional traumas that could cause such, but the extent and combination seemed awfully convenient.

"There's no explanation I can give you. I remembered the skills I used to survive when I needed them. What I did felt natural. I have not questioned 'why' until now. If you are dying of thirst and come across a pool of water, are you going to question how it got there? The memories will return, or they won't."

For the sake of his people, Larron had to wonder if what she did not recall was a danger. He knew how this conversation would go with his current party.

"This could be a trick of Kahnlair's," Geelomin *would argue. "She may have willingly endured the injuries to infiltrate their group and undermine the security of the Woodlands. Amnesia is a convenient excuse to avoid providing any details about herself."*

Thanon would shake his head. "It is more likely the result of torture. She needs our help, and we need to keep her safe from whatever might be after her."

"In addition to that, she is an elf. We cannot abandon our kin." Bealaras would add as Palan would nod his agreement with the latter two.

Geelomin would roll his eyes. "Correction. She appears to be half elf and half fairy. Both of which are impossible as far as our recorded history knows."

Palan would then hold up his hand. "Does that not make it less likely she is a plant seeking to infiltrate our group? It would make more sense to send someone we would not question so...specifically."

All of the imaginary arguments were valid. Larron would keep an eye out for pursuit in case she was escaping an enemy, but he did not honestly expect one. As for infiltration, the guise of a *fairy* had to be the least effective choice possible. Anywhere she went, she would cause a sensation, simply by existing. There was no chance someone with wings would escape questions, speculation, and disbelief; to the rest of the world, the fairy simply did not exist.

He would also consider the possibility she was telling the truth when she described a kind of physical transformation. There were too many scenarios in that direction. He would not kill or turn away one of his own people. He would be hard-pressed to make such a heartless decision with one of the other races. Larron was taking a risk, and it was her life he was risking. She already knew enough about them to give them away, and if she started to severely hinder their progress or risk their success, he would have to kill her. She could not be left alone and alive with any knowledge.

Perhaps, he thought, *she would have been better off clean, bandaged, and left on her own before she regained consciousness.*

CHAPTER FIVE

They stopped for the night. Larron gently helped her from the horse, and she watched with appreciation as they efficiently set up camp. She did, however, insist on helping to brush her mount. Her name was Moonshine. She was a beautiful silver-gray mare, with whom Annalla had found a pace and stride that worked for them both. Moonshine seemed to understand her rider was injured and was careful with her footing.

Throughout their ride, she avoided the easy jumps others made over obstacles and looked for the least winding path through the tree trunks without urging. Allowing someone else to take care of Moonshine after such consideration would have been ungrateful, and the mare made the task easier by following Annalla's orders instead of making her walk around.

"It would seem you know horses quite well. Though, I am surprised she follows your commands," the one called Palan said as he moved the heavier supplies over with the rest. Palan was the one with the red tint to his hair. The auburn color complemented his milk chocolate skin and the lighter brown of his eyes. He had returned to the campsite shortly after they stopped for the day, so he must have left some marker she missed for the location during his scouting.

"She is a very clever animal," she smiled over at him. "I'm impressed she can carry so much in addition to carrying me."

"Moonshine is one of the pack horses we brought. You can see the difference in how much taller and broader she is than the ones we ride. Though, I have heard humans have a breed of horse that is even larger," his tone was loving, and he stopped for a moment to pat at Moonshine's flank before continuing to unload and move items.

"I don't know that I could ride a horse much larger around." In fact, she could already feel her muscles straining in new ways from the ride today.

"I believe they are used mostly for farming and hauling, but Larron would know better than I. Did she work for you today?"

"Yes, we found our rhythm," she said with a smile and stroked Moonshine's flank herself before returning her attention to him. "You work with horses?"

It was a guess, but he lit up. "Not recently, but I was a horse trainer for several decades about a century ago. Riding every day makes me want to take it up again. My Kelley is one of the fastest we have with us for this trip. It is why we can range ahead so well."

His eyes roved over the clustered animals, and she could see pride in them. Looking back at her and Moonshine, he chuckled. "I imagine you will be sore tomorrow, unless you have been riding much of late."

She curled her lip. "Ugh, probably, but I'm not sure I will be able to tell the difference to be honest. It can't be worse than all the other aches and pains."

Even though she was facing him, it felt like his eyes went to her wing joints, and he paled a bit before responding.

"Yes, your injuries were extensive. I am surprised you are moving much at all. You must still be in pain."

"It's not too bad if I move slowly. Less than it has been, but I do feel more tired," Annalla hesitated before she smiled teasingly. "By your expression, I assume you're not usually patching up injuries."

"Ha!" his eyes went wide, and he slowly shook his head. "No, not at all. No offense, but your back was disgusting. I hope to never see such an injury again."

The reaction was so real and horrified it had her laughing again.

"The fatigue you feel is likely the medication our Commander gave to you. It is meant to encourage the one healing to *rest*," Geelomin said with a stern look at the two of them as he handed her another small piece of bread and dried meat. "Rations."

He acted the most distrustful of her, though it was more protective of his companions than aggressive toward her.

She looked up at him from the food. "I can survive on less if you cannot spare full rations."

"You cannot regain your health with no food and little water, especially still fighting the fever. Our pace may be slow, but you will need to be able to move fast if there is need." The tone in which this was said brooked no argument, like a parent correcting a child on basic facts.

She nodded obediently and took the food. "There's water nearby. I can hear it. Maybe we can take the empty water skins and fill them in the morning. I can go early, before we head out."

He paused and turned back to her, tilting his face to scan the forest. "I cannot hear such. How far do you believe it is?"

"Half hour, there and back, but I'm not great with distances or time... Well, actually, I'm pretty terrible at judging distances so far. Everything seems to be further away in this forest, but maybe I'm just slower than I think I am." She was babbling, trying to compensate for being a burden to them by being helpful. It still translated to her babbling.

Geelomin turned toward the fire. "Commander, there is a chance a source of water may be nearby. We will need more before we quit the forest."

"Is it along our path?" He asked, and Geelomin looked at her and raised an eyebrow.

"You are heading east," she shook her head when they confirmed and instead pointed south. "It is that direction."

Larron looked from her to the direction in which she pointed, pausing as though listening for something. Probably seeking the faint trickle that became clear to her ears when the horses stopped moving for the day.

"Hmm. I do not hear anything. Palan," he looked to the probably younger man and received a quick acknowledgement, "you have spare boots with you. Do you think we could add enough padding for them to fit Lady Annalla?"

Palan looked at her feet thoughtfully, tilting his head and scrunching his nose. "Probably not to fit well, but we can make it close enough to be functional. I will grab them."

"Geelomin will go with you in the morning," Larron said as Palan turned word to deed and grabbed a bag from the supplies.

She nodded and began eating as boots and socks were brought over, feeling a little better about her contributions, and about the companions settling in around her.

***

Footsteps. Someone approached the spot she was sleeping, waking her early. Her eyes popped open and she fluidly rose to a ready stance with one hand reaching over her shoulder and the other toward her hip, grasping. Geelomin froze and held up his hands while his eyes missed nothing of her movement.

"You favor long knives, I see." Geelomin commented.

Annalla relaxed and tilted her head. "Pardon?"

With a nod toward her shoulder, where she had been reaching, he responded. "You naturally reach for them in the standard elven carry, likely with a backup knife or sword at your waist. Bealaras carries long knives."

She looked over to where Bealaras lay with his gear and thought about wearing the weapons as he did, crossing her back with the handles in easy reach. Then she thought about the feel of Larron's sword in her hand. Should one feel more natural than the other if she favored it? She seemed to know what to do with the sword just fine when she held it.

"Maybe. I can't say one weapon feels more familiar than another."

"Fair enough," he said, though she was not sure if he was conceding the point or dropping the subject. "We should move out when you are ready. I will collect the water skins."

She only had to put on her new shoes, and they were moving before the sky lightened. He allowed her to set the pace and direction, and she eased into a steady walk. This time it was the injury in her leg from the trakin slowing her the most. The fever made her tire quickly, but she could push through being tired. It was a milder form of the exhaustion she became used to recently.

Palan's boots remained much too large for her and slid around, but her feet were well insulated from the movement. It was better than walking through the unforgiving brush barefoot again. Larron had bandaged her feet along with the rest of her when he treated her injuries, and she remained thankful she had been unconscious when he was cleaning the dirt out of those cuts and scrapes. She would live with the oversized boots.

Most of their walk was spent in silence. He did not seem the type for idle chatter, and she suspected he was on alert in case she was leading him into some sort of ambush. She was content to allow it. Talking for so long the previous day felt odd. Good, but odd. From time to time, she stopped to listen for the water to make sure their periodic side-trips around dense thorny bushes did not divert them from their course. The leaves might be withering in the heat and drought, but that did not thin the thorns or branches.

"If we do not turn back soon, we will delay the group's departure."

"The undergrowth and my leg slowed us. I'm sure you will start to hear it anytime now," her tone was as conciliatory as she could make it.

She already said she was not great at judging distance, so that was on him for assuming otherwise, but she recognized they would not make it back before the others were ready to leave at this pace.

It was still a few minutes more before she thought Geelomin heard the flowing water. Though he said nothing, his pace quickened, and he did not rely on her for direction any longer.

How he could have missed the noise before was a mystery to her, but she would ponder that question after she was off her feet. The latest injury screamed at her for being foolish enough to take the long walk, and they still had to walk back.

When she cleared the last of the bushes behind him and came within sight of the stream, she was presented with a hidden oasis amid the desolate forest. It was no raging river, you could jump from side to side without effort, even straddle the tiny stream without getting wet if you were careful and had the leg strength to push back up. Along with plenty of water was what looked like clusters of potentially edible plants.

If she were still on her own, she would have eaten them there and then. Instead, they completed their water collection in more silence—not that she expected him to become a conversationalist now—and Annalla went to collect the roots growing in the wet ground after they were done.

"Are you certain those are edible?"

She shrugged at him. "Pretty sure. Someone in your group will know though... Right?"

"That is likely. We should hurry back. We will already be later than expected." Geelomin looked at the sky and then her leg. "I will carry all of the water skins. You bring those plants."

Her stubborn independence bristled at the idea, but she knew he was right. The added weight would slow her down, and her leg protested just getting back on her feet. She nodded and handed her half of them over. Part of him must have wanted to rush back to his companions with all haste, but he was ordered out here as her guard, one way or another.

She was again allowed to set their pace, and she did so with as much speed as she could manage. Even so, it was nearing an hour after they left when they returned, only to find the area empty.

"I still hear horses nearby, and there is no sign they were attacked," she whispered to Geelomin as she edged closer to him. "They would not leave you behind, would they?" Leaving her behind? She was not so sure about that.

A small smile pulling at the corners of his mouth was a surprise to her when she looked away from the trees to see his face.

"More likely they are acting cautious should we have been attacked and led our assailants here under duress." He walked further into the tiny clearing, now devoid of any evidence their group had camped there, slowly and with his hands held out to the side. "My apologies for our tardiness. It seems the fairy hear as elves see, and our objective was a further journey than anticipated."

When no one responded he indicated with a hand wave she should join him.

"What do you mean 'the fairy hear as we see?'" she asked at his side, no longer whispering since he had spoken loud enough to be heard. Her only response from him was a look of mild surprise.

"You speak Jularian." Larron answered off to the right, a statement rather than a question. He was giving her what she was beginning to think of as his 'assessing look,' as he and the rest emerged from hiding. That look of his always felt as though he knew more than he was saying, or hinting he knew more than she. The latter was not difficult right now, but it still made her bristle.

"No, I don't. What is Jularian?"

"It is the language of the elves, and you responded in Jularian to something said in Jularian. I would qualify that as understanding and speaking our tongue. Outside of our Woodlands we speak what is known as 'Market.' It is a common language used for trading that developed over the ages as our realm intersected with others. As to your first question, the sight of elves is greater than that of other races, so I would guess he meant the fairy have a similar advantage with hearing. Of course, that is basing the abilities of an entire race upon one individual." He turned from her to ask Geelomin, "You were successful?"

"All the skins are full, and she found roots nearby we brought with us to supplement our supplies if they are safe to consume."

Larron nodded his approval and looked at the forage she held out for inspection. "Those will be fine. We have packed and are ready to leave. There is bread at the top of your packs to break fast. You will need to eat as we ride, though, as I would have us on our way."

As Geelomin moved toward his horse, Annalla snicked her call and Moonshine stepped closer. She attached the skins she took back from Geelomin to Moonshine's baggage, making sure it was evenly weighted. Larron again offered his help to mount, and she was quickly on Moonshine's back, with her morning ration in hand as he strode away to his horse. This time, she fell in beside Larron as they headed out.

"I feel like I'm missing something with how you reference elves and fairy between each other," She gestured to the rest of the group. She was not fond of feeling this way.

"In what way?"

She scrunched her face and attempted to keep bitterness from her voice. "Mmm, like just now pretending something is new as some sort of joke. Or comparing the two is some form of sarcasm. I don't get the joke or the sarcasm. I have to say that I feel like it is all at my expense."

"Ah," he said with a nod and a shrug that did not earn him any forgiveness. "It is neither a joke nor sarcasm you hear, but likely some level of discomfort. We are beyond our experiences. You are literally the embodiment of concepts we long have believed impossible. And yet, here you are."

That answered nothing, she thought grumpily, but snorted out some air and tried again, her voice flat. "Assume you are talking to someone with no references for what you are talking about. What does any of that mean?"

Larron looked at her, and finally seemed to realize she was feeling hurt and insulted. "Fair enough. You will likely have noticed you have wings, while we do not."

It was not a question, but she nodded anyway.

"Only two races of people in Elaria have ever had functional wings; the fairy and the vampires. It is lore among the elves that the vampires were too strong for the fairy to fight and drove them to extinction thousands of years ago.

"Maybe that means you are a vampire, but vampire wings resemble those of a fly or bat, while yours resemble a butterfly's instead. Based on your appearance, fairy makes the most sense, but we are baffled as to how that is possible when no fairy has been seen in all these millennia." He raised his hands, the reins held loosely in them, with another shrug.

Annalla touched her lips in thought. "I'm guessing being a vampire would be a bad thing based on how you said that."

"For the sake of simplicity at this moment, we will go with 'yes.' The vampires are allied with darkness and plague the good races of Elaria still today. Vampires subsist upon a liquid diet requiring the blood of living creatures. While animal blood can sustain them, they prefer that of the peoples of the world *and* that it be from a living donor."

She looked over at him, "You mean they drink people alive? And I'm assuming it is not some simple, willing donation, but ends up with the donor dying."

"Correct."

An uncomfortable fact about a race she was either part of, or that drove her own race to near extinction.

Raising her hand, she spoke louder. "At this time, I would like to point out that I have *not* been drinking blood."

"What about the rat you told me about yesterday?" Thanon called from behind them, and she could swear she heard him laughing. She had liked the young elf, but now regretted answering his questions around the fire last night about how she survived in the forest before meeting them.

"I ate that, I did not drink its blood. Thank you very much." She called back, earning them a laugh from everyone in the line. If they were laughing, hopefully it meant they did not believe she was going to start drinking their blood and murdering them all.

Even Larron was smiling, and quickly set her mind at ease. "I do not believe you are descended from vampires. However, I believe you can better understand the comments we make upon your fairy lineage. Yes?"

"Yes." She was quiet for a bit, and started to feel alone in the world, even around these people she was starting to like. "What do you think happened to the fairy?"

When he looked at her again, there was sympathy in his eyes. "They cannot be gone from the world, Annalla. You are proof enough of that. I do not know where they might be, but perhaps we can seek them out together."

It was inexplicable to feel so relieved at a vague hint he might go with her on such a search, but she did. It was something to hold onto amid all the unknowns.

"The path is growing close."

Caught up in her own thoughts, she failed to notice the change in their surroundings with the path they followed becoming closed in by surrounding bushes. He moved his horse ahead of hers on the trail. They went on in silence as the path continued to shrink before expanding and then shrinking again.

At times there was a comfortable amount of space between them and the walls of thick brush on either side, and at others their legs and the flanks of the horses were pushing past new growth. The hours wore on, the path wound on, and she could feel their progress bearing more north than east. Finally, when they came to the next area with room to maneuver, a halt was called from the front.

Larron dismounted and squeezed past the sides of the riders in front of him to confer with Palan, who had returned early from scouting. "We are no longer following the old path."

"No. It continues in this manner, leaning north and without room to move, for miles ahead." He looked away, and she imagined he was looking toward where the path should be. "Those thorn bushes we always had to prune away from the direct path in this area took over. There is no place for us to set camp tonight."

"Why don't we just go straight east?" Annalla squeezed in behind him and pointed past the bushes he looked over.

Palan was the one to answer. "You do not want to go through *that* brush if you can avoid it. Becoming tangled in it is worse than being a feast for swamp midges."

"But a mile back down the path, it's less than half a mile wide. Don't you think we could probably cut through before dark?"

"We have been stuck in this winding alley for less than a day and cutting through could cost us more than that. Without a place to camp, we will lead the horses through the night and ride in the morning. If there is still no end by midday, we rest the horses while attempting to forge a path through the thinnest section."

Larron turned to her with an apologetic look. "I am sorry to ask you to walk again with your injuries and illness still healing."

"You mean for one night, with a full stomach, and none of said injuries leaving a trail of blood behind me? I think I can manage."

He smirked at her sarcasm. "Very well. Bag the horses and take your own meals. We eat as we ride."

They did, travelling through the leafy corridor in silence while eating their mid-day meal. Even though cutting through was her suggestion, she was pleased he opted to continue upon the tendril of a path rather than forge a new one.

A few times during her solitary trek through the forest, she ran into these plants, and they were not pleasant. Even the smallest scrape from their little clingy thorns left a painfully irritating rash. The first time she walked through a thin section was more than enough to learn the lesson to avoid them. It was probably worse than she remembered. Her experience with it might still be somewhat dulled by the rest of her aches and pains at the time.

Instead of turning firmly in the direction they wanted to go, the thin opening available continued to twist and turn, shrink and grow, and extend beyond seeing with only a few blockages. When the sun set, they stopped briefly to feed and water the horses as best they could, then they were walking and eating their final meal. Progress was slower in the dark. The eyesight of the elves allowed them to see enough to remain on the path, and the horses followed without protest, but they would not risk their mounts' footing by riding.

Annalla also suspected they were holding back for

her. She was nowhere near recovered—she had no doubt she would be bleeding, sweating, and panting by the end of the night—and she had no desire to slow them further.

Was it just this morning I was walking an hour for the water? She asked herself.

Compared to her solitary trek at the beginning, this was simple, but she was spoiled with enough to eat and the ability to ride instead of walk. The mind was an amazing thing. Her earliest memories were of pain, all-encompassing pain for which every movement was torture, every small bite and sip of water a reminder of a need not to be fully satisfied.

It was her mind providing escape, driving survival before the desire to give in. She knew it hurt, remembered wondering if that was all there was to life. Pain was still her constant companion, but it had eased. Surely, those first days were worse than this trek through the darkness. This pain was nothing in comparison, but the further they went into the night, the more her aches and injuries called for her to stop. The stab in her leg screaming with every step.

Survival drove her on again, to put one foot before the other, but there was something else there too… Fear. It was an emotion only on the periphery before, part of the vague notion she could die and what that might mean.

There was more to lose now. Comfort, safety, a connection to something and someone more. Things she had no knowledge of days before, and still only a small taste of them as she came to know these people, but they were enough to be afraid of losing them.

How slow would they allow her to go before leaving her behind? How much generosity would they expend before deciding she was not worth the effort? The image of those creatures coming to devour her was at the forefront of her thoughts, and she did not want to go back there to face that again. Determination and fear drove her beyond the pain.

She took only the one rest Larron called in the middle of the night for the horses. It was not until the sun rose that he called another halt, and all her strength went into not falling to the ground where she stood. They were tending to the horses, and Moonshine had been walking all night too, but leaning on her horse was the only thing preventing her from collapsing.

"Sit down."

The gentle voice in her ear made her shiver and jump slightly. "I can…"

"I will not abandon you to the wilderness." *Is my fear so close to the surface he can read it so clearly?* "Sit down. Rest. Replace the bandage on your leg. I will bring you your next dose of medicine."

As usual, she only needed to be told twice. Annalla grabbed the closest bandage and plopped to the nearest bit of open ground. Her calf wound had opened again, and blood dripped down her leg and into the socks given to her, but most had been absorbed by the bandage. She removed the soaked fabric before replacing it with a clean one. Her bandage might not be as professional, but she was happy with the effort.

Larron handed her three little leaves along with a blanket. "As we cannot build a fire here, you will need to chew and suck on them for a while and drink some water. Keep them in your cheek as you sleep. You can spit them out when you wake."

"Thank you." She squeezed his hand as she said it, her tired mind uncertain if she thanked him before. The leaves were bitter in her mouth, but she knew they were the thing fighting off the fever continuing to slow her down. She needed to not be slow and wounded, so she ignored the taste.

"Of course," he smiled and held her hand in both of his before she curled up with the blanket beneath her head. "Try not to threaten me with my own sword upon waking if we have the horse carry you while sleeping again."

An exhausted chuckle carried her into sleep.

CHAPTER SIX

"She lasted the night." There was respect in Geelomin's voice as his four men stood together looking over at her sleeping form. Larron watched them all as he repacked their medicine kit.

"Part of her is terrified, but she buries it deep," Bealaras commented before turning wistful. "Strength and fragility. Another day and time and she would be a wonderful subject."

"Perhaps she will return to The Derou with us and sit for a portrait after the war," offered Thanon. The optimistic statement was followed by a more realistic silence. The war was not going their way, and an end to it right now would most likely mean a victory for Kahnlair's forces, not theirs. With their Woodland dying, none of his people could deny that. "I like her."

Larron finished his task and came up behind the group. "As do I, Thanon. She will already be visiting The Palonian Woodland, so I do not see a reason you cannot invite her to ours as well when all is said and done." He patted the young elf on the back and looked at the sleeping fairy with a water skin dangling from her fingers. "The horses are ready. We will tie her to the horse again. She needs sleep, and we need to keep moving."

He made sure the release lines were within reach of her hands before they started off, just in case she woke before they removed them at their next stop. He hoped she would sleep through midday. She wore herself out maintaining their pace through the night. None of them would have said no to either a slower pace or more breaks. All the stubborn woman needed to do was speak up and ask.

Bealaras could call it strength, but it was driving Larron to no end of frustration that she would push herself to exhaustion. There was no reason for it, as she was no longer on her own or on the run from trakins. His team was concerned for their people and would give their lives if necessary, but she did not even remember who her people were. Perhaps that was it, though, their determination driving her as well. If they were willing to sacrifice themselves, were they also willing to sacrifice her?

This frustration at her not taking care of herself was more than he should be feeling for a stranger. Would he sacrifice her for their mission? Every part of him that made him an elf rebelled at the idea of killing her. It would be murder. They might be in a war, and it might be necessary to protect his people, but unless she acted against them, it would still be murder.

I would do it, should it become necessary, I would not let it fall to one of those under my command. Though something in me would die along with her in the act, I would do my duty and see my people safe.

He hoped it would never come to that. He hoped she would choose to remain with them at least until they found known allies. She was too much of an unknown at this point to release upon her own volition in an area of which they had zero recent intelligence.

With a sigh, he forcefully turned his thoughts to the land around them. There were many times he traveled through this forest over the centuries. It was never the most scenic or welcoming place. The large nettles they found themselves trapped in were common to the undergrowth and persisted no matter the weather extremes like the summer they now faced. They could grow in almost no sunlight, which made them perfect for the thick canopy of this forest. The deep shadows and dense growth were nothing new.

Stories about the evil places of the world filled with unnatural shadows, coming to life, and consuming unsuspecting innocents without leaving a trace were mostly, but not all, human fables and superstition. These lands belonged to the elves, and as his people were mostly content to remain within the Woodlands themselves, the superstition and the unwelcoming forest at their border were welcome deterrents to those who might seek to encroach upon their territory without invitation.

This forest was usually dark, but it was a fair warning and not even a taste of what would await trespassers within a Woodland. Elven Woodlands were more aware than other forests, an awareness originating from the natural connection of the Woodlands to the elves who lived there.

Most people could intuit when a place was off, but they might not recognize all the small signs they were picking up to make that determination. Not much had changed in this forest looking out at it now, but it was enough that even the unobservant would sense the danger. There had been life before, beyond the trees and plants hemming them in. The rustling of the leaves or bushes of small animals moving about. Fluttering and chirping of birds among the branches. Still subtler sounds of insects.

Annalla had enough bugs on her at first to show those were still around, but even they seemed to be in hiding. Trakins could do that to a forest if left unchecked. They were from another realm and settled in here well enough so long as the population was kept in check. In better times, the elves would have taken care of the packs before they became so numerous. Now, there was no one to spare for such concerns. The forest was suffering as much as his people were as a result.

"Commander!" Palan called out from ahead. His voice betrayed only resignation, no hint of concern.

Larron dismounted and made his way to the front. "Is there a problem?"

"There is no natural exit to this path within range, but only a short way ahead is the thinnest place in the eastern wall I have found. It is about as wide as the location Annalla pointed out yesterday. I wanted to return before you passed it. Turning the horses around is challenging." The last was said as he scratched the back of his neck and winced.

They would all be wincing soon. He wanted to sigh and grimace at the thought of going through the nettles but forced his features to remain neutral. "No use in putting it off any further. Lead the way."

He saw where Palan's scratches came from as he turned Kelley again in the lane, helping push the scraggly bushes away from the horse with his body to give her more room. As promised, it was not long before Palan called a halt. They hobbled only the lead horse. The others would remain where they were.

All the elves gathered thicker clothing from their packs to cover exposed skin despite the heat. Hacking through the tangled mess would mean walking and striking into those stinging branches. They could be armored for battle and the thorns would find skin. This was going to be unpleasant.

His party carried two blades meant for this purpose—their weapons were better saved for an enemy—and it would only be safe for two of them to work in such close proximity. The path they needed to make was one just wide enough to squeeze the horses through. It would be overgrown within the season, but it would also remain a clear marker of the time and place of their passage for that duration as well. Larron allowed himself a sigh. No good options, but they would persist.

While Palan and Geelomin took the first round, the other three started relieving the horses of as much of their burdens as possible. There was not enough room to set up any sort of camp, but they could brush them down to prevent sores and blisters and allow them some rest after their extreme efforts over the last day and a half.

Annalla had not even stirred when they put her on the horse, but as he slid her down into his arms, she was instantly awake. He froze in place, defenseless with his hands full. There was a moment of tension before he saw recognition set in and she relaxed enough to yawn the remnants of sleep away, naturally resting a hand on his shoulder and the other on his chest.

"Started early?" She asked, looking at the sky and nodding toward the two chopping at the brush as she blinked the last of her drowsiness away, at ease in his arms.

"It was necessary. No, you will not be taking a turn." He said anticipating the offer before she finished taking the breath to speak and doing his best to look stern and commanding. Larron usually did not have to try for commanding, but she seemed to delight in creating conflict with him.

She pursed her lips and looked down before staring back at him. He saw the moment she realized he was still holding her. Annalla froze, her eyes widened, and she moved to be put down all in the space of a breath. His hands followed for balance, but he let her go. He awkwardly stood straight and held his fisted hands at his sides, unsure what to say.

"May I have something to eat?" The question was not what he expected as she took a small step back to stand against Moonshine.

At his nod, Thanon brought over the morning ration she missed earlier. The hunter had been hovering and now had a grin on his face Larron chose to ignore. "Go eat. I will take care of Moonshine this time."

"Are none of you going to sleep?" she asked Thanon. The two of them moved toward where Bealaras sat in a part of the path they left clear.

"As long as we can sleep tonight, the rest is enough for us. The walk was not an exhausting effort for only one night." Thanon's response was not meant as an insult, and Larron was relieved to see she did not interpret it as one and simply nodded at the statement.

"So, can I ask what you all do back home, or is messenger your regular job?"

Thanon raised his hand slightly, always happy to talk. "I work as a hunter."

"What does that entail? Just bringing back food each day?"

"That is the primary responsibility I had, but bringing in game took up the least amount of my time. I sometimes acted as a border scout when ranging further out. The largest amount of time was spent monitoring the animal populations to ensure they maintain healthy levels."

Annalla raised a skeptical eyebrow at him. "Did you go alone?"

"Usually. That is the way it worked, but I did not mind the time away. The Woodland was my companion. It would take me out of the Heartwood for days or weeks at a time, but I never left home."

"I'm surprised by that. You don't seem like someone who would enjoy solitude," she said thoughtfully.

"Most people are surprised. I talk to everyone."

"All the time," Bealaras added flatly, eyeing his companion. "Some relished the silence upon his departure."

"I know you all missed me enormously," he smiled widely at his friend and turned back to her. "I need both; companionship and solitude. I could never be a traveler, though. That is too far away from home for too long. Unlike Commander Larron."

"You travelled much?" she twisted to look over at him.

"I am often away."

"Travelers like our Commander are rare," Thanon added in a somewhat awed tone. "Those are what we call the elves who enjoy visiting the different races and societies in the realm. They are the ones who bring back knowledge of other people and how the world changes around us. Their stories always sound like great adventures."

Larron nodded and spoke as he continued to brush. "Most of the elves are content to remain in our home Woodlands, but I find myself becoming restless if I remain in one place overlong. I have often acted as an ambassador, which enables me to serve my people as I travel. When I am home, I serve in our guard."

"So, leading this little group is pretty standard for you."

Larron tipped his head. "Just so."

"What about you, Bealaras? Wait!" She held out her hand. "Let me make what is sure to be a horribly wrong guess."

Annalla crossed her arms, propping her head up with one hand and leaning forward as she squinted at Bealaras, her scrutinizing gaze inspecting him. Bealaras stared back, seemingly unbothered by the scrutiny, with a small smile on his face.

"I am a painter."

"Gah! You weren't supposed to..." She widened her eyes and her words trailed off, eyebrows raised. "A painter? Really?"

He nodded and smiled at her surprise. "Really. I have traded a number of my works for income, but I am coming to believe I have limited my art too much by not travelling outside the Woodland before now. Our home is beautiful, but there are so many aspects to life I am missing."

"What do you usually paint?"

"People are my primary subjects, most often in scenes of elven life. I have done portraits, but those are usually only commissioned for children. We have only had three born in my lifetime in The Derou."

"Eight now," Larron commented. War always coincided with higher birth rates among the bonded, and five more were born in the last twenty years.

He looked away in thought. "I had forgotten. I am usually not called upon until at least a few decades have passed, and I have not been back to the Heartwood much of late to see them."

"Children are not common then? I suppose that makes sense in an immortal race."

Bealaras shook his head. "More than that. We are

sterile until we find our life-mates."

"Love at first sight?" her tone was full of wry sarcasm.

"No," Larron smiled and laughed at her tone. "Some life-mates know each other for centuries before they are ready to acknowledge the bond, or before the bond is ready for them. I heard one bonded pair refused the bond because of a lingering dispute between them. I will not even pretend to understand what a bonded connection is beyond being deeper in our physical selves than our link to the earth and Woodlands. It alters the pair physically over a period of time to enable conception. Bonded friends have tried to describe the relationship aspect of it to me, but there are things only experience can convey."

"So, it's like a geas that you either accept or have to fight for the rest of your life?"

He shook his head. "The pair who refused it did not have to fight anything, they simply chose not to follow that path for their lives. A bond is simply one path through the forest of our lives, and we can choose to live how we will. However, the bonded relationship is the only path that leads to biological children. Rejecting it is not a choice made lightly."

She still looked uncomfortable with the concept. "Are any of you bonded? Or is that a taboo question?"

Thanon laughed. "Not taboo, but we generally do not ask unless one is interested in becoming lovers with the person they are asking." He laughed again at her rising blush and exaggeratedly wiggled his eyebrows before sending Larron a darting glance when she covered her eyes and theatrically groaned in response to his antics. "Since you are asking, none among us are bonded."

Larron felt his pulse rise a moment as he watched her

roll her eyes before he voiced a thought he previously mentioned to Geelomin. "I wonder why the word of a non-elf life-mate would not have been known across the Woodlands. We celebrate our bonds, and any children they bring."

"Is it not allowed?" she asked cautiously.

"It was never an issue," Thanon said. "There have been inter-racial romances and relationships, but not many. The stories about them are usually tragedies though. Not because we dislike them, but...they all die."

Grabbing some food and joining them on the ground, Larron added to that thought. "Immortality is a mixed blessing. I have formed great friendships with others in my travels, but eventually I move on. When I return, those friends are old or gone, and it is their families and stories of me that remain. Relationships are allowed, but the elves are counseled by their friends on the pain that will follow for both parties involved."

Thanon continued, "As a result, the relationships are rare to start, and there has never been a life bond. At least, until your parents. Obviously."

"Maybe they were not sure a mixed-race child would be welcome?" She shrugged, but her nonchalance was an affectation not fooling any of them.

Larron stopped and held her eye. "I do not, and will not, believe any elf would worry about his or her child being accepted and welcomed." Elves adored children and doted on any brought into their Woodlands by friends, be they elf or not. Elven children were so rare, each one a blessing.

"What if the elf didn't know? Could my father have bonded and left without knowing about me?"

All three of them were emphatically shaking their heads. "Not the way you are thinking," Bealaras answered. "From everything we know, the bond does not mean instant fertility, but a slow progression toward fertility. It varies by elf, but nothing short of six months has been recorded. The process is physiological, not magic. By the time an elf can father children, he will know the bond exists. If your father was the elf side of your parentage, he would have had to either choose to leave his life-mate, and tell no one, or have died before being able to tell his Woodland of you."

Larron tilted his head at a new thought. "You do not know how old you are?"

"I don't feel old, but no. Why would that matter?"

"As no fairy have come to the Woodlands—we would have noticed—your elf parent is likely a traveler like me and they met on one of the journeys. While travelers are rare, being immortal means the younger you are the more it narrows the parental possibilities. I keep my Woodland informed of my travels. They might not hear from me for a year, but I will not wait two years to send word. We keep track of our people, so we would know who may have gone missing during or around a specific period of time. I know of two travelers missing from the Derou in the last century. We can ask at The Palonian as well."

There was a nervous light in her eyes. "But, if I am also immortal, I could be over one hundred years old."

"Or any age, yes."

She took a deep breath and sagged a little. "This is all a lot to think about."

"Would you like to hear more about the Woodlands?" Thanon offered into the silence.

He could see her appreciation for the subject change as she looked at the eager elf and responded. "I assume they are not simply forests your people live in?"

"A *different* forest, and even more than that. We have grazing meadows for the wild and domestic herds. Some of them are fenced off and planted as crop fields and gardens, but we make sure to scatter ours enough not to push out the animals. A couple small wetlands have been cultivated to serve as water retention and filtration that feed both irrigation as well as the lines to our homes. If we wish to impose a change on the land, like expanding or shrinking the area of a wetland artificially, we first look at the records and watch the area for a year to identify potential impacts before proceeding or not."

"How long do you monitor them after a change is implemented?" She seemed genuinely interested in the answer, rather than asking to humor Thanon's enthusiasm.

"A full year at the same level as the preparation year. It then gradually eases over the next decade until the area is back on a standard rotation only. Of course, that is assuming there is no issue. If something starts to go wrong to a level that looks unrecoverable on its own, then we step in to adjust and mitigate the impact. The close monitoring is usually two years after a correction before it begins to ease."

"And your people are okay with changes taking that long?"

Thanon nodded, "It takes patience, allowing events to progress as they will, but patience is very much a part of our nature. You will see that our society is much the same way; each prospers according to their own will and in their own time, but still eventually benefitting the whole. When you have many centuries, it is easier to allow someone to find their place rather than forcing them into something quickly."

"Are your leaders not inundated with complaints about things taking too long or people not contributing and taking food and stuff other people worked for?"

He looked at Larron before responding, receiving a gesture that meant he was free to answer as he willed.

"Everyone is given what they need, and we trade things we want or not. There are so few new people at any time, that it is easy enough to work out disputes without any leadership authority as you might recognize it.

"We have a king, succession usually based on birth, but there have been exceptions. However, our king lives much as the rest of us. Everyone does their part to work the land, and provide food and shelter. The times our king is above us are when a decision will have a larger impact on more lives. Trade agreements, interaction with other leaders, larger armed conflicts. Thinking about it in comparison with what I know of the other races, we lead simple lives and have the time to dedicate to each problem as it arises. No crime of our own and a love of life. That is why our Balance takes such pleasure in death and destruction. Order and chaos."

"Balance?" She asked, her forehead furrowing. "I'm afraid you've lost me again."

"Yes, nature loves to maintain balance."

Annalla raised her eyebrow and tilted her head. Larron could feel the sarcasm oozing off her even before she started to respond. "Ooo-kaaay."

"It might help to discuss a fundamental understanding of Elaria," offered Larron, who had these conversations with humans often enough and was suppressing a chuckle at Thanon's attempt. "The balance Thanon refers to is the balance between good and evil and other opposing aspects of nature. This balance is most apparent here in Elaria."

Larron looked away for the right place to begin. "Different realms are governed by different...we will call them 'concepts' or 'powers.' This is the realm of Elaria, an essential realm. Here, balance is maintained by the seven essential elements and counter-balance creation. Races in Elaria emerge with a natural inclination toward good or evil.

When one emerges, so does another with the opposite inclination.

"Gilar are the Balance for the elves, and both of our races are said to have emerged at the same time. None of the originals now remain, and the records are only stories and lost to time. By nature—I am simplifying heavily here—we are good, and they are evil, as demonstrated through our influence on each other and the rest of the world by our actions.

"That does not mean we are not corruptible nor that they might not be able to oppose their worst desires, but it is more difficult for one of our two races to switch sides. There also seem to be different degrees or methods of good and evil, as not all good societies emerging in Elaria have been as free of internal conflict as the elves, which could also be a result of many other factors.

"Not all the evil races crave destruction without purpose as much as the Gilar either. It is nowhere near as simple as I am describing it, and there continue to be philosophical debates on the definitions of good and evil throughout the societies dwelling hereon. I will not claim every decision by an elf is going to be good rather than evil, as life and the concept of morality is infinitely complicated and personal, but the basic concept is sound as applied in general to natural balance."

She nodded as he spoke. "I think I follow you. The vampires were the balance to the fairy."

"They were, or are, yes." He could not read her thoughts from the question or behavior. There were likely too many to process, so he was simply seeing her 'thinking' face.

"The gilar are lizard-like people, aren't they?" Annalla asked.

"Their appearance is reptilian," he confirmed. "You

remember seeing them?"

She shook her head and frowned. "No. Not any specific memory, but when you named them, I knew what they looked like. I also know how to fight them." The last was said with a fierce look, filled with an anger she probably did not recognize internally. That much anger was from personal experience.

He glanced over at the two cutting through the brush before meeting her eyes again. "That knowledge will likely be necessary before we reach our destination... Take some rest. I am going to relieve Geelomin. Thanon, you will take over for Palan in another half turn."

***

Annalla shifted away as they traded out and drifted off for a short nap, thinking about everything she had learned. None of the elves seemed to think her parents would have been ashamed of her, at least the elf parent. Their relatively easy acceptance of her heritage made it easier to believe, but it also made her forgotten life more of a mystery and more frustrating.

It makes no sense! she thought. But then, it did make sense. They were either ashamed or dead. The remaining questions were around what happened during her childhood. Who raised her and where? Gilar played some part, she knew that from the image that flashed in her mind when Larron mentioned them.

Rustling of bags woke her up sometime later, and by the position of the sun, there were only a couple of hours until they needed to make camp. Only three elves stood around her. If they were packing up, they must be close to breaking through to the other side. Otherwise, they would be preparing to roll out their bedding to sleep here. It would be a matter of coaxing the horses onto the small path they created to get them into open forest.

After putting back on the borrowed boots, she rose without a word and started helping load the horse's packs. The additional padding continued to make her feet boil in the hot weather, so she had taken to riding without them. Unfortunately, they would be walking for this part, and their path was carpeted with thorns.

"How are the boots working?" Palan asked with concern at her side.

These elves welcomed her. She would make that be enough. "Stiflingly warm with the extra cloth, but I thank you for the use of them."

"I would say we should try to find shoes more suited to you at the first village, but Larron believes the few settlements between The Derou and The Palonian are likely abandoned by now."

"Because of the trakins, or the larger conflict?"

"I imagine both, especially in this region. There are not many large settlements in the area, and they would want the safety of numbers. Are you ready to try this?" He asked as he handed her a jacket of sorts. It was more of a thicker shirt than a jacket, but she could wear it over the thinner shirt she already put on after the last bandage changes for her back.

She scrunched her nose and asked, "I'm taking all of your spare clothes, aren't I?"

Palan laughed and looked over his shoulder before speaking in a conspiratorial whisper. "No, you needed something larger this time, so we grabbed one of Geelomin's shirts."

Annalla shook her head. "Bealaras I'm not sure about,

but I swear you and Thanon are trying to get me killed."

The grin he gave her could only be described as mischievous. "Geelomin likes you, if only because we bother you now instead of him."

"This is not considered bothering him?" Annalla asked dryly, not expecting an answer as she settled the thick and hot cloth over her shoulders. Steeling herself, she looked at him again and took a deep breath. "Let's get the horses through."

There was some initial protesting, but Palan talked and coaxed his horse slowly forward. The training and breeding of the animals held true, and the rest followed. Blankets extended to cover as much of their flanks as possible, but even with that precaution the horses would still become plenty scratched. Even Annalla's sides were tugged at by the branches the elves could not trim back without shears or a lot more time.

Her exposed skin, less with the jacket—Geelomin had seen, but made no comment yet—was scratched and nicked despite her best efforts to avoid the thorns. It must have been the same for the others, but they ignored the sting to focus on the animals. All of them returned from their turns at chopping through the nettles bleeding in several places, but no one gave any indication of the serious irritation they must have been experiencing. It was a calm she hoped to emulate.

As soon as they were in the clear, relatively speaking, they mounted up and set out east. Progress was still slow. They might not have to chop their way through nettles, but there was no clear path to follow through the dense underbrush.

If they were fortunate, they would run across an old game trail or two to speed their way, but there was no guarantee based on the general lack of game in the area.

Annalla was glad for the resupply of water earlier. Her escort might have known where the path crossed streams, but she personally knew how scarce water was in the forest right now.

"This looks to be a suitable place to camp for the night. Palan, Thanon, we will need the salve," came Larron's orders.

The clearing was large enough to resume their nightly fire. Trees were packed densely around them, even the brush was dense, but that small clearing felt like an open plain after seeing nothing but thorns bracketing them.

Two of the elves pulled out small canisters of a greenish-yellow paste. They each took tiny amounts and began a detailed inspection of the animals' hides, dabbing a bit on each scratch. Only when all the horses were taken care of did they do the same to themselves, and each other for the places they could not easily see or reach. That is when Annalla finally breathed a true sigh of relief. The sickly colored goo took the irritation down enormously. It felt cool and clean and even a bit tingly, and she could feel herself melting into the comfort.

"That stuff is magic, but I'm afraid to ask what it is."

Palan returned from packing the canister away again. "This is from the sap of a tree growing in The Derou. It must be refined for this level of efficacy, but can sooth most rashes or skin irritations even when used in its natural form."

"Including insect bites?" She wondered if they used it on her wings where the insects got at the joints, but those were probably worse off for other reasons.

"I believe most, but I cannot say for certain."

She was the one to pass out food this time, having completed taking care of Moonshine first tonight.

"Will it heal the scratches too?"

Larron answered her. "Not directly. The sap helps prevent infection, but it is not a healing agent on its own." That probably explained why she was chewing on the bitter leaves he kept giving her instead of using this stuff.

"I can't believe I'm tired again already."

"The medicine will contribute to that. It is a good sign, I think. You are finally allowing your body the time to heal properly and for the medicine to finish with the infection," Larron said, with a look she thought of as "grumpy."

She sighed before yawning. "Let's hope it's only a short time."

***

Morning dawned, and she knew the fever was gone. It was like a painful fog lifted from inside her head and she could think clearly.

How did I not notice before? She thought in wonder.

Her energy was up, and she smiled and felt like she could fight her way through a whole, big pack of trakins. Then she sat up and was abruptly reminded there were still injuries healing all over her body as muscles and bones protested the abrupt movement. Annalla had never felt more out of shape. She might be healing but remained frustratingly weak.

Walking and riding was good, but she was inspired to test her abilities further. Her companions gave her more clothing as they continued, not all from Palan as she first thought, so she changed into a lighter set and padded barefoot to a small clear area.

Starting from a neutral stance, Annalla let her mind form a simple routine designed to stretch and strengthen without over stressing any muscles or joints. Pushing her abilities could wait for another day. She opened her eyes and started to move, slow, but steady through each position, flowing through each stance. No flips and kicks, she needed to build back up strength and muscle control before she could push for more.

"Do you see it?" She heard Geelomin quietly ask someone, who only grunted in response. Her focus remained on the routine and her body moving through it.

"See what?" Thanon asked.

Larron must have been the grunter. "The forms you see have the basic structure of an elven weapons dance. She has had basic training in our fighting styles."

"More than that," Geelomin emphasized. "I think she can Dance. This is perfectly weighted to someone at her level of recovery. I would have assigned this routine in training, but I would have had to walk most trainees, even many soldiers, through it. She has more than *basic* training. She has skill with a blade and is likely a master."

"You are both masters," his voice conveyed a shrug.

"No, Thanon. Blademaster is a teaching title given to me in the guard, not indicative of a level of skill I possess. Larron is the only master among us."

Silence reigned for a beat, and she knew they continued to watch her. She was not shaky yet, but her muscles were beginning to strain, so it was good she neared the end of her planned routine.

"Good. We need fighters," Thanon stated, and she heard him turn away. "I will get the food out."

Another grunt. "Let us start packing as well."

The routine ended back in a neutral position, and she stretched out to cool down. It had not been strenuous enough for her to sweat much, but she would need to start pushing it if she continued to heal this well so she would build muscle tone and agility.

"You are feeling better." Thanon reached across, handing her some food as he stood on the other side of the horse while she changed into her riding clothes.

"Starting to, anyway. My back still hurts, and I know I need to stay careful of my ribs. I'm not back yet, but I can see a way now." She smiled at him, then frowned a bit. "Why do you need fighters?"

He tilted his head in confusion for a moment before her lost memory clicked for him. "Ah, right, you do not know. We are at war. We have been for decades now, and we are losing."

Thanon's words were so matter of fact, that she nearly overlooked their import and weight. "The Derou are at war?"

This was the most subdued she had seen Thanon, as he shook his head, his eyes downcast. "No, the *world* is at war. The good and evil Larron talked about, it is never at peace in Elaria, the binary nature drives conflict. This time, though, they are not simply poking at us and lashing out violently for fun. Something stirs the dark not only to attack, but to end us."

"And they haven't had that goal before? You would think that the goal of evil would always be to end good. Didn't the vampires drive out the fairy for that reason?"

He winced, but she was not worried about any insensitive comment. "I do not know that I would phrase it in that manner. Good and evil are not driving forces. They are opposing sides of a larger balance. The gilar enjoy killing us too much to want to see us eliminated, if that makes sense.

"They love chaos, destruction, and death. It is probably some sick game to them. The vampires took their own game too far, and the fairy paid for that. We probably should have acted then and taken the vampires more seriously. The races have never acted together in the past, though, on either side. Conflicts were contained, racially and regionally. It does not forgive the inaction of the elves. The irimoten may have been too young a race at the time, but we should have known help was needed."

She saw the problems that would have kept them out of the fight. Regional conflicts could be over before allies arrived or even received word of a problem.

"The current war is not contained." It was not said as a question, and he slowly shook his head confirming her guess and leaned folded arms on Moonshine's back.

"They have never cooperated, trusting each other and working together is not in their natures, even within each race. Somehow, Kahnlair has all of them working in his name. Gilar. Windani. Vampire. His first assaults included all three fighting together almost seamlessly with each other as well as with humans and magai. Large settlements in the western half of the continent were completely eliminated before any resistance could be raised, many before we even knew a resistance was necessary."

Annalla felt like she should know more of the races to which he was referencing, but for the moment she would think of them as one group of 'other races' and ask later. "And you think I can help?"

"I am not asking you to save us all by yourself, Annalla," he said seriously before smiling at her. "Everyone can help, and we can use all the help we can find. Eat up, or you will be eating in the saddle again."

He grinned bigger and winked at her before walking away, leaving her wondering about his sanity. It was good he was not expecting her to save anyone. She needed their help simply to save herself.

CHAPTER SEVEN

Nearly two weeks later they were still trudging through the dark forest. According to Palan, it wouldn't be much longer, but the heat had not let up in all this time. Instead of simply shading them from the sun, the dense canopy trapped the heat of the day and turned the air into a sauna. Even the perfectly coiffed elves were beginning to look a little baked, sweating in the heat of the day.

As each day wore on, her hair and clothing stuck to her damp skin, made worse by the humidity that never eased. Each morning she woke with salt and dirt stuck to her skin, and the borrowed clothing she wore was crunchy with salt lines. She would have given or done almost anything for a cool soak in a deep, clean pool of water. There was at least the comfort of having enough to drink, if not enough to bathe, with their store of water replenished fully at every tiny stream.

Time, food, water, and rest allowed her to heal. Some of the bruises might be yellow tinged, but the pain was gone. Where small cuts had been, only reddened skin remained, and the larger lacerations were well scabbed over—her leg itched like crazy—and on their way to becoming scars. Only her ribs still ached if she tried to do too much and push too hard. They were tender, and she had to be careful not to break them before they completely healed. Her energy was back up, and even with the heat she kept up without needing rest every few hours.

"Annalla, you would be such a joy to paint in motion." Bealaras said as she sat down far enough from the fire the heat could not be felt. Having just finished her nightly exercise, she was plenty warm. Both morning and evening she went through different routines now. Geelomin identified most of them as variations on elven weapons 'dances,' and she was increasing the complexity and difficulty a little each time.

"I am starting to doubt your eye. We are all covered in dirt and sweat. No one here is worth painting at the moment. If you tried, people would likely be able to smell us through the canvas."

"Ah, you honor me. If I could but be so talented..." He trailed off.

She shook her head, smiling. "Tell me Bealaras, I can see it with the hunter and tracker, but how does a painter become a soldier?"

"Everyone contributes what they can in times of war. Painters often notice details others might overlook." He turned up his hands. "It happens I have been able to turn that talent into an asset as a scout. I will admit I would prefer not to fight, but I will not deny my people my skills when there is need."

"That's it? You simply joined the army without hesitation?"

He sobered and leaned forward with his elbows on his legs.

"The Derou is the closest Woodland to the desert in

which Kahnlair keeps his main stronghold. While most of his attention has been focused to the south and the Kingdom of Ceru, where the settlements were more spread out, The Derou has had no support from our allies against attack."

Bealaras pursed his lips before continuing, "To say we have been decimated would be grossly underestimating the losses we have suffered. We sent a contingent to the allied forces in the south early in the war, but our home was besieged shortly after. Nearly a third of our number have been captured or killed."

He looked her in the eye, and she saw the horror and pain he felt bared to her. "Not a third of our soldiers, but a third of our total population. Friends and family. Gone. I cannot afford *not* to fight with the rest of my people."

She reached over and squeezed his hand, knowing the gesture insufficient. "I'm sorry, my friend, for all you have lost."

Returning the squeeze, he nodded and stared into the fire, still holding her hand.

"What has you two so somber over here?" Palan asked as he sat across from them.

"The heat," she stated simply when Bealaras made no indication he wanted to talk more about that subject. "So, is it only proficiency that determines what you do as a profession?"

Bealaras smoothly ran with her shift from their difficult conversation and pointed to his companion. "Not normally. Take Palan here as an example, and you see our professions are our own choice."

Annalla dramatically threw up her hands and rolled her eyes. "You know, you don't have to make cryptic statements and wait for me to pull information from you piece by painful piece." They were not as good at being *mysterious* as they thought. "But I will bite your hook again and ask the logical question. Why, oh clever elf, is Palan an example of this?"

Palan smiled at her sarcasm and raised his head proudly, fists on his hips even, as he remained seated. "I am what most elves refer to as a 'flitter.' I shift from one occupation to the next as the whim takes me. Usually, I try my hand at something new every few decades or so."

Most of that sounded like he was reciting a standard definition. The last bit, though, was more serious, so she guessed that piece was more about him specifically. It did not surprise her. From everything she had seen, he was interested in everything and nothing, and was friends with everyone, but few people knew him well. Thanon and Bealaras were probably becoming two of his closest friends.

One eyebrow raised in curiosity, she asked, "How long did you work with the horses?"

"Mmm," tilting his head back and forth, he thought about it. "Only about fifty years."

"Only..." she blinked her eyes at the oxymoronic statement.

That earned her another big smile, and he laughed before adding, "Most elves do not look at or even consider learning a new profession for centuries. Flitters are like travelers. We both go against a norm of elven society."

So did my parents. Maybe that is why I fit with this group, she thought. "Are they negative terms, then, flitter and traveler?"

"I suppose one could take offense. The tone it is said in is often playful, and one could mistake it for mocking, but I do not believe that is the intent. I am who I am. Why would I take offense to the truth?" Annalla was not so sure of herself, but Palan seemed to take it well when Bealaras alluded to what might be considered a peccadillo.

Annalla was finding her nature seemed to be less forgiving. "I suppose it helps when you have the patience that comes with immortality to reason it out and view it in such a way. But some people still might mean it negatively."

"I like to think that if you own a term, 'mixed-race' as a completely-unrelated-to-anything-here example, no one can turn it negative unless you allow them to take it from you."

While she only gave him an unamused look, Bealaras laughed and threw a pinecone at him, hitting him in the chest before it bounced harmlessly to the ground. "Palan, maybe subtlety should be your next skill to master."

He grinned at his friend as he booted it away, but he turned back to her. "Annalla, like our fearless leaders, you worry too much. Do not doubt your own level of patience. Even Geelomin has admitted you must have it in stores to learn all those exercises you practice. You must know by now he is not easily impressed...by anything...at all...ever."

She had to chuckle at his grumbling. "Thank you. I've been working on it."

"Yes, your efforts at being less irritating have been noted." She heard Larron approaching from behind her and Bealaras even before he spoke.

"I figured if you were willing to make the effort, I could at least try." She smiled up at him sweetly, fluttered her eyelashes, and clasped her hands before her.

He schooled his features well enough but could not keep the laugh from his eyes before he scanned his elves. "Thanon is on watch again. I suggest everyone take their rest."

"Yes, Commander." They set out their blankets to lie on. It was too warm to need them for cover, but the padding was nice.

"Annalla, what do you think you would choose to do if you were in our Woodland?" Palan asked as they settled down.

She did not have to think about that for long. "I would be a good fighter."

"I do not doubt you have the skill, but I also cannot say that I could see you as a soldier taking orders in the guard."

Ignoring Larron's barked laugh, she responded, "Maybe I would travel and guard caravans of goods instead. I'm sure I could find some use for my training."

"Definitely. If you are as good as they believe, you would have no trouble there." She heard the humor in his voice. "Good night, Annalla."

"Good night, Palan."

***

Larron woke to the touch of a hand on his shoulder and instinctively reached for his weapons. It was still dark. He looked up to see Annalla staring into the woods to the south.

"Trakins," she said without being asked, sensing he was awake now and alert.

"Thanon?" *Was it still first watch?*

"He should hear them soon."

"Defensive positions," he called out more loudly. Three other bodies sat up and scrambled for their own weapons. "Thanon, to the south. Let us know when they are near."

He moved over to their piled gear. "How many?"

"I'm as bad with determining numbers as I am at distances. More than six, less than twenty. If I had to guess, I would say closer to the middle."

"With that many they will try to surround us, watch your backs." He grabbed a machete from the supplies and handed it to Annalla.

There were no questions. He was pleased to see her calmly take a position within their defensive circle around the horses. She accepted the crude weapon and held it as though she was no stranger to the feel of a blade in her hands. It should not have surprised him with Geelomin's assessment of her skills.

No blade would be out of place in the hands of a master. Even had he not believed her story about taking on six trakins by herself, he had been on the receiving end of an attack when she took him hostage. Skill, talent, it was more than training. She was a natural fighter. Training would have simply amplified such abilities.

"Sixteen," Thanon called down before his bow sang. He would join them in a moment to provide cover with Palan, but the forest was more closed off here. "Fourteen. They are circling."

No sooner had the words left his mouth and they were under attack. Larron could not see what was happening behind him and did not dare try to look, nor was it necessary. His people were capable, all of them, and he trusted them to watch his back. Instead, he focused his attention on the thing coming toward him.

They were one of the ugliest species he had seen, and one of the most dangerous. Their fore and hind legs were like metal, and Larron could only deflect the first attack before facing another. Trakins worked as a pack by instinct, so they fought as a unit and were less likely to get in each other's way as a group of fighters might when merging different units.

Block. Block. Stab, one injured.

Dodge. Block. Slice, one down.

Each moment was composed of legs and teeth and how to meet or avoid them.

"Bealaras!" Annalla shouted from his left. "Larron, shift left to cover. I need to help him."

"Go!"

He would need to cover more ground, but there were fewer of the creatures by this point. At a break in the fighting, he stole a look. Bealaras was on the ground, bleeding high on his back and at his right ankle, with Annalla standing guard before him. It looked as though a trakin had started to drag him away.

She traded the machete for Bealaras's long knives and was defending against four trakins with relative ease. The group changed their strategy. The weakest prey was identified, and they shifted to focus on escaping with it, leaving the others for a later attack. That might have been a wise tactic against another animal herd or pack, but Larron had options.

"Thanon, concentrate fire on Bealaras's position."

Geelomin and Palan shifted slightly as Thanon peeled off to the other side and quickly started firing around Annalla. She did not even flinch as the first arrow struck home, crossing in front of her eyes. As that creature fell, she took the head of another and removed the leg of a third.

He missed what happened next to face a trakin attacking from his right. It made a springing attack, but he saw the movement at the edge of his vision. The leap brought it within reach quickly with zero ability to maneuver. Momentum brought it down on his raised sword, impaling the creature's heart.

Larron scanned the woods around him for more, but even the sounds of the attack died away. Only the nervous breathing and shuffling of horses could be heard.

"Enemy status?" Larron called out.

"Three," from Geelomin.

"Two," counted Palan.

"Six plus the first two taken down," said Thanon.

"Three more over here, stand down." They dealt with all sixteen.

"How is Bealaras?" Larron asked as he grabbed the meds pack and crossed to him. Geelomin took his sword from him and would clean it as Larron worked on Bealaras's injuries.

Annalla had already removed or moved clothing to better expose the injuries. "Flesh wounds. He'll recover."

His initial assessment tied with hers. The wound in Bealaras's back was a puncture stopped at the shoulder blade, the bone protecting him. His ankle was messier; torn in the attempt to drag him away, but it was not beyond repair. Were it not for the sedative effect of the trakin wound, he would have still been up and fighting with them despite the injuries. Though it would be best for his recovery to have him avoid walking for a while.

"This was different from the last time I fought them. Shorter, simpler," Annalla said offhand, more to herself and sounding a little confused.

"You were not alone, exhausted with fever and malnutrition, in pain, or unarmed this time. Most other people would have died in your first conflict with the trakins. The odds were in our favor here."

They would have prevailed in this situation without her, as they had before, but their victory was further assured with six defenders.

"And I have been training again. I'm stronger now. What do you need me to do here?" she asked at the same time Geelomin approached. Maybe she could have been a good soldier taking orders after all.

"Thanon and Palan are scouting for a new campsite. I will begin packing," Geelomin turned to her. "Good work tonight."

A tiny widening of her eyes was the only betrayal of surprise she gave at the compliment. Larron restrained his amusement as diligently and nodded at Geelomin's back. "Help him. The horses will not rest if we remain here."

He continued to work on cleaning and wrapping Bealaras's ankle while his unit made ready to depart. The two scouts returned shortly with the location of a small clearing nearby they could huddle down in for the rest of the night. They would leave the horses packed with most of the gear. A few extra hours would not harm them.

"Help me with Bealaras," Larron asked Geelomin as he finished. The two worked to gently pile Bealaras on top of his horse.

"We are becoming experts at this." The sardonic comment was surprising from the stoic soldier, and he paused in his work to look over at him. Geelomin glanced over when Larron paused and pursed his lips against a smile as he continued working.

"I do believe you have been spending too much time with Annalla. She is clearly a negative influence on all of you."

"Hmm. We both know you did not select this unit for its discipline."

Larron scanned over the people around him. No serious recent romantic relationships, no close siblings other than his own, so no distractions for them or those left behind. Their skills were not in question, and Palan had been to the Palonian before, but of all with similar qualifications, these were the four volunteers he selected.

"I expected you to be disciplined enough for all of us." He said, rather than acknowledging the implication of an expected suicide mission.

"Heh," he chuckled. "Thanon and Palan are both legends in their own ways for their antics. Those stricter than I have fallen to them."

Larron grunted and shook his head with a smile on his face. "Are we ready?"

"The last of the items are being packed now. I will put out the fire and follow if you are ready to leave, Commander."

Giving the go ahead for that, he spoke to his group of disciplined troublemakers. "Let us move out."

It was only about ten minutes later they were grabbing their blankets and squeezing into the tiny area clear of trees and bushes for the last hours of sleep.

"I can take this watch," Annalla said as Geelomin caught up to them. "Without room for a fire, it might help to have the earlier warning I can give."

Larron watched his Lieutenant purse his lips, then shrug in a non-committal response that was as good as a recommendation from him. "Very well. Thank you."

She grabbed a bow and quiver Thanon held out to her as he settled down shoulder to shoulder with Bealaras and Geelomin. No one even paused to question whether she knew how to shoot.

***

The fight had been easy. Only one came at her when the attack started, and it quickly lost its head. The second crept forward moments before there was a flash of movement to

her left, and Bealaras was toppled by the trakin literally
jumping him before he could raise his knives against it.

By the time she dispatched her own opponent, he was
being dragged off and she had to expand their circle. Before
the creatures focused on the two of them, she dropped the
cumbersome blade and picked up Bealaras's long knives.
Light and elegant, these were a master painting in
comparison to the crude, cave drawing substitute Larron gave
her.

She was quickly surrounded, but the cold focus
remained as she blocked every attack, spinning and circling
around her fallen companion. Without remorse, she took
every opportunity to deliver injury or death with those
elegant knives. Part of her mind registered when Thanon was
ordered to break off and help them, and she heard the
bowstring release an instant before the arrow thunked into
the body near her head.

It was irrelevant before it fell back to the ground;
dead, no longer a threat. With an archer to aid her, she was
no longer held to looking for opportunities to strike but was
instead able to create them for herself and for Thanon. When
the last one fell, she stood poised for another attack until
Larron called for them to stand down.

Her familiarity with fighting unnerved her. The
exercises she knew were enough to tell her she had training,
but even the best trained could freeze in actual combat. For
the first time she could remember, she felt completely at
home, completely comfortable with a situation.

If her memory returned, would she like the person she
was before? Would she be able to reconcile who she was
with who she thought she was becoming? At least without
her memory, she was able to help people. She was forming
friendships, but they might be at risk from the real her,

despite her heritage being on the good side of the balance they talked about.

"You are doing it again."

"What?" Annalla shook herself out of her reverie and looked up from Moonshine's packs.

"Worrying about something over which you have no control," Bealaras answered. "I might not be alive were it not for your actions. We underestimated you at first, and you could have killed Larron. You could have sacrificed me to maintain the defensive perimeter, but you took the more challenging path to save my life. The person you are worried you might be would not have worried about collateral damage."

"Maybe I just think my odds are better with five of you around instead of four," she said with a forced smirk, denying her thoughts had been anywhere near that direction.

"Naturally," he smiled and turned to go, but turned back to her, suddenly more serious. "You have issues with abandonment."

Annalla blinked and slowly turned her head to him. He was not joking now. "Excuse you?"

His smile was sympathetic and unafraid of her glare. "Do not be insulted by the truth. I am correct in this. Though we might not know from where it originates, it drives you to question yourself."

She did not like the way this conversation turned. With crossed arms and raised eyebrows, she responded, "And what is it you think I have issues with specifically?"

"Your parents would be one example, and being dropped in the middle of nowhere to die is another."

"I have no idea what actually happened with either of those situations." Her voice rose in pitch, exasperated. How could she have issues with something she did not even remember? *I should make that point, that is a good one,* she thought, but he was already responding.

"Which is part of the problem, Annalla," he said, giving no ground, and running on before she could speak again. "You are still worried we will abandon you, and not knowing why all of this happened to you makes you wonder if we will find a reason we should."

"Why would I worry about something I can't even remember?"

"You can imagine," he seemed unimpressed with her argument.

"So now you're saying I'm imagining things?"

Bealaras sighed at that. "Now you are being intentionally obtuse. No, you are not imagining things, but you can think of any number of horrible reasons someone would leave you. Then you take those reasons and link them, no matter how tenuous, to something real about yourself." He paused.

"Oh, don't stop now. Everyone is loving the insight into my mind here." *Did they all know? Did they all see?* Her panicked mind raced. She knew her face was red, and her heart was racing…and that her tone was unfair.

"No one else can hear me unless you draw them over with theatrics. Their ears are not so keen. There is no need to be defensive either. This is an understandable reaction to what you face, but it is also an overreaction. I am trying to tell you that unless you outright betray us, not one of us will abandon you, so stop punishing yourself." She could not look at him directly, but she heard the pain in a voice no longer calm when he continued. "It hurts me…us…to see you this way."

They might not be able to hear the words, but she knew curious ears were turning their way. The argument had not gone unnoticed. Embarrassment flared again, and she wanted to say something to hurt him for doing this to her. Annalla turned to look at him to do just that, and found him braced for it, ready to take whatever she needed to give.

Bealaras was the most sensitive of the group, often the ear Thanon and Palan went to when they needed a serious talk. She did not doubt his words, and while she might not like his analysis, it came from his heart. A heart she was about to hit while those soulful eyes looked at her.

The fight went out of her, and she let out a deep breath. "I'm not happy with you at the moment."

"That is fair," he smiled tentatively and mounted up. His leg was still healing after only a couple of days, but the injuries were not as bad as they originally looked. "I will take your anger over more brooding. Staring moodily into the distance does not suit you, my friend."

As he rode off, she wanted to stick her tongue out at him, but decided it would not benefit her to follow through on the childish impulse. She saw Thanon and Geelomin both riding away with Bealaras, the former literally shooing Larron—his Commander—in her direction.

Cowards. The thought cheered her a bit. Larron made it over, stood next to her, and patted Moonshine.

"The breeze is a welcome change."

She blinked. It was not another lecture as she expected to hear, and she could not stop herself from looking at him sideways. Seeing the look, he shrugged.

"Your quarrel is none of our concern. Geelomin does not care. He simply did not want to be the one pushed over here in my place. Thanon wants to know, if only so he and Palan can gossip tonight. You should talk to me about something, though, so I can pretend to know something he does not and keep it from both of them."

She turned to face him with her back to the others. "This does not seem very 'leaderly.'"

He ducked his head closer to hers to hide his smile even as the move would have him looking sympathetic to their observers.

"It is absolutely leader-ly, especially for this lot. Thanon is far too nosey for his own good, and Bealaras will know exactly what I am doing... You need to speak more if you are supposed to be confiding in me."

He was inviting her to play with him...with them. The realization struck her after a moment as the smile continued to dance in his eyes. Larron was a good leader and knew his people, so he probably knew what the argument was about. Instead of being worried, he was joking with her. She was completely out of her element but searched around for something to talk about.

"Um... Are we expecting to cross a river?" *Ugh, boring.* Something in her scolded.

Larron did not seem to notice her internal complaint. "From where the original path exited the forest, the river would have been less than a league distant. Do you hear it?"

"Maybe, but that does not sound correct. I'm not even sure it is water yet because the noise is still so faint, and I don't think I could hear it that far away."

"We suspected we were too far north for the crossing. Further north it is rough water and closer to the forest."

"That would make more sense. I will let you know if I get a clearer picture..." she trailed off and looked around. "Am I supposed to be angry with you or happy now?"

His laughter invited her to join, and he held his arms open. "I believe you are supposed to be so grateful for my sympathetic ear you cannot help but offer to hug me." His tone was not even close to serious now.

"Bealaras probably deserves a hug more than you."
She poked him in the stomach, wondering if that would bring
the "Commander" side back.

His arms dropped before he held one to his chest
dramatically. "You wound me."

With another laugh he walked backward toward his
horse before spinning to mount up. Annalla gave off an
exasperated sigh and shook her head, feeling very confused
but lighter than she had been, before she too mounted and left
the small clearing.

***

Full dark, and the moon was not set to rise until nearly
morning.

Kahnlair was another shadow in his dark cloak
moving between the rocks. This was one of the places in the
desert where stone projected from the earth and was not yet
worn away by the frequent sandstorms. Some of these places
hosted pinnacles of rock stretching toward the sky. Some
were nothing more than a collection of stepping stones you
could not rely on to remain uncovered. Most fell somewhere
between the two extremes, as the one he now walked within.
Here, wide slabs of stone reached the height of two men.
They were large and relatively flat, lying close together.
Crevasses between them were, at best, wide enough for his
shoulders without having to turn sideways.

It was dangerous to travel these passageways, as they
were the preferred nesting grounds for sand vipers. Those
born in the desert knew to stay far away from the
labyrinthine crevasses. Those who ventured within died a
quick, painful, death at the fangs of the snakes. He combined
this natural protection with spells of his own, surrounding

this specific area within the stones. They were more than enough to keep any of the foolishly curious from venturing so far from his main city. If the snakes did not prove to be an additional precaution, he would have destroyed them simply to remove the annoyance.

The very thought of doing so brought a glint to his eye. Turning a predator into prey was one of his favorite hobbies, and the only reason he occasionally traveled with his army into battle. People were always afraid of death on some level, but that was rarely the fear driving them.

That is especially true with the strong ones, he thought to himself.

They willingly give their lives for something, even if only to show him they do not fear him. There is always something. Even if they do not know what it is themselves, there is always something to make a person's skin crawl. Something to make their pulse quicken until the sound of their heart is practically audible across a room. Something to make the sweet stench of fear and self-loathing rise from them. That is when it is time, when they become his. In that moment, when someone so strong finally breaks for him, is a feeling of pure ecstasy.

Nearly a month passed since he had last taken pleasure in breaking one of his opposition. His followers could satisfy his needs for a time, but they were either too accepting or too weak. It was most often a combination of failings in those still within his desert city. The strongest were keeping the humans and elves busy elsewhere, playing with their hope and desperation on his behalf.

Sending for a prisoner was an option, but they were usually weakened or broken by their captivity. He would probably need to rejoin his forces to find someone worthy of his efforts. Although, there was a rumor of an elven king recently taken captive and held in one of his camps. The sense of duty taught to them and impressed upon them over the centuries would likely keep one going for a long time. Perhaps meeting the front lines would not be necessary after all, so long as this king was not fed to the gilar before he could be identified. It would have to be a decision made later. Kahnlair wrenched his focus to the matter at hand. He reached the entrance and turned his full attention to the stone wall at his side.

Where there had been only stone, an opening appeared in the wall of one stone block. It was as narrow as the crevasse between the stone slabs, and low enough his tall frame had to stoop to enter, but after about a hundred paces, the tunnel opened and became high enough to stand upright. At this same point, the floor began to slope down. There were no diverging passages. One path, always leading downward and deeper into complete darkness. He would create no light in this place. It would serve no purpose.

He had attempted to create a globe light during his first endeavor into the tunnel, but the walls absorbed every ray. The globe itself could be seen, but nothing else was illuminated. The same held true for more mundane sources of light in every following experiment. On he walked, through the field of black, knowing the way by feel and feeling, until the walls disappeared. His skin prickled in awareness of the immense drop to either side and the massive cavern before him.

In the distance, the blackness became distorted by a single point of dark blue, his destination. Several times along the way the path made sudden turns, but some deeper feeling led him through without allowing him to falter. Finally, the descent leveled out. His feet touched softer earth, and he was standing in front of a circular pool.

Without hesitation, he removed his clothing, folding them neatly and setting them on the ground. The dark blue light hovering over the center of the pool called to him. It always called to him. It was a flame, but darker than any blue from a natural fire. Nearly indistinguishable from black, only after so long in darkness could one identify it as light at all.

With his clothing removed, Kahnlair stepped into the pool, and the blue light shimmered on the ripples created by his entrance. It was a liquid with the thick consistency of blood, and it looked as black as ink in the dark light. As he moved slowly forward, the liquid deepened to his waist, his chest, and just as he reached the pool's center, it caressed his lips.

This close, he could see from what the hovering flame originated. It was small, no longer than his hand was wide, and in the shape of a flat, elongated diamond. The piece itself held no significance in its design or construction. What continued to keep him enthralled and returning to this place was the inscription, and what its presence provided him. There, staring back at him, was the symbol for the Goddess Mephoria.

Since her imprisonment, this symbol was thought to have ceased to exist and ceased to be possible. No one could remember it, write it in any form, or speak it. Even staring at it now, he was incapable of saying the word aloud, and when he left, he would forget it completely.

He always knew what was held here, but only staring at this piece could he think the true name, only here would his mind form the symbol. That, and his feeling of invincibility here and simply *knowing* it to be the truth, were enough to convince him this belonged to her, was part of her.

It was his destiny to have found this cavern, and he would continue to patiently finish her work in the world. His enemies would fall only when he was finished with them. He would become a god worthy to be her partner, and his name would raise greater fear than hers ever had. Standing in the thick pool beneath the symbol of the Goddess, he whispered a prayer.

Slowly, he tore his eyes away and made his way back through the water toward his clothing at the pool's edge. As he rose from it, the thick liquid slid from his body, leaving him clean and dry. Once fully clothed, Kahnlair took a small vial from a pocket and bent to fill it with the liquid from the pool. The Blood of the Goddess, as he referred to it, did not kill in small quantities, but it could enter the body and cause a most exquisite pain.

In the light, his victims would see a small vial, filled with perfectly clear liquid, but they would never appreciate the gift he gave them with that sight.

Only the incredibly strong willed survived long enough to see this substance. They did not comprehend the honor he bestowed upon them, none of them were worthy of her Blood the way he was. If any were, it would have slipped from their bodies as it did his, instead of boring into their skin. Their pain would become his power when they broke for him.

Kahnlair slipped the full vial into his pocket and began his walk back to the surface. Once again, his mind turned to contemplating where he might find someone strong enough, someone with whom he could savor the effects of the Blood, someone who might satisfy the growing need within him.

CHAPTER EIGHT

"Hold it like this." *He instructed calmly, his mouth next to her ear as he crouched to match her height. "Remember to set, nock, and draw."*

His body was held to support hers and his hands were gently guiding. In her peripheral vision, she saw he was an elf and much taller than she. He towered over her and had to lean and bend to match his arms to her own. Even that awkward position was achieved with natural elven grace. His blue eyes and golden blond hair sparkled in the afternoon sun, and so much joy flowed from him she felt infected by it despite her frustration with their current task.

"The string is too tight. I cannot pull it back far enough."

She held an elven bow and arrow, adjusted only slightly for her stature, and together they faced a target set a moderate distance across an open meadow flowing with knee-high grasses and flowers. It was a beautiful day with few clouds in the sky, and a light breeze to cool them just enough for comfort. She would need to remember to account for the breeze in her aim. At this distance, it would not be an issue if she had a longer draw.

"This is another reason we do your strength training, Annalla. It is not only the heavier weapons that will require your muscles to be strong. A loose bowstring has no power behind it, and you will need that power in a fight. It can serve for both greater distances and accuracy, and for penetrating armor. For now, I will assist some in drawing with you, but I expect you to master this on your own as with all the others."

His words and tone brooked no argument, but there was also patience and understanding in them. She did not question why she must learn these things. It had always been so, and the lessons were as much a part of her life as eating, sleeping, and traveling.

. There had never been any fighting she was aware of, not even bandits on the roads they traveled, and it seemed peaceful enough wherever they went. Despite this, the first reaction to a place or person, ingrained in her through endless training, was always a threat assessment.

What were the dangers, and how could she eliminate them if it became necessary? What were the escape routes and how could she most efficiently reach them? Preparation and anticipation had gone from thought to instinct years ago, before she could even remember thinking differently.

"I understand."

"We are facing the target, so draw. Good. Sight along the arrow, taking into account wind, distance, angle. Steady. Inhale. Three...Two...One... Release."

The arrow sprang off the bow string at their smooth release with a twang and shot through the air to hit at the edge of the target.

"Not a bad first effort today. Let us try again."

It was high praise, and she let herself smile. She had more training with blades now, and such imperfection would not receive any praise in that field of study.

For the rest of the afternoon, she shot at her target until her arms felt as though they would not be able to move for days—though there was little chance of that being allowed—and she was only doing half of the draw! Despite the work they put in, there was also a great deal of laughter, and she knew she felt deeply for this elf.

"This will be the last one before we pick up and return to camp."

It shot away toward the target but was well off the mark. Her arms were too tired to hold anything close to a steady sighting. The two of them collected their gear from where it was set off to the side as they practiced and moved to gather the spent arrows from the target and surrounding area. He stopped at the edge of the straw target and began pulling the embedded arrows free, while she went to gather those that missed.

If only he had helped me target as well, none of them would have missed, *she grumped to herself and stomped further into the grass.*

As they had shot, she noted where each fell and was thankful for those mental exercises now. It would save her the time of trying to search them out, since he would not let her leave any for lost.

As she bent to gather the first shaft to the right of the target, a brief, wet spray hit her face and arm. All the training took over, and it was but an instant before the warmth of the spray and sounds registered in her mind as danger. There would be no rain from the clear day. Her arm was not coated in water, but in warm, red blood. She turned in a defensive crouch in time to see the elf's head complete its fall to the ground with a sickening thump, and a hideous lizard creature holding a bloody blade in its hands standing over him.

"NOOOOO!" She screamed.

Annalla pulled her blades from her pack in a smooth, practiced motion and tried to jump at the attacker, but something grabbed her from behind and placed a hand over her mouth. The hold on her tightened when another pair of arms was added to those holding her back, this time around her legs, then something wrapped around her waist. As much as she tried to thrash, and scream, and bite, they would not let go.

All her training failed her with these phantoms appearing out of the air. The one holding the bloody sword gazed at the dead elf and then at her. It smiled, began to laugh with its scaly lips stretched to reveal yellow teeth, while those holding her shouted in her ears, mocking her pain and heartache.

"Stop, Annalla! Quiet!" The voices hissing at her lost none of their urgency with the lack of volume. "Wake up!"

Her eyes snapped open to discover three elves holding her down, one with a hand over her mouth to quiet her screams. She was drenched in sweat and her few lingering wounds throbbed from her struggles against their efforts to subdue her.

Taking deep breaths, she tried to quiet the pounding of her heart, still her shaking, and she looked around with wide eyes to regain her bearings. Recognition was not instantaneous, but it came back quickly as she looked at Larron and his companions staring at her from where they wrapped their arms around her body.

She swallowed and held as still as she could against the arms holding her. Mumbling through the hand now only loosely covering her mouth, "Sorry… I think you can let me go now."

Larron hesitated, then nodded at Geelomin and

Thanon, and they gently untangled themselves to stand with Palan and Bealaras watching. Annalla sat up and closed her eyes, trying to shake a foul taste from her mouth and the image of death from her mind.

"Nightmare?" He sat close enough their arms touched and waved the others away to sleep or maintain watch, then handed her a clean cloth. She took it and wiped the sweat and tears from her face. "Would you care to share what had you calling out in the dark of night?"

She did not, but his question was more an order than a request. He also, she acknowledged to herself, had every right to question her about it. They were in hostile territory as far as they knew, and it was immensely dangerous to have someone shouting their presence and position to the world. Annalla took her blanket and wrapped it around herself, still shaking but steadier now that she was not caught in the memory.

"An elf was teaching me to shoot a bow. I think that is why I have been exercising as much as I can. The proper use of a weapon requires strength." She wandered between thoughts, but he nodded.

"It does. Do you know who the elf was?"

"Someone I loved; my father, I think."

He had to be, right? How many elves could keep her birth a secret if they reacted like these five and held the same beliefs? And it did not sound like most travelers travelled together. *Was it memory? Imagination?* Either way, it was likely churned up by the conversation from earlier in the day.

"This is what frightened you?" he prodded into the silence when she did not continue.

Shaking her head, she continued in a whisper, "At the end of the day, we went to retrieve the arrows from our target. Something attacked. It just came out of nowhere. I

125

saw his head fall to the ground, and the creature just stood there and laughed. I tried to get to him, tried to fight like I was taught, but there was nothing I could do, and I was just a child." She felt like a child again now. Her words came out rushed and un-poetic, but they came. "I'm sorry about the noise I made."

She buried her head in her arms and felt a comforting hand on her shoulder pulling her into a side embrace. "It was a nightmare. Your father may yet be alive."

Her response was a mirthless laugh, and she leaned her head against his shoulder as tears threatened again.

"It felt so real, Larron. I don't think it happened that way exactly, but part of me *knows* that is the way he died. I watched it happen, I know I did." Saying it felt right. Maybe she was grasping, but this felt like the truth. She watched her father murdered.

"What did it look like, the creature that attacked him?"

With a deep sigh, she tried to regain her composure without pulling away from the comforting embrace. "It was a gilar."

"Gilar." She could discern nothing from his tone. "You did say you knew their form. Do not worry about the noise. I will switch to an overlapping watch rotation tonight."

"I'll let you know if I hear anything. I don't think I'll be getting back to sleep."

She felt exhausted, as though she had run miles without stopping at a full sprint, and her eyes were gritty, but she was not going to be able to settle despite it all.

"What did he look like? Your father?" he asked instead of trying to argue and convince her to sleep.

"Most of it was fuzzy, like trying to remember something from childhood that is more about emotion than thought or images, but he was an elf, long and lean like all of you, but with blue eyes and blond hair. More of a golden blond than mine."

"That might fit Anor's description from the Derou, but the coloration you describe is more common of the Palonian elves. The Derou are frequently darker with the range of browns you see in our party, including Kayden, the other traveler I know of going missing from our home."

She shook her head as she raised it from him. "Those names do not sound familiar."

"I am sorry for your loss, Annalla." She started to shake her head again, but he gave a brief squeeze to the hug. "*When* does not matter. Loss lingers."

"Thank you." She met his eyes. "Do you mind if I stay with the horses for the night?"

He rubbed her back once before standing and pulling her to her feet. "No. Do as you need tonight."

Wanting to avoid either accusing or worried stares, she walked over to the sleeping horses and sat on the ground nearby. Moonshine was the only one to stir at her arrival, and she sleepily came over to gain additional attention from her rider.

Annalla scratched her nose while she looked over them. Except for Larron's stallion, all were mares. It was still odd to think they would ride a stallion into a war, but she had seen no behavior to dispute their claim his training would hold. Or maybe she did not know much about horses and was making wild assumptions.

Along with her silver-gray mare, there were three brown with a few patches of white, Eagle, Fleet, and Holly, two black, one with white feet, Dancer and Shadow, two cream, Falaro and Kelley, and one grey, Storm. Larron's stallion was the dark grey called Dusk.

All were magnificent and knew how to move with their riders. As Annalla healed, Moonshine gradually shifted back to finding the easiest path for herself, rather than the one that would most spare her rider. The cluttered forest impeded them up to this point. She could only imagine how they could move over open ground when given the chance, even those meant for hauling.

She patted the horse's nose as she thought back on the previous day. Shortly after leaving in the morning, they managed to find a game trail to follow. Palan left signs to indicate his scouting showed the trail lead in the general direction they wanted. It was far from a straight road, but the twists and turns were made up for by the fact they could travel faster and with fewer obstacles.

Maybe it was only in her mind, but it seemed the forest steadily eased its hold. There was a faint breeze stirring the leaves around them where, before, only the stagnant, hot air had been. The sunlight was even a little brighter in the middle of the day.

Palan returned early from scouting with word they would be under an open sky before the sun set. There was a collective sigh of relief and shared smiles as they took a deep breath of open air and saw the last rays of the setting sun playing on the scattered clouds instead of smothered by the forest canopy.

The change in their surroundings was tangible, as though a blanket lifted. They could also see the rapids of a small river a short distance away as they set up camp at the edge of the forest. There was no fire without the concealing canopy. However, new dangers could not detract from open sky, crisp air, and change in scenery. Maybe the change in scenery had brought on the nightmare. The open land here reminded her of that meadow. The talk with Bealaras probably had not helped.

She had to hope the nightmare would not be a recurring event. Looking over the horses again, she fought to turn her mind to something more productive. The pack horses were still heavily burdened, but that was likely because they shifted some of what Moonshine would have been carrying to the others. Even the riding horses carried provisions along with riders until recently. Even with everything loaded into the supplies, they were probably going to have to re-provision somewhere. She was taking a fifth again as much of everything, and anything they hunted would not stay good for long.

"They said the villages were probably gone, Moonshine. Do you think there might still be someone to trade with out here?" Moonshine pushed against her hand again but had no answers before she tucked her head to doze, leaving Annalla with silence in the dark.

No one spoke of the nightmare as they packed in the morning. Her companions seemed to be letting it go unless she wanted to bring it up. She did not and would, in fact, rather fight off the trakins again than talk about it. If they were simply biding their time before asking, they would find that out fast enough.

The ford through the river was almost a day's ride south at their normal pace, and it was far too dangerous to skip that journey and cross where they camped next to the forest, so they kept to the river line and headed south. With no tree cover, the summer sun beat down on them. Annalla was still too grateful to be out of the stuffy forest to complain about the sun just yet. She was certain that would not last long as her skin heated beneath the unforgiving rays.

When they arrived at the ford, it was running low enough to easily cross and presented a perfect opportunity to refill their water supply from a clear running source. Annalla could make out the impression of a highway overgrown as it led off across the open land on the far side, and when they arrived on the other side and dismounted to fill the skins, she could see a smaller roadway leading south.

"There is a village a league or so south," Palan said when he saw her looking in that direction. In this area, he would be remaining with the group and not scouting ahead again until they reached The Claws. "The river is deeper there, and they use it for trade. That river port is most active in the spring and autumn."

Larron nodded. "It was not large, more of a trading outpost and community center for the local farmers, and it was without defenses."

"You believe it is no longer inhabited?" Geelomin asked Larron, who tilted his head in agreement.

Palan looked over at the two of them. "You still mean to detour there first?"

"Yes, a couple hours is a fair price for the chance we could buy prepared supplies."

Annalla looked between them, confused. "I thought you packed enough to reach the Palonian?"

All three looked at her as though she was crazy, so maybe she was mixing up the entire trip with just their journey through the forest.

"We did bring enough of the travel bread to supplement the entire trip, as it keeps well for close to a year and balances a limited diet," Geelomin answered. She had wondered why they rationed the bread so sparingly when they carried so much of it. "However, we will need to either buy or hunt for additional food along the way."

"A cart would have been necessary to provision the entire trip," Palan added.

And there she saw the problem, "And a cart would have never made it through that forest."

"Exactly. Along with not allowing for much stealth. That path has never been reliable, as it is not used frequently enough. I think we stopped around ten times for supplies and more than that simply to stay the night in a village when I came this way previously. North Riverton was one of the supply stops."

She stopped her nod and turned back to face Palan. "North Riverton? It's called North Riverton?"

"It is." Larron answered and smiled at her, like he was waiting for her to ask the next logical question. The smile warned her to stop, but she continued.

"Is there a South Riverton?"

The smile grew. "Not on this river. I shall tell you all about it on the way to North Riverton."

Everyone groaned around her as they started south.

"What is wrong with South Riverton?" she asked Palan before he could move off.

"You do not ask a traveler about geography unless you want a long answer filled with many stories, anecdotes, and much history. You planted this garden. Have fun," he said and kicked Kelley ahead with the others, leaving her staring after them.

Larron trotted up beside her, looking at the backs of his unit ahead and chuckled. "Do you actually want to know?"

"You baited me to get rid of them," Annalla accused him, and she did not have to wait long to understand why he did.

"I took the opportunity presented to me, yes." He studied her. "I wanted a chance to ask how you are feeling today. No one will push," he added, "but any one of us will listen."

She read the sincerity and concern on his face, and knew his words were true. Over the preceding weeks, Larron and his elves had joked with her and supported her. They were all becoming trusted friends. They were nosey to a fault, but she appreciated them all.

"Thank you. I'm tired today, and what I dreamt does hurt, but part of me already knew of and accepted his death. Maybe things will change as I learn or remember more, or remember more clearly exactly what happened, but I'm okay for now."

"Alright," he accepted her word, and that in itself meant so much.

After a few minutes of comfortable silence, she smiled at him. "I might not want the full history, but how many Rivertons are there?"

***

Five. There are five Rivertons in the human kingdom on three different rivers. He told her about how each was named, how they were similar and how they were different. Annalla laughed with him and asked him questions about some of the different regions. Larron's eyes roved her face as she laughed, and he was glad to see some of the strain and shadows of last night fade. The nightmare came out of nowhere, surprising them all. He wanted her to not only seem happy, but actually be happy.

"You should take me on a Riverton Tour trip after all of this is done so I can see them for myself," she teased.

He saw Geelomin send Palan ahead to scout the town as the others stopped. "I would be happy to do so. Ours will be one of the oddest celebration tours, but the more noteworthy as a result."

"The bards shall sing of it for centuries to come," she joked, then looked ahead at the little settlement. "Hmm, maybe only if you commission the song and pay them to sing it. It might need to be a large commission to compensate for the size of the village."

"If *I* pay them?" he asked, wondering when he became the backer of this expedition in her mind. While he would do so in a heartbeat, it ran counter to her independent streak.

"I suppose I will have found work by then for income to contribute to the cause," she considered as they approached Geelomin and Thanon.

Geelomin acknowledged Larron and addressed Annalla. "You will receive income from the Derou for this journey."

"You guys rescued me and are letting me tag along. I hardly think that will earn income from your king—or whoever manages the finances."

"If that were true, you would add nothing to our mission and only require additional resources. You contribute to our tasks and help defend us with your skills. As a contributing member, you will be compensated according to the value of those contributions in our reports," Geelomin stated in response. There was clearly no doubt in his mind that it would happen, and Larron agreed with the assessment.

"Huh, that's good to know."

"Do not become too excited," Larron cautioned, as she would likely receive the income as an elf. "Elven compensation is often barter or trade in a Woodland. We have coins, but it is usually held centrally and exchanged for when leaving the Woodland or trading with others. It is a financial structure far different, and far less officially structured than those utilized by humans and dwarves."

With so few people leaving, limited numbers of young or infirm, and no elderly, their society could operate much more effectively with little to no monetary compensation. He could take with him as much coin as he wanted whenever he left the Woodland to travel, and he often sent back purchases anyone else could have if they found it pleasing. His house was not large, so the few things he kept for himself were generally small trinkets to catch his eye and remind him of a specific place or person.

"We may proceed," Geelomin stated when they saw Palan emerge between two buildings, and he heeled Dusk forward.

"No one is with him," Thanon said, grimacing as he looked over. "I imagine someone would be with him if there was anyone in town."

"Yes. It is likely empty of people." He thought they would discover quickly enough if those people left it alive or dead.

There were few homes in North Riverton. As he had said, it was more of a trading post and community center where the local farmers gathered and sold their crops. It had an inn for traders coming and going as well as for the infrequent elf passing through. A general store and gathering hall were off to one side while the storehouses were closer to the river, where a dock stood high over a currently retreating river.

"It is difficult to tell, but I do not believe anyone has been here for two years at the least," Palan said when they joined him at the edge of town. "While the overgrown gardens could have happened quickly, within a year, the level of disrepair makes me believe it has been longer."

"That is around the time we lost contact with the

councils, but the timing is vague," Thanon said.

"An attack would have left more destruction in its wake," Geelomin commented.

Palan nodded agreement, "Abandoned is more likely. Everything seems to have been packed away or stored neatly and boarded up."

Larron nodded. "The similar timing likely indicates an increasing threat level in the area driving several divergent results, including our communications cut off. Split up. Look for food items they missed in their packing. No breaking down doors or other such destruction but scavenge what will be useful and we will make note of it to repay."

Larron headed straight for the general store, thinking it would be the place most likely to have something of use in too great a quantity for the people to take with them. He noticed Palan heading toward the storehouses. The rest of the group would not know the layout and could explore.

As he approached, Larron saw the townsfolk had boarded up the doors and windows of the store as Palan stated. It was all done from the outside, so it was most likely to keep animals and weather from getting in and destroying the structure rather than an attempt to keep people out. The effort would serve them well if they could return within another few years, as the thatch was well laid and might only need minor repairs and a new ridge by that time, at least on most of the buildings he could see in this section.

He circled the building, hoping to discover an easy way in. They could remove and replace boards, but one already loose would take less time and he could potentially replace it better than he found it. It would be nice to be able to help preserve this place in return for anything they might take.

While the back door proved to be just as well

boarded, the cellar door was not boarded at all. It was, unfortunately, probably latched from the inside. A slide bolt would be a problem, but if it just dropped in, he might be able to work the latch up and out to fall out of the angled cover. Sliding his knife blade between the doors, he slowly moved it up the crack toward the middle of the door. When the blade finally met resistance, it was not as he expected, and Larron grimaced. Rather than feeling solid wood, it felt soft and gave easily.

"Rotted," he muttered to himself and rose with a sigh to test the heavy door. The thin, pulpy wood tore like precious paper, and the door opened easily.

"I thought you said no breaking doors." Looking over, Larron saw Annalla laughing at him as she came around the other side of the store's exterior.

He shook his head. "It was effectively already broken."

Her smile grew smug. "Uh-huh."

"They used sapwood as a latch, probably thinking it would work fine on the inside, but moisture can enter between the doors, so it rotted out. It was probably useless after no more than a season."

"…Uh-huh." Now she was struggling not to laugh again. Larron pursed his own lips attempting to look unamused as he stared at her.

That did make her laugh. "You're not as good at the stern face as you think you are."

He made a 'hmm' sound, but did not comment, so she shook her head and continued only slightly more seriously. "It was likely replaced regularly when there were people here all the time. Most of the buildings are boarded up like this one. Thanon and Geelomin worked a board off the inn's door and are checking that out. Palan can see inside most of the storehouses. Want some help here?"

Opening the other door fully and letting the sun light the stairs down, he smiled and held his hand toward the stairs. "After you."

They both had to hunch in the tiny cellar with a ladder leading up to a wooden trap door in the opposite corner ceiling. Barrels lined one side, with shelves on the other containing a handful of cheese wheels. Whatever was in the barrels was more likely to be good, but they could not carry so much liquid, nor did they need or want alcohol along this journey.

"We have no use for taking the wine or cider, but the cheese has a chance of being edible. If you want to pack those, I will see what is on the main floor."

While she nodded and went back out, he moved to the ladder. It was built of better wood than the latch had been. He found some luck when the trap door at the top had neither latch nor lock, allowing him to enter the main floor easily.

Dust had settled on the shelves and counters, and there was evidence of rodent activity, which he followed to an overturned grain sack in a back room. In the entirety of the store, only one set of shelves held any food items. He suspected they finished loading the rest and simply decided it was not worth another crate or could not hold one more.

Fruits and vegetables pickled and preserved sat in a few jars. Dried foods traveled better, but they could consume these first and discard the bulk quickly enough. When Annalla finished with the cheese, he handed the jars down to her, picked up the scattered bits of cloth scraps strewn about—not good enough for the effort of packing for the townsfolk—and followed her out. The scraps would at least do for additional bandages once cleaned.

He walked back to the cellar doors after they packed

away the last of the jars and looked at them.

"Trying to decide how to latch it again?" Annalla asked him, seeing where his thoughts were.

"Sliding it into position like I was trying to slide it out is the best option, but we do not have a good option to use for a latch."

Annalla leaned closer to the door and looked at the catch. "A piece of the boards might work. Let me see if they have put back the one they took off the inn door." She ran off as she called over her shoulder, "Wait here!"

"I guess I will wait here then," he said to no one.

Her head poked around the corner briefly before disappearing again. "I heard that."

When she returned, it was with Geelomin carrying a plank of wood and machete. They compared the thickness of the board and it looked like it would fit well, so it was an easy cut to trim off the bottom quarter.

"Anything?" He asked Geelomin as he propped the piece in place in one closed door, positioning it to easily catch with his knife.

"Dried herbs, but they were so old they crumbled to dust at the slightest touch. We did find another blanket and a bedroll for Annalla. Thanon is packing them now."

He started to gently close the other door. "That is something. We collected some jarred produce and questionable cheese."

"My favorite kind, Sir." Larron raised an eyebrow at his lieutenant's dry humor before working his knife in.

"Commander!" Palan called from the other end of the little street. "There are some chickens gone feral roosting in one of the storehouses."

The piece caught and settled as Larron considered their options. Looking at Geelomin, he asked, "Does the inn still have a working kitchen and a table and chairs?"

Smiling back at him, his lieutenant nodded. "It does. We have not put any of the boards back yet either."

"Palan," he looked briefly at the cellar door he just closed and briefly regretted locking up the cider so soon instead of watering some down for a meal, "take three of them. We will cook them at the inn and have ourselves a mid-day feast."

Everyone perked up at that. They had not eaten at a table since before leaving the Woodland's bounds, nor had fresh meat in just as long. The time it would take was only slightly longer than a normal break, and if they ate more now, they could go with a smaller supper tonight with any leftovers they took with them.

If it were not risking too much, and the beds were remotely functional, he would have suggested a night at the inn. As it was, the cooking fire was as much as he was willing to risk right now. He would want to be well on their way from this location by nightfall.

Working together, they had the stove fire quickly stoked, an old pan from a dusty shelf on the stove, and some plates cleaned off. They feasted on pan-fried chicken and pickled vegetables, joking and laughing while the hobbled horses lazily grazed in the adjacent field.

An hour later, the borrowed tools were washed and put away, the food was packed, and they were riding again, cutting directly across the fields to meet up with the highway leading toward The Claws.

CHAPTER NINE

With open land spread around them, the sun beat down. Thanon had noticed Annalla's pale cheeks turning pink their first day in the open, and unearthed a dusty old straw hat for her in his exploration of the inn. They simply covered their heads with cloth. Everyone kept their eyes out for enemies who might see them miles away, but even the new challenges could not dampen their spirits.

Despite the empty land before them, they continued to travel at an easy pace for the horses. Pushing them would waste their energy in a sprint when this was a marathon, and the pack horses were not built for speed. Still, each day they devoured leagues of rolling meadows and fields gone fallow stretching to the horizon in every direction.

The encroaching weeds and grasses were dry and brown without active irrigation. Infrequent bushes along the road they travelled had exposed leaves burnt on top from the relentless sun. She could hear the shushing of the grass blades brushing against each other whenever a breeze rolled through.

"Shouldn't we see more villages like North Riverton along this highway?" Annalla asked as they passed a cluster of about three buildings set a mile to the north late in the afternoon.

Palan shook his head. "Most are around this size. The farmers around here are primarily self-sustaining and trade only a portion of their crops cooperatively. Larger towns are unsustainable in the area, as it would not be able to support that many people."

Her brow furrowed. "Why don't the villages grow into the unclaimed land?"

"This is elven land, not unclaimed." Larron slowed to join them. "The triangle of land between and around the Woodlands belongs to the elves. Our treaty with Ceru allows for humans to work the lands, but there are limits in place, and the Ceru guard will help us enforce those limits if necessary."

She was not as certain of humans holding to a treaty after generations passed. There was no one around to enforce these rules, and an ancestor three times removed could not possibly predict all the challenges one would be facing. It would be so easy to have people start to justify bending the rules a little more every year.

However, it did not sound like this treaty was a recent development from the way they described it, so maybe the deterrents were effective enough.

"What would you do if Ceru did not help?"

The look Larron turned on her was one of uncompromising power. This was an ambassador who knew the strength of his position and that of his people. "We would expand the Woodlands and reclaim land that was once ours. The Woodlands would close to outsiders and mean death to any who might try to enter, and any aid we give to the lands of men would not only be revoked but turned actively against them."

"You help with their crops," she said, starting to understand some of the nuances of how the elves helped the humans in Elaria.

"Among other things, yes. Our connection to the land is our greatest strength and asset. The Auradia Woodland also hosts most of the royal family at some point in their lives, so the rulers have an appreciation for what our civilization offers and provides."

"That…" she paused, "is much more manipulative than I expected."

"We have fought the gilar for millennia, long before humans came to Elaria. Good does not mean peaceful nor naïve, and the land is as important as the people. One cannot exist without the other, so we will protect both with the same ferocity."

This was important to him, and she was certain it was a point he shared and emphasized with humans around Elaria in his travels. Annalla wondered to herself how many of those humans failed to grasp the gravity of this conviction.

"How do the humans see you?" she asked him, "When you travel, I mean."

Larron looked at her and smiled, no less fierce, but she could tell he knew what she meant with her question. She wanted to know if the people he visited knew what elves offered, and what they could take away.

"Most often, I am a blessing come to visit, and I am invited to stay. The people there know a plentiful harvest will likely follow this year or next. Barring a weather disaster, of course. One elf can only do so much directly."

Her eyes narrowed. "And the times you are not welcomed are the reason, barring accident, that travelers most often go missing."

He was somber when he nodded. "They know either a

blight or their King's justice will follow any breaking of our agreements. Being rid of the elf is thought to be easier than facing consequences for their actions. I am thankful it does not happen often. There are few travelers with the level of combat training I possess."

Annalla felt her lip curl with disdain. "You have been attacked and escaped... How often have you followed those your people lost and served justice to those responsible?"

She knew he had done so. She knew in her heart he had followed after those gone missing and found people who would murder to take what was not theirs. His jaw was hard, and he swallowed against the memories that must be pushing at him of people lost to human greed.

Larron took a breath and looked over again, only somewhat composed. "Only for those I found the guilty party. For the rest, it was a blight on their crops and a report to the King." She watched that thought calm him a little. "Annalla, in all my years of travel I have never known a King of Ceru to take the murder of an elf lightly. They pay, and they pay with what matters to them."

Palan was looking between them, unsure of what was going on at that moment.

Maybe some elves remain naïve, she thought to herself, but also acknowledged that Larron was not one of them. If he was satisfied with the justice served, she could trust him.

A tilt of her head conceded the point, and she changed the subject. "I'm going to exercise my wings tonight."

"You are nowhere near ready to fly," was the immediate response of the party's medic, and she smiled at his concern.

"Of course not, but I need to start exercising the

muscles there, or I never will be."

He grunted, and Palan rolled his eyes as they smiled at each other.

***

The first night trying her wings more than just stretching them, she flexed a handful of times and felt them droop further with each pass. Even after that limited work, her back ached so much the next morning she groaned trying to sit up.

Pulling herself into the saddle was even worse, but not enough to admit wanting help after his warning the day before. It would still be some time before she was flying, but she would work through the aches to get them back in flying shape.

If she was even able to fly on these wings. They were the shape of a butterfly's but seemed far too small proportionally to allow her to get in the air. Taking the size of a butterfly's body in comparison to its wings meant her wings would need to be twice as large to be of any use.

The thought crossed her mind, more than once over the last few days, that her elven half might have caused her wings to be smaller than they should. She could very well be a crippled, grounded fairy. If their size proved not to be an issue, however, by her estimation she could be taking her full weight on them before they left the mountains they approached.

Referring to what the elves called 'The Claws' as mountains was being generous in her opinion. Perhaps millions of years ago, when the elven race itself could be considered young, but time and elements had worn them down to nothing more than large, craggy hills.

Elven sight was not enough to make them

distinguishable early on, barely peeking over the horizon. Less than two full days' ride away, characteristics of the landscape could finally be made out. A weathered down mountain range might bring an image of a smoothed rise in the earth covered with soft, green growth, but The Claws ran contrary to that in every way.

Their name came primarily from two features Palan described to her in a detailed recollection, the first being the jagged terrain. The rock the mountains consisted of was not the type to smooth from the elements. Instead, it cracked and broke, and slid and crashed, creating a sharp and treacherous path at best, lethal at worst. The second feature lending credence to the name was their orientation. From one wider range running north to south, four more stretched out to the west as would claws from a paw.

What the range lacked in height, it made up for in breadth and dangerous footing. The next step in their journey would be to cross those jagged peaks through one of the less frequented passes. Going around would add months to their trip and the main pass was too well known and likely guarded as a result. To reach the pass they wanted, they needed to travel south of the closest claw, and move along the foothills, until they were nearly two thirds of the way to the base range.

This pass was used less often both because it required more time in the barren range, and because the entrance was difficult to find and access for anyone who did not have prior knowledge of it. They would then travel the rest of the way to the base range within the claw, finally following the meandering path through to the other side. It would take them an estimated two weeks in the pass because the horses would be led instead of ridden for most of the crossing, and they expected sections requiring them to tread carefully or even seek alternate paths.

The first jumbled rocks of The Claws came upon them quickly, and they skirted to the south to remain clear of the slopes until they needed to enter the pass. It was three more days of riding along the gradually growing foothills since that point, and they would soon be scanning the passing rocks for the elusive entrance.

"What are we looking for exactly?" Everyone had started looking at the grey rocks rising to their left more frequently at some signal she missed, or maybe it was simply as Larron looked more often.

Larron scanned the clifftop again, along with the land before them, before answering, "This claw has a massive depression about a day back containing a large reservoir of water. That lake slowly drains out through the claw before spilling over the side and creating a stream leading off into the trees. I believe it feeds a pond to the southwest."

"And we go up the waterfall?" she asked.

The uncertain hum in his throat was not encouraging. "There should be a deeper gully past the stream that will put us on the best path to the pass."

"Wait, should? As in, it is not always there? Or you are not sure? I thought you and Palan have both made this trip before."

He shook his head. "Only through the main pass to the south. There is usually no need to travel this road. This route is more a trail than an actual pass, and it is a dangerous crossing. However, it is less known, and the main pass has a number of ideal ambush locations."

"We are trading risks," Palan added. "Our horses will fare better than others on this trail, and we have a better chance of surviving an ambush here because it limits the numbers either side can bring to a fight."

It made sense if they could mitigate the known terrain risks in this area. The risk of gilar or other enemies was less certain. While they had not seen evidence of the gilar this far north because most of the fighting was in the south, the lack of current intelligence made that a risky assumption. The further they travelled away from their Woodland, the more they risked running into unexpected enemy expansion.

Palan rose in his saddle. "There is something ahead, about a mile. It might be a streambed, but it does not look like there is any water."

The rest rose as well and squinted into the distance. "It could be the marker, dried from the harsh summer," Thanon shrugged, "we will find out soon."

Less than a half hour later it was nearing mid-day, and they were on their horses standing around what was clearly a dried streambed bending away from the claw.

"This is approximately where I would expect it." Larron looked up again at the group, having come to some internal decision. "There is likely a fair camp location where the dry bed is better surrounded with trees and brush, we will find that first and set up camp for tonight."

He turned Dusk toward the trees, and they followed him in a line along the stream's usual path. Larron continued to scan the forest as they travelled, looking for a good location for whatever he had in mind. He did not stop again until the scattered trees grew thicker.

"We are going to need to quickly re-provision. The trees will offer some protection for us to dry meat tonight if we can find and take down game today. We should forage as well. Thanon, Palan, you are hunting. Geelomin and Annalla can forage for us. Bealaras and I will cut grass for the horses. Return by nightfall. As we will have a fire tonight, I want an overlapping watch patrolling a perimeter as people return and overnight."

A flurry of activity followed, with equipment and baggage pulled from the horses. It was not only set down, but cleverly hidden around the selected area so you would not know it was there if you had not seen it stashed.

The pack horses were given long leads on light tethers that would not hold them if a threat attacked, but effectively told them to remain in the area. And one by one, the party dispersed in different directions on their appointed assignments. Annalla helped with unloading, but the speed with which it was accomplished left her standing around watching toward the end. As with their time at the inn, the party was moving quickly, not comfortable to remain in one place longer than necessary.

Geelomin broke her out of her thoughts when he handed her two empty cloth bags. "Do you have a preference? South or south-east?"

She shook her head and grabbed them from him.

"Take Moonshine to search south then. If you are not sure something is edible, but it looks like it could keep for a while, bring it back. Thanon knows the most about what is and is not safe. Watch the sun. Commander wants us back by nightfall." He hesitated, "Will you be able to navigate back on your own?"

Annalla looked around at landmarks and the forest around them before nodding. "Yes. I'll be fine."

He took her at her word, mounted his horse, and headed south-east. She saw Moonshine had been divested of the last of the equipment the horse usually carried and was placidly munching on dry grass as she waited.

"Off we go, I guess," Annalla said to her horse as she mounted up and turned them south.

It was not long before she came across a patch of

wildflowers. There were a good number of dandelions mixed in, so she headed over. The ground turned out to be too hard to dig, having baked firm in the long summer, so she settled for ripping all the greens off and stuffing them in one of the bags. By the time she collected all of them she could reach and headed out again, the first bag was already about half full.

It was filled completely with the next patch she came across of the prolific flower. Instead of picking the next patch, she noted its locations but kept moving in case there was more of a variety to be found to fill her second bag elsewhere.

She and Moonshine meandered back and forth in a southerly direction as she peered about for anything standing out. The tall, broad leaves of grass clumped in one area had potential, and as she drew close to the plants, the smell confirmed another find. The scent of onions was distinct and pungent in the area.

Leaving the tiny ones alone, she started pulling some of the larger leaves and working a few of the larger bulbs up out of the hard earth. She left the oniony smelling area with a sense of contentment as the aroma followed her out, wafting from the bag tied to Moonshine. Onions were a great find because they could last longer than a lot of other plant items.

Her next find, as the shadows grew, would not last as long, but it would be so much sweeter. An enormous blackberry bush tangling up between three spread-out trees dominated the space in front of her like some thorny plant monster.

With the harsh summer, the berries appeared small and were probably more seed than berry. It looked like birds had picked over a good portion as well, especially on top, but there were still some to be found of a fair size.

Annalla decided to move some of the dandelions out
of the first bag and fill up the top of both bags with the
berries, hoping the leaves would give some cushion to keep
from crushing the fruits too badly on the trek back. With her
mostly full bags in hand, she plodded over to the best-
looking area and started picking the easy to reach berries,
circling to the right.

"Little sucker." She swore under her breath a half
hour later at a thorn embedded in her right tricep as she tried
to reach around to gently remove the branch without further
scratching herself. The movement caused another three
dangling branches to grab onto her and her clothes as she
twisted. That was saying nothing of the thorns clinging to
and poking her through her pants. "Ow, ow, ow! That's it.
I'm done."

No one was around to hear her announcement other
than the horse—who was most definitely watching and
laughing in her too-knowing, horsey way—and no one was
around to help her extricate herself from the bush either.
When Annalla pivoted where she stood and looked back at
how far she had delved into the thick of the bush in her berry
hunting misadventure, she grunted, sighed, and assessed the
best path forward and out.

***

Palan materialized out of the scattered trees in front of her.
His greeting halted with his hand half raised and his eyes
widened as he scanned her from head to toe. "Oh, my lord.
What happened to you? Are you alright?"

"I don't want to talk about it," she said with barely
contained frustration. "Aren't you supposed to be hunting?"

Ok, not so contained, she thought to herself.

His lips twitched like he was holding in laughter.

"I found a small herd of deer and was able to take one down. It is being prepared now, so I am on patrol with Bealaras. You are the last to return."

She nodded and continued toward camp, leaving him to melt back into the sparse trees. Before she was out of hearing range, she heard him laughing before he called out to her, "They should have something for you to put on those scratches!"

Annalla snarled and nudged Moonshine to a slightly faster walk. As she entered their camp, a fire was going with a rack set up around it. Strips of meat hung to dry looking like they had first been coated in salt and herbs. She dismounted and took Moonshine over to the other horses as the others called out to her, trying to hide behind the animal's bulk.

Their elf eyes were too fast, though. "Annalla, what..."

"Not a word. Not one word," she interrupted irritably as they started their questions. "I swear I will not hesitate to murder you all."

There was silence as she took care of her horse, put away the saddle, and brought her two bags over to Larron, avoiding looking at anyone's face the entire time.

Thanon resumed preparing more meat for the rack, Larron stood and walked away, and Geelomin pulled a large skewer from the fire. It looked like Geelomin was preparing dinner, so she pulled her bags closer to her, grabbed one of the light bowls they used, and started ripping up leaves for a basic salad of dandelion, onion, and blackberry.

Geelomin passed her a plate with a large portion of roasted venison on it, to which she added some of her greens and passed that bowl. Larron did the same for his plate as he sat down next to her, but then he handed her the little canister she remembered seeing before in the trakin forest. The one after they got through all the nettles.

"I thought I said 'not a word,'" Annalla glared at him, but her heart was not in it, and the canister was tempting.

He had the audacity to smile charmingly and lift a verbose eyebrow before setting the canister next to her and then slowly reaching up—as though she were an animal that was going to bite him—and plucking a little, dried husk of a blackberry branch from the back of her sleeve near her shoulder.

She sighed. Her head dropped into the hand not holding her plate.

Thanon sputtered off to the side once, then twice, sounding like he was choking, and finally could not contain his laughter any longer and just started roaring. Annalla buried her burning face in her hand as Larron, and then even Geelomin, joined in the laughter. She felt her lips curving in a reluctant smile as it continued. Clearing her throat, she raised her head high and continued eating as they slowly got themselves back under control.

"They aren't even good blackberries," she complained to Thanon later as she helped him finish the racks that would dry most of the meat overnight.

He smiled at her and asked with wonder, "Then why did you go so far into the bush?"

"Hmm. I think it was the thought of something sweet. Jerky and bread are filling, but can you imagine fresh, ripe, juicy blackberries right now?"

"Pie? Or tarts?" he added with enthusiasm and a small moan of longing. She joined him with a wistful sigh.

"The fresh meat was nice though. And I didn't know you brought spices with you. I thought we were lucky to find anything, even spice dust, back at the inn."

"Two small bags of salt for just this purpose, and the spices for cooking are all in one small pouch that does not add much weight. It would absolutely be different without the pack animals."

Larron joined the two of them around the fire after they cleaned up and all the remaining meat hung to dry. "Are you feeling better?"

She rolled her eyes at him. "It was more irritating than anything else. You forget how clingy those bushes can be and they make you pay for it."

"You look like you lost a fight with a raccoon or fell off your horse into a thicket in training," Thanon added unhelpfully.

"Thank you for that, Thanon. What would I do without you here to serve in place of a mirror?" Her tone was wry as she glared at him.

"I do believe I hear Geelomin calling me to take care of something over there," he said, tongue in cheek, and darted off.

Larron bent his head to catch her eye. "You are alright with their teasing?"

"I deserve it after this."

She smiled easily and bumped his shoulder. It was easier to accept the jokes now that she was no longer mad at her own stupidity. Being honest with herself, their playful banter helped her get over it. If it had happened to anyone else, she would have been participating along with the other side of things, poking fun at whoever had gotten themselves into a harmless scrape. It was all comfortable and good natured, and it made her feel more welcome in an odd way.

"Thank you for asking, but I should be concerned about you all thinking I was actually threatening murder."

"You would not murder us. You need us." He winked at her.

"Well, there is that. I'm also fairly sure Geelomin is starting to warm to me since I threatened murder." Her volume was pitched just loud enough to carry across the small camp.

"I do not recall any mention of murder beyond a request for assistance in tracking down a troublesome raccoon that escaped your skill." The lieutenant raised an eyebrow and Thanon let out a gleeful chuckle as he stared.

There are too many expressive eyebrows tonight, was her first thought.

She muttered to Larron, "Everyone thinks they're funny now."

He looked down at her, half laughing and eyes dancing. "I do believe you started it."

She laughed and pushed his arm. "Fair enough. I am going to sleep before I get myself into more trouble."

The three of them said goodnight to her, and she knew that either Palan or Bealaras would wake her for her night shift at patrol. Hopefully they would not also feel the need to comment on her misadventure.

***

"We will travel closer to The Claws from here. Remember to look further up the hills for a gully that stands out on the nearest slopes," Larron said the next morning as they rode from their stocking-up camp.

They proceeded as ordered, all peering intently into the jumble of rocks when they neared, while at the same time keeping a watch for enemies. The sun was well past the point of mid-day before Bealaras called out.

"I believe I have found it!" The entire group stopped and looked forward to where he pointed.

Annalla could barely discern a small dimple at the top. Managing to reach it would be an effort. Though, she supposed this one was closer and wider than the chips in the hills they passed thus far. It did not, however, appear to be any sort of path.

Gentle foothills turned sharply into steep mountains. Between them and that spot were jagged rocks, steep slopes without firm holds, sharp rises and drops, and numerous other obstacles. It would be difficult for them to make it up that slope. She could only think it would be near impossible for the horses, and they needed the horses. A slip on that climb would likely be fatal.

"Yes, this is as the messenger described. Making our way over this rise into the pass will take at least half a day. We will camp down here again, but no fire tonight. Let us also scout what we can before nightfall."

They rode to the pass sighting together and dismounted to stare up at the steep climb. Larron ordered three to scout the slopes, specifically looking for a safe way to lead the horses up. Geelomin, Bealaras, and Palan each took a direction, left, right, and center, and started climbing.

She watched their forms move, then pause, move, then pause. The pauses were likely stopping to view the next series of steps they would need to take on their path. It felt like an eternity of sitting, watching, and waiting for one of them to reach the top while she paced and fidgeted.

"I know you have the patience to stand watch, silent and immobile for hours, Annalla. Why so restless?" Larron asked her, looking up from sharpening one of the machetes with a curious head tilt.

She scrunched her nose at him and thought. "I'm not

sure I would describe it as patience. More like focus, determination."

"Stubbornness," Thanon helpfully added.

"Hmm, thank you," she said sarcastically to his large grin and shook her head. "Anyway, this feels more like inactivity. Travel is doing something. Guarding is doing something. This is just waiting for others to do something."

"We even rushed you through our meal at the inn and pushed for a quick forage yesterday." Larron nodded, "It does feel like time is precious. However, I would argue this is not so much a matter of patience, as it is about trust and control."

"How so?"

"Would you be as impatient at our delay if you were scouting?" He smiled at her thoughtful silence. "Trust them to find a way, and control what is before you."

What was before her? Annalla looked around at Larron and Thanon taking care of small tasks to prepare equipment for the climb or future use. There was plenty of time for them to complete their activities, so they did not really need her help. Her eyes settled on the rhythmic stroke of Larron's whetstone across the blade. There was one weapon she alone could hone.

After a quick change, she stepped into another exercise routine. Aware of the task ahead for the next day, she made sure this was a light one and would not tire her much, but she stretched and worked on her range of motion, including that of her wings. Methodically going through the motions was calming and distracting enough to see her through until they started a cold meal.

Palan returned not long after. His body language was not encouraging.

"There was nothing passable in that area. I would

have had to free climb a short distance to reach the top myself. The horses could never make it, so I turned back. There are some dangerous alternatives I bypassed today that we can explore further if we need additional options."

Larron nodded without showing any disappointment. "We will hope the others have more promising news."

Bealaras was the next to return, though his report was marginally better.

"It is a winding route up the slope. I believe the horses could successfully make the climb as long as we do not push too fast. Though, I would prefer not to take this path if there is a better option. In most places, one misstep by elf or horse would quickly lead to death."

Word upon Geelomin's return was much the same. "I was able to gain the top and spy a way down the other side. If there is no alternative, the horses might all make it, but not fully laden. The way is not nearly firm enough, and we would need to make several trips to bring everything to the top. I do not take comfort in our chances for making it up and down several times without losing any of the mounts and supplies."

"We will follow Bealaras then. The path he found is not ideal either, but it does not require several crossings," Larron said in response, as Bealaras's nod confirmed the statement.

Everyone else also nodded their agreement or understanding as he spoke. In a list of poor options, they would go with the least terrible. It seemed this might become a pattern for the decisions they would make regarding their trip through The Claws.

The next morning, they all took extra care lashing down the baggage so it would not shift the slightest on the horses' packs, and they spread more of it to the riding horses as well.

Larron spoke again as they reached the base of the slope and dismounted. "Check the bags one last time before heading up. Bealaras, lead the way when you are ready."

It was only a few moments before they took the reins and led their horses after Bealaras toward the rocks. Those with a pack horse following behind did so with the thinnest of lead ties possible, hoping that if one fell it would snap before taking both and potentially the person guiding them.

The path upon which Bealaras led them had one of two features at any given point. It was either a hard, narrow ledge with a drop that would leave anyone who toppled over lame or dead, or an unstable slope of rocks growing steeper with each switchback.

Annalla was more grateful than ever Palan had lent her the boots. She might have new calluses because they did not fit, but it was still preferable to walking on rocks as sharp as blades. Her feet would have been destroyed and leaving a trail of blood after the first few steps. It was the horses suffering whenever the sharp rocks made it past their shoes and hooves to the soft flesh above.

Despite the pain, they faithfully followed their riders up. The sun rose past mid-day and continued its blistering path. At the more dangerous places, Bealaras slowed their pace and passed back a verbal warning, but they continued without stopping to maintain the steady progress working for them. There was danger with every step, but she was beginning to think the level of the threat in The Claws was exaggerated. That was until they reached the top, near the dimple at the crest of the ridge.

Stepping from one side to the other was like stepping from a closed room out into a gale. The wind picked up and blew dust, and even smaller rocks, about. The blow would come and go, but it came from above and to the east, as though the surrounding cliffs scooped it up and funneled it down into this section of The Claws. It was more than enough force to knock the unprepared or incautious off unsteady footing.

She was thankful for all the exercising over the preceding weeks, as even with that preparation, her legs were burning before they reached the top. An entirely different combination of muscles was being used to climb, stop the periodic sliding in the scree, and maintain balance on the slanted stones.

By the time they started down the treacherous descent, Annalla's body was cramping, and she was limping again, as the endless hike aggravated injuries she thought healed. She insisted on bringing up the rear when they started up, and she was slowly dropping back more from the horse in front of her. If she fell, she would not be taking anyone with her. Hopefully, she would not pull Moonshine, the only one behind her, down as well.

The distance between her and the group steadily grew on the descent, and she was glad they would have little visibility to look back past their horses on the narrow way leading east—at least until she was so far behind as to be enough above them to be seen over the horses.

There would be no point in them stopping to try and help her, because they would not be able to safely reach her, and neither they nor the horses could carry her. As they crossed over, she had spotted where the path should become more stable, where it became an actual path with firm, stone footing and not simply the least dangerous place to walk. It was visible for a brief period before it disappeared behind the people in front of her.

Further down the slope, she could see that path again

when the others had pulled far enough ahead. Enough scree sat above their trail that the dust and gravel picked up by the wind was pelting into her. It was not painful at first, only irritating on her already scratched skin, but it gained momentum and force every step of their descent.

Little bullets of rock struck with stinging force, and she had to protect her eyes and cover Moonshine's. One by one, the elves before her moved on to the stable ledge and passed around a bend to be hidden by the covering, hill-side wall. They would make better time now. That also meant they would be pulling away from her even faster.

Focus, Annalla.

Allowing her focus to waver would only lead to a wrong step and see her at the bottom well before them, but not in any shape to continue on to see the Woodland they were headed toward. She and Moonshine kept their own pace, calmly and carefully testing each step before placing their weight fully upon it.

The wind continued gusting, less forgiving of their pace and punishing them for each moment they remained exposed. Its invisible force rushed down at them in a sudden gust, throwing the smaller rocks and pebbles against their bodies. It was a quick attack, but when she looked up in the direction from which it had come, she saw this time was different. At least, the result was different and far more dangerous.

Smaller rocks at the top slammed into others positioned precariously on the slope. Quicker than she could blink, a rockslide started, and they were still much too far away from the small ledge the others had disappeared on for her to reach it, but Moonshine might.

She did not see it build in size and momentum, though she heard it start to roar, because when she saw what had begun, Annalla was already slashing through the harness holding the supplies to Moonshine's back with the hunting knife Larron had given her one morning. As it fell to the ground, she slapped Moonshine on the rear and ordered her to run.

The horse took off toward the ledge upon hearing the shouted command, scrambling for purchase among the stones breaking off and sliding away underfoot. It had taken only seconds. Without the burden, she might be able to keep her footing and make it to safety.

Annalla gathered the harness and stuck her head and arms through the loops to lift it, just as leading pebbles from the slide began to hit. Glancing over one last time, she watched as the horse dug into the shifting gravel, almost as if in slow motion. Moonshine's hurried steps were causing another rockslide below, but she would make the ledge so long as she did not falter. Annalla's gaze turned, satisfied, from the horse to look at the mass of rocks and boulders bearing down on her.

CHAPTER TEN

Steep rock walls continued to rise at their sides as the ground flattened out before them. Larron released a quiet sigh of relief when he heard Bealaras call out that their destination for the day was in sight.

The path had been every bit as dangerous as he warned, especially on the descent into the pass. With the wind working constantly to speed them to the distant bottom, they were lucky not to have lost someone. To move right or left of the thin trail, marked only by the stone collecting where it was marginally less steep, would have been dangerous.

It had grated on Larron to be forced to rely on his ears alone to tell him if anyone met with disaster. Amid the sounds of the constantly shifting scree all over the mountainside and their own steps loosening rock, it was near impossible to know for certain. Every moment was spent straining to hear those before and behind him, dreading the sound of a screaming elf or horse would reach him as one of his team fell to their death on the jagged rocks below or buried and crushed by rock from above.

Fighting against gilar or trakins was something he

could address head-on and do something about personally. The dangers of the Claws were passive and more unpredictable. His need for control here was nearly as strong as Annalla's that had her pacing and fidgeting yesterday. There was no doubt in his mind this hike would not be the last of its kind as they crossed the Claws, and his nerves would become frayed every time. Even the main pass he traveled a few times before had two such locations. He could only imagine how many this spur would have along their route.

"Just ahead is where we should camp. It looks well protected," Bealaras exclaimed ahead, as he was the first to step onto the flat and solid ground of the trail.

Larron heard the others laughing and could not help but smile with them after that climb.

"Unburden the horses and check their hooves, first thing. We do not want any of them coming up lame."

He turned around to watch everyone step into the level clearing one-by-one, seeing them all for the first time since beginning their ascent. Bealaras was already down. Palan followed Larron's horses, then Geelomin and Thanon. He watched, waited for a minute or more, staring as his face grew numb and his vision blurry with dread.

"Where is Annalla?"

"It was a difficult climb. She may have needed to rest along the way." Geelomin did not sound convinced as he, too, peered back up the trail.

He frowned at the thought her injuries were still not healed enough for such strenuous activity. He watched her exercise and often joined her and others. He would have sworn she was well enough to make the hike without stopping.

Larron had not wanted to allow her to take the rear

position, but—as Thanon eloquently pointed out—she could be incredibly stubborn, and she was a fair judge of her own strength. Those dances were well known to him, and they were not for novices.

Perhaps knowing her own strength is exactly why she insisted on taking the rear position, he thought to himself with no little anger at both of them.

How far would she have to have fallen behind for him to miss hearing her fall? Guilt, loss, he refused to acknowledge the stabbing sensation within his chest as he thought of her lying broken upon stones. They waited longer.

"I am heading back up. Take care of Dusk for me." He turned and handed the reins off to Geelomin.

"No need," Thanon said. "I believe she is coming now."

Everyone turned and looked again at the path from which they emerged. The clop of horse hooves was distinct and approached quickly, though they could not see far enough up the path from the angle of the trail to make out Annalla's and Moonshine's approach.

She could not be running fast enough to stay with Moonshine at that pace. Why would she be riding her on dangerous footing?

"Take up your weapons. Something is not right."

With weapons in hand, they took up defensive positions behind cover, waiting for her to appear and warn them of the trouble that must surely follow. Moonshine's pace slowed. There was no way to be certain if it was at a command from Annalla, or if she simply caught the scent of the other horses.

Larron's heart stopped, and he held his breath, in the moments before Moonshine trotted into the open. Nothing followed the horse, not even a sound of pursuit. Slowly, they relaxed their defensive posture and cautiously emerged from concealment to stare questioningly at the horse. Moonshine was alone, and the supplies she carried were gone along with Annalla.

She saved the horse. Larron knew what happened and closed his eyes.

"No." He breathed out and took off running. Some measure of training reasserted itself enough for him to bark an order over his shoulder before he was out of range. "Stay there!"

***

Another gust of wind raced the landslide thundering down on her. Annalla could see its progress by the cloud of dust kicked up in the wake of the tumbling rocks and boulders. The wind pushed the finer particles in the air ahead faster. With its greater speed, the airflow would overtake the slide and reach her just before she was crushed. The timing had to be right for her desperate, insane idea to have a chance of working. She waited in a crouched position, staring down the face of oncoming destruction.

Almost there. Count it down.
Three...two...one...Now!

With all the strength remaining to her, she pushed off with her legs, throwing her weight and that of the supplies she carried into the air. In the same movement, she lifted her arms and snapped open her wings.

When she thought of this plan, she imagined her legs pushing her far into the air where she would hang majestically at the apex long enough for the wind to gently catch her wings. She would drift away from the slope and glide gracefully down to triumphantly land where her friends waited.

That…is not how it happened. With all the equipment she was carrying, her tired legs elevated her maybe two feet off the ground. There was no floating or hanging in the air. Gravity grabbed her at the top of those two feet and pulled her back down. Annalla's toes were nearly touching back down before the wind caught her wings. The opposing forces had her gritting her teeth to keep from screaming from the pain shooting down her back.

The wind threw her violently into the air, away from the slope, and out of the path of the rockslide, a moment before it passed. Only one of the smaller boulders clipped her foot as it bounced and tumbled below before she rose above.

Her jump saved her from one death, only for the air currents to throw her about like a leaf in a storm. Forcing her joints to work through the agony, she strained to control her heading. Annalla tried to angle her trajectory toward where her companions had been heading, but the attempt was brief and ineffective.

She was nowhere near strong enough to push through and move against the wind, especially when she had no idea how to move in the air. Opting to ride with the wind instead, Annalla flailed about with her feet and the hand not holding the supplies. She dangled like a pendant on a string, afraid to lose any altitude by moving her wings too much. Eventually, the twisting and jostling turned her back to the wind.

Through her wings, she understood every nuance of the wind currents. The one she rode was forcing her toward the face of a distant cliff. She could also sense a backdraft pushing out and slightly to the side. Her only hope of not being smashed against the cliff like a swatted bug was to reach this alternate draft. Unfortunately, understanding the currents did not translate to an ability to effectively navigate them.

Leaning and angling with strength borne out of sheer determination, Annalla struggled against the once-saving wind now trying to destroy her. She felt like a fledgling bird flapping too-small wings in a futile fight against gravity. Her pulse raced, and panic gripped her stomach tighter every moment as the stone wall loomed larger until it was all she could see.

She closed her eyes, but it changed nothing. The opposing draft alone would not be enough or in time to slow her momentum. Gentle pressure against her skin told her the rock wall was right there. She positioned her legs to roll along its length to absorb the impact even as she opened her eyes again.

All at once, her knees buckled against the pressure as she slammed into the stone and the reversing current tugged hard on her wings. At least one waterskin burst when she hit, but no bones broke. Agony lanced through her as wings and body were pulled in multiple directions until the wind finally spun her off in a northeasterly direction.

The first spin around crumpled one wing against the rockface, so she dropped about fifteen feet before the lift caught her again. Another struggle to right herself ensued before Annalla regained her balance on the air and was no longer spiraling.

She was heading back the way she had come, this time along the opposite side of the canyon. Finding where her companions were remained the goal, but she was willing to settle for making it to the ground without breaking something.

Minutes added up, and the wind she rode began to die down. Without healthy wing joints, she knew she could not actually fly. This had been a haphazard glide enabled by the strong winds, and without them, she started to drop quickly.

As she passed a bend in the rocky landscape, her elven sight provided a clear enough view of the group in a clearing to the southeast. They were standing with weapons drawn, staring at Moonshine.

She made it down!

She spared a moment of glee for her horse before her rapid descent brought her own situation to the fore. Her course was well downhill from them. Depending on how quickly she came down, it could be well past their position. Annalla struggled around, wiggling like a worm on a hook until she found she could perform a controlled swing of her legs to push her momentum in a shift to the side.

It was awkward and exhausting, but it moved her closer to her friends. The shifts also took her out of the main wind currents, and she started to drop faster, which was good for her aim but bad for any ideas about landing. Not remembering ever having flown or landed before, she could only guess on how to go about reaching the ground without breaking her legs. Her lack of control was not going to make this easy.

Shock registered on Geelomin's face when he noticed her in the air, and he yelled, "Vampire!" at the others.

Annalla's eyes went wide, and she started flailing about again, waving her arms and legs, as though it might help them see it was her as they took up their bows on his command.

Geelomin *finally* took a second look and immediately yelled again, this time for them to stop, and she let out a sigh of relief. He said something too quiet for her to hear, which sent Thanon running up a trail leading away. Three elves started waving her over to them in unison. Annalla rolled her eyes and groaned before pointing to where she was headed.

Their path was along the top of a canyon wall. There was still an enormous drop below her, and she was heading straight for the side of that wall. By her best estimate, she would hit about ten or twenty feet below the ledge with about a sixty-foot drop to the still very steep slope at the bottom. There was no updraft down there, so Annalla was unsure if her wings would catch her again, or if she would simply plummet.

Push off or cling? She asked herself. She was moving slower this time, but the memory of smacking into the last wall was still fresh in her mind. *Push off or cling?* She asked again as the wall grew closer. *Push off or cling?!*

Even using her hands and legs to slow, Annalla smacked into the wall, hitting her cheek against the rock, and getting grit in her eye as the rest of her body smacked hard and jarred back a fraction. For a moment she was stuck there, suspended, but a moment was all it lasted before she fell.

Annalla scrabbled at the rock in a panic. Her left palm scratched open on something before the fingers of her right hand caught on an edge of rock. Momentum pulled her from it, but the brief grip slowed her enough to grab onto another edge right below it. Breathing heavy and shaking, Annalla dangled from the fingers of her left hand, blood trickling down her wrist and her eye watering.

Her wings hung limp down her back, the muscles not even responding when she tried to lift them again. She looked down through bleary eyes trying to blink away the grit. There were no footholds she could see, and the supply packs wrapped around her were in the way of her turning back against the wall where she might get her right hand on the edge as well. Annalla fumbled around for the knife to cut the straps, but she could not find it amid all the leather and pouches.

I can hold on, she told herself as her fingers started to ache. *They will not take long to get here, less than a half hour for certain.*

A soft breeze blew. She felt her body sway a fraction and her grip shift. Her fingers tightened as she sucked in a breath, but she had to relax them again to delay her hand cramping up for as long as possible. Falling from this height would not likely be immediately lethal, but the broken bones and internal damage it caused would mean death just as surely.

Annalla knew her wings were useless at the moment. They felt like lead weights pulling at her, and the only thing she got from trying to lift them was more pain. The best thing she could do right now was to literally hang on and wait for her friends to help her. Anything she tried was more likely to break her grip and send her plummeting, so she needed to rely on others, to trust them to help her.

Needing help was not a comfortable position for her to be in, and everything in her wanted to take action, take control, just like Larron said.

She waited, holding on and trying not to move. Her hand started cramping after a time, and she knew she was close to losing muscle control. Another minute, maybe two, and she would need to risk trying something, or she would be dead either way.

They will come, she thought again, even as she looked up at the ledge and tried to think of a way to maneuver her body around and up enough to grab it with her other hand.

Because of the supplies, she would need to pull higher to compensate. If she was not strong enough to lift herself, she might need momentum to gain the leverage, but that would strain her hand more at the start. It was her best option, though. She did not think she would be able to pull herself up on strained fingers without the movement.

Annalla slowly stretched out, preparing to swing her weight over and up. There was likely to be only one chance at this, and she closed her eyes to whisper confident words to herself.

"I can do this. Hold. Swing. Lift. Grab," she breathed. "Four simple steps, and my right hand is up there to give them more time to find me." Another breath. "On three…"

"Annalla!" a voice called from above. Still too far down the trail, but close.

A shaky breath escaped her as she started to ease out of the stretched position slowly.

"Thank you," she whispered before calling out. "Here! I'm here!"

Palan's head popped over the side and scanned for her, so she called out again, barely refraining from waving around to get his attention. The movement would not help her precarious hold.

His eyes caught on her, and he shouted back at someone. "Another half mile. Go!" Looking back over at her he called down, "We are close, Annalla, hold on!"

Her arm was screaming, but it would only be minutes now. She had to hold on just a little longer. All her concentration went to forcing her hand to maintain its grip. Dimly above her, she heard something about "another ten feet." It might have been Bealaras. Another moment passed, and Palan was calling her name.

"Annalla!" He called again, "Annalla! Grab the rope! Annalla!"

She had not realized she closed her eyes until she was forcing them open again to see a rope dangling a foot away from her against the rock face. There was no time for any methodical planning. She kept her movements smooth, but quickly shifted her weight around, wrapped the rope around her arm a couple of times, and grabbed it before letting go of the rock and trusting her entire weight to it.

As her fingers released, she gave a small cry of pain. Her cramped hand would not open or grip, so she dangled from one arm on the rope, but it held. Annalla pushed aside the pain in her hand and worked to wrap her legs around the cord even as she felt them pulling her up.

"Slow, slow," she heard Palan say, and she looked up to see him at the edge just above her. "Give me your other hand, Annalla."

Swallowing thickly, "I can't move my hand."

He met her eyes. "That is alright. I will take your wrist. It is only to help you over the edge here."

Annalla nodded and stretched out her aching arm for him to wrap his hand around her wrist and gently pull until Bealaras grabbed her other hand and the two of them lifted her over and away from the edge to where Geelomin was braced with the rope.

She collapsed against them, crying, and hugging them close.

"I was dead… Another minute, and I was dead." They awkwardly patted her shoulders. "Thank you for coming for me."

"Of course we did," Palan stated in a way that clearly said he thought she was daft to think they might not.

"Annalla, can you walk?" Geelomin asked. "Your back is bleeding, and we should make our way back to camp so you can receive treatment."

She wiped her eyes. "Help me up, please."

When they did, she stood and vividly remembered the large rock hitting her leg, which felt like hours ago, as the bruise throbbed. Taking a step to test it, she limped forward.

"I might need a hand."

"That will take longer. Climb on my back." Geelomin stood in front of her and squatted down slightly.

"What?" She blinked at his back, not comprehending, and saw him sigh.

"This is the fastest method that will not further damage your wings. Climb on."

Palan and Bealaras were obviously laughing at her, and Palan said, "Do you need assistance?"

"No." Annalla waved him off and hopped onto Geelomin's back, wrapping her arms around his neck as he grabbed her thighs. He stood and immediately started striding down the trail at a quick pace, leaving the other two to fall in behind him.

"My leg is not that bad," she said to him, hoping it was true.

They would need to walk most of the coming days, and she was certain after this incident Larron would absolutely not be okay with her at the back of the line anytime soon.

"I'm sure it is just bruised," she concluded confidently.

"You are probably correct, but it is growing darker and there are people back at camp who will worry over you until they see you safe again."

That quieted her protests. She knew how worried she had been over her horse alone.

She saw the flickering of a small fire when they came around a corner. The truth of his words hit when Thanon cheered and Larron came running over. Geelomin settled her on her feet before they walked further into camp.

Larron gently placed a hand on her cheek, and she stilled. He visually catalogued her limp and the blood on her shirt. "Are you alright? Is anything broken? What happened?"

Her heart skipped and the pain left for a moment at his touch and the concern in his eyes. She quickly buried the feeling and gave a wry grin.

"So many questions," she groaned theatrically. "I'm fine considering the circumstances. I don't think anything is broken, but I may have crushed some of the supplies." Her answers were said slowly to avoid breathing deeply. "You might need to patch up my back again."

"I need to look. Can you take off the shirt or do we need to cut it?" He was in full medic mode. She started to respond, but he cut her off. "Actually, it would be better to move you to the campsite now." He nodded at Palan and Bealaras as they moved into camp as well.

She winced as she walked, and he steadied her with a hand under her elbow.

Goodness, that hurts.

Every step pulled at her back, and she shortened her steps.

"I did not think you were yet capable of flight," Larron said as they approached the fire.

It hurt to laugh, so it came out as more of a rough, short bark.

"I am most definitely not able to fly. That was the fairy equivalent of getting down a hill by tumbling head over heels the entire way." She responded as Larron helped her to sit slowly after setting out one blanket and handing her another.

"Shirt."

Trickles of blood down her back told her the scars had torn open before Larron even had a chance to look at them. While they discreetly turned their backs, she started to slip off the shirt, but stopped when she tried to lift it. "Nope. I need help. I need someone to pull the shirt over my wings. Let me just get my arms and head out first."

Annalla pulled her arms in and slipped the loose front over her head to let it go behind her as gently as possible before she held the second blanket to her chest.

"Okay, maybe two people to help." She said as she tried to scrunch her wings up to a size that could fit through the shirt's holes, but her muscles remained unresponsive. Annalla fought back tears at the thought she might never be able to use her wings again, never be able to feel the wind currents.

"Geelomin, you take the shirt." Larron said as he saw her struggle and handed her something before kneeling at her back. "Chew this, it is for the pain."

Annalla popped the leaves in her mouth and chewed. She felt his hands move to gently support the bottom of her wings as he worked to accordion first one, then the other, and bring them straight back.

They were careful, but it took forever, and she was clenching her teeth together so tightly her jaw hurt by the time they were done. She did not even notice when they both departed, before Larron came back. He took a quick look at her ankle and calf before sitting behind her once more.

"As far as I can tell, the rest of the injuries are only scrapes and bruises." His hands were warm upon her back, a pleasant contrast to the cool salve he applied to the torn skin around her wings. "These are inflamed, but they do not look as bad as they were in the forest. If they healed from that, this should be no problem. You are going to need to restrict their movement again though."

His words brought tears of relief to her eyes, and Annalla finally relaxed a fraction. If his hands lingered, if she leaned into the touch, they both pretended not to notice while he worked.

"Did you see anything below on your flight?"

"No movement. Though, I must admit my concentration was not on the ground much beyond this spot. I have no idea what may lie ahead. The wind took me back west, not east."

"That is fine. You should rest tonight. We will cover your shift at watch." Larron must have also sensed Thanon lingering nearby, as his next comment was to him. "It appears you have supper for Annalla, which will also help. I will leave Thanon to aid you until you fall asleep. I should attend the camp."

"Thank you, Larron."

He looked at her as he stood. "Always."

Thanon sat beside her and watched Larron walk away. "He thought you were dead and still ran back to find you. I had to shout to gain his attention when I caught up enough to see him ahead of me. You had us all scared. Palan told me how close it was when they were running to you."

"He cares about his people." She looked at Thanon seriously. "It scared me, too."

She could tell Thanon thought about hugging her but settled on squeezing her hand after considering her injuries. He gave her a tentative smile. "I know. Palan told me you cried all over him. I think he is traumatized."

"Ha! I don't remember it that way at all." She laughed with him.

"Do you remember Geelomin giving you a ride like a child?"

"I'm certain *that* never happened. We would all be traumatized." The two of them shared equal grins, and she held up a shirt to him. "Help me put this on backwards so I can eat."

He held up the button-down shirt so she could slip her arms through, and he closed only the top couple buttons for her to avoid aggravating the treated wounds. She was glad for the help. Moving her arms strained overexerted muscles and the reopened injuries.

"What was it like to fly?" he asked as she started munching on her rations.

"Terrifying...and awesome. Though it wasn't really flying, and it hurt because I should not have been flying yet. I was worried I wouldn't be able to fly again because of reinjuring the joints, but Larron thinks they will still heal fine."

"That is good. I wonder how much you can carry. I would love to be able to fly."

"We'll see, Thanon. If I can carry people, I will take you on a flight with me." She chuckled at the elf's enthusiasm but could not completely stifle a yawn. The painkiller was starting to dull everything, including her thoughts.

"I will allow you to finish your meal so you can rest. I heard Larron tell you 'no watch' tonight, and you know he is telling the others."

"Yes, Sir." She yawned again. "I think resting tonight is for the best."

CHAPTER ELEVEN

They were five days into the barren terrain, having already crossed frequent ledges and loose slopes countless times. Her leg was feeling better. The bruise had given her the most trouble in the first couple of days. Larron wrapped it well, but even with that it became swollen after walking on it the first day.

Unfortunately, she could not ride any longer each day than anyone else. If that were not the case, she was certain Larron would have had her up on Moonshine constantly, whether or not the rest of the group was walking. She would have felt like some useless ornament. Annalla was simply glad the terrain drove more of their lack of speed than her own limitations.

It was mid-morning when the sky flared and a clap of thunder followed, rolling in from a distance. Looking behind them, a dark line could be seen in the sky at their backs quickly moving in from the northwest.

"Wow," Annalla whispered and slowly shook her head as another flash of lightning lit up the distant clouds. "That is going to be on us fast."

"Rain will make our footing problematic," Bealaras

added from his position in front of her.

Not to be left out, Thanon peeked his head to the side to look back at them. "More...*more* problematic."

She could almost hear Bealaras roll his eyes. "Yes, thank you, Thanon."

Larron looked back at the group. "We knew the weather could become an issue by setting out so late in the summer. The lightning is an added risk though, so we will look for a location where we might wait it out and hope it is not an extensive storm front."

Before midday, they were caught in a torrential downpour with a cacophony of thunder and lightning bursting around them. They had to move even more carefully, feeling every step, as visibility was reduced to a few horse-lengths ahead.

Solid stone was not too bad. They only had to watch their footing and make sure they followed the path of the person in front of them. The slopes with loose rocks and gravel between some of the stone ledges were an entirely different story.

As they crossed the open slopes, water poured down over and beneath the loose footing, moving smaller pebbles within the current and putting sideways force on everything. Sometimes the wind tried to help push them down the slope, and sometimes it tried to topple them flat against the hill.

The horses were reduced to moving only one foot at a time and bracing between each step. Their guides were not in any better shape. Forward progress slowed to a crawl, and Larron decided to push through their normal break hoping to find any sort of shelter.

After another such slope, the sturdier path that followed widened enough for three across, with a drop to the left and a cliff wall to the right, so Annalla moved up to walk beside Bealaras.

He looked at her, took a second look, and winced. "I am sorry we do not have an extra cloak for you to use."

"Do I look like a drowning rat?" She asked with a wry grin as she futilely blinked away the rain streaming down her head and face.

"What?" He yelled over the pounding rain, so she shouted her reply at him a second time and he smiled at her. "Perhaps, but a lovely drowning rat."

"Ha! Always with the flattery." Her grin widened. "We might have to settle for stable ground if we do not find a better place to stop for the night soon. This is the widest ledge we have had all day."

He stole a peek toward the sun. "Yes, within the hour, maybe two at the very latest."

The group made better time on the broad, stable path, but it was nearly an hour later before they slowed again. She heard a halt called from the front. Looking around the horses ahead, Annalla could just make out Palan's figure through the pouring rain. He must have stopped or returned early, knowing they would need to cut the day short with the weather beating down on them. He was currently conferring with Larron, but their words were muffled by the volume of the storm.

Palan's horse stood behind him beneath an overhang—if one was being generous with the description—created by the cliff wall. About four feet up, the wall started to angle out, jutting out more sharply about three feet further. It resulted in an abbreviated, sloped ceiling extending approximately five feet over the path and provided marginal shelter. Larron finished talking to Palan and waved the rest of them forward.

"Ring the horses around us here," He announced

loudly. "We will stay between them and the wall tonight. Remove the supplies as well. If the weather remains this bad, we will try to wait it out tomorrow as well."

"The fodder is going to mold with this much rain, even if it is kept closer to the wall with us," Bealaras sighed.

"At least we don't have to worry about water anymore," Annalla noted.

He stopped and stared at her as she passed him as though he could not comprehend. She could not help laughing at his stupefied expression. He might not remember the drought, but she would certainly not forget the feeling of dehydration sapping her strength more every day. Nor the taste of water that was more dirt and silt than liquid that she needed to suck the moisture out of to have even a hope of surviving.

Finally, he shook himself. "No, we no longer need to worry about water."

The five elves wrapped their cloaks about themselves after the horses and supplies were positioned, while Annalla used one of the spare blankets that were part of her original bedding as a cover. The cliff wall did little to stave off the rain, as the howling wind blew it in unpredictable directions, but they were already thoroughly soaked from the walk.

She tried to sleep. They bedded down with their heads toward the wall, rotating the bedrolls to scrunch together as they rotated who was on watch. Every time exhaustion tried to take her under, another clap-boom of lightning and thunder split the sky above them and rattled the mountain's bones. Horses shied away, she and those on either side of her jerked awake, and the cycle began again.

All of them were bleary-eyed when a grey morning came. Three elves sat opposite Annalla and the rest against the wall with her as they ate their cold meal together.

Larron wiped water from his face. "Thoughts?"

"Our supplies will last us for a seven-day delay, more if we tighten rations now. We do not endanger ourselves on slippery and shadowed footing if we wait a while longer to see if this will break," Palan offered.

"I propose we move on today despite the rain," countered Geelomin. "We know not what other obstacles The Claws will put in our path. Additional delays should not be discounted. We need to hedge against the unknown."

"True," Palan agreed. "If the season's rains are upon us, it could lead to further delays, and we do not know the condition of the pass ahead. My concern is that moving in this storm could make this entire discussion moot. Losing a packhorse would mean our supplies are immediately reduced. Or one of us could slip and fall. Best case there would be that we delay for recovery."

He did not need to speak of what the worst case would be. The death of one of them might simplify the supply situation, but no one considered that an acceptable option.

"Risks," Geelomin acknowledged. "But the weather was anticipated, we should not allow it to dictate our actions without an overwhelming threat to our safety."

Annalla was staring out at the storm, but she felt Larron look past Thanon toward her. With a break in the conversation, he called her out, "Annalla, what would you have us do?"

She glanced over at him and scrunched her face. He knew her well enough by now that his only response was to raise an eyebrow. Thinking back to her gliding flight gave her an idea, but it was only a rough idea. She was not certain of her ability to read or interpret anything accurately based on her limited insight into the air currents and reading them.

It would be an informed guess, but that might be more information than anyone else could offer on their current situation.

Setting the blanket she was wrapped in on Thanon's lap, Annalla took a deep breath as she stood and spread her wings. It still hurt, the new damage still in the early stages of healing, but it was less every day. At least she could open and close them now without needing assistance, so she could change her shirt unaided.

Closing her eyes, she tried to listen to the wind on her wings like she had in the air, hoping it would come to her again. Up there she knew the currents, knew where they were headed and relative strength. Once she was in the air, it had been instinct. On the ground, it felt forced.

A storm is simply air currents on a grander scale, right? she wondered as she let the rain and wind pound into her body.

"This storm will last more than a few days still as best I can tell. But I'm still a novice at this, and still injured," she offered. "Though I do not like that I am deaf to what is ahead of us, nor that travel will be slower over the slippery rocks, I'm not sure our supplies are enough to wait out this storm and any storms or other delays that might follow."

"How can you know how long the storm will last?" Bealaras asked, curious, but not questioning.

Grabbing the blanket, she wrapped her wings and cuddled back into it. The lingering warmth of summer kept her from freezing in the wind, but it was certainly not warm. Now she was soaked and freezing again.

"I don't know for sure," she answered. "When I took my glide the other day, it felt like I could read the wind somehow. I tried to do it again here, but it's confusing. Like reading a map you don't have a legend for. If I had to describe how this storm feels, it's like it came from the northwest and hit a barrier, but wherever it came from is still throwing force against that barrier. Like it slowed but has not given up and will not for a while."

"How certain are you of a few days?" Larron caught her eye again.

She shrugged. "Half sure?" Annalla held her hands palm-up, indicating that too was a guess. "I'm more sure of at least three days, less certain from there, but could be between four and seven."

Larron looked around at the others.

"It could be similar to our affinity to flora," Thanon offered, which made the rest of the elves look thoughtful.

"We will see to the horses and then head out mid-morning, stopping by the early evening as soon as we find a relatively reasonable location to sleep." His decision was made. "Palan, adjust how far you scout ahead, and plan for an early camp each night, especially if you find an ideal location. I will take a delay for something resembling a cave for a night out of this rain. We will make shorter days and try to end our travel before this murky, grey light becomes too dim for safety."

***

Once the supplies were loaded, they mounted and pushed away from the wall and out into the full pour of the storm. They followed a path that kept them at the lowest point as much as possible to avoid becoming a target for a random lightning strike. Days became short and constantly wet and gray, while the nights were long and uncomfortable.

Annalla was miserable. A blanket offered no protection from the rain, and her every moment was spent in garments heavy and clinging with water. It also helped the colder temperatures coming with the new season seep into her, sapping her of energy, denying her sleep, and making her teeth chatter.

She knew it could be worse. The temperatures were not too low, and she withstood them far better than she feared. Even so, as the days wore on, it became increasingly difficult to keep her focus against distractions. Her awareness narrowed to each next step in front of her.

Annalla could feel the eyes of her companions upon her. Every single one of them was torn between duty and compassion. Maybe they could rotate cloaks to share the burden. Maybe just one of them could trade off with her.

She suspected Thanon had asked Larron about it at one point. They spoke quietly enough that she could not hear them over the pouring rain. Their voices were audible to her, but the specific words were lost in the cacophony. Annalla only thought it was about her as Thanon nodded subtly in her direction at one point. Larron had closed his eyes briefly, looking in that moment like he had been punched in the gut, and shook his head.

Annalla knew why the decision was made. Their mission was important, and the five of them were more important to the mission than she. Annalla would have made the same decision as Larron because responsibilities came first, no matter the personal cost. So, when they stopped and she had enough brain power to think, she tried to ease their minds and joke like she did before. She nodded, met their gaze, and tried to make them understand she cast no blame.

Fortune held with them through the treacherous days on the slick stone. None of the horses came up lame and no one was injured. Throughout the morning, five days later, the rain gradually lessened. The infrequent, distant thunder and lightning disappeared entirely. Eventually, a clear sky passed over their heads to cease the downpour.

It took her a while to notice, still trapped in her tunnel vision of putting one foot before the other to keep moving forward. Finally, as more water dripped off her and was not instantly replaced, she looked up from the ground. Moonshine, also drenched and dripping, caught up to her as she stopped and nuzzled her cheek when she poked her head over Annalla's shoulder.

"Yes, girl. At last. I hope it stays dry for a while too," she said with a comforting pat before moving again, both of them a little lighter.

Later, at one of the rare wider areas of the trail they followed, Larron dropped back to where Annalla was riding and raised an eyebrow. "Five days?"

"In my estimated range." She could not restrain the smug smile tugging at her mouth.

"Can you tell how long the weather will remain clear?"

She lifted her face to the slight breeze chilling their damp clothing and opened her wings. Annalla suppressed a shiver at the cold running through her before the wind seeped in deeper.

"The wind has lessened here. It is difficult to judge what it might be at a distance... Two, perhaps three days before more rain, or it could pass us by entirely to the north." Smiling shyly now, she shrugged, "It was a guess, not a prediction."

"Fairly specific for a guess. You based it upon some form of knowing."

She tilted her head back and forth. "I don't know that I would call it *knowing* exactly, at least not for the outcome. It is the wind currents I am reading, and it was much easier when I was in the air.

"Storms, like the one we just went through, have different pressures, it flowed differently from what I felt before and since. I think something just clicked into place when I was gliding. I could feel the way the air was moving up there, and it stayed with me in a limited capacity. I was guessing on my estimate though, I really just thought it would be more than two or three days and picked numbers."

Her eyes widened and she snapped her head back to look at him. "Did that change your decision? I should have been more specific about what I meant."

Larron looked at her, face serious for a worrying moment before he smiled gently. "No. Any more than a day longer was too long to wait. Palan was correct about the risks of moving, but Geelomin and I made plans for this trip together. He was more aware of my preferences and expectations for this leg of the journey."

"Okay, good. How is our progress?"

"I am much less familiar with this route, but I believe we passed the midpoint yesterday or late the day before. That would put us around two days behind a crossing with zero setbacks. It depends greatly upon the weather, but we will likely leave The Claws in eight to eleven days more."

She did the math in her head. "The latter could put us close to your provisions estimate. Are you going to start rationing?"

"No." He shook his head. "What we just went through was a heavy storm. They are not unusual, but it is also not commonly frequent. Most weather we face should not be that extreme and will not have the same level of delays. If another of a similar magnitude does arrive, then I might consider rationing."

"We may be able to stay on the lower end of that

estimate if the sun dries out the rocks today."

"And you. And the horses."

"Ugh," she groaned. "Now you're just being mean. This blanket, and the rest of me, will probably never be dry again."

"We will be taking care of the animals at the next rest. You should change into something relatively dry at the same time."

"Yes, and wring out these clothes. Maybe I can hang them from the lead rope the next time we have to walk the horses."

Larron laughed at that. "We did not bring clothes pins with us, but you are welcome to try. I believe you would spend more time gathering fallen garments than they would spend hanging, though."

Annalla gave him a wry grin. "Hmm. I will have to give it some thought."

"You are not feeling ill?" It was a question he asked her every day it rained, quietly and away from the others.

"I'm still not sick. You are worrying too much." Every time he asked, she again tried to convey her understanding of the situation. She was not angry or upset with any of them.

"You should have started sniffling the first time he asked," Thanon said from in front of them. He remained bitter on her behalf. "He probably would have given you his cloak."

She smiled at the thought, but did not want him to remain angry at his commanding officer. "But then I would have had to keep pretending for days."

"Not necessarily. If it was clear the cloak was helping…"

"Are you crazy? Who would bandage my next

injuries, which you *know* are going to happen, if our medic is sick?" she asked with a laugh. "I know my priorities, Thanon, and I am far too accident prone to risk my personal physician's health."

"Huh," he grunted reluctantly, "I suppose that is true enough."

Larron sighed and shook his head dramatically. "No respect." The tone was serious, but his eyes were laughing with her and silently thanking her.

***

The sun dried the rocks that day, but they were back to walking the horses on uneven footing only a couple of hours later. Larron was disappointed the terrain did not exactly hold to Annalla's optimism. She did change clothes but decided not to dangle them from the lead rope and instead lay them out on rocks to dry overnight as they slept.

That first dry night, she even bent enough to request her removal from the watch rotation. It was a request he could, and did, easily grant. Annalla was the most worn from their recent weather, and he knew she needed a full night of sleep to regain her focus and vigilance.

Cliff walls around them at this leg were tall enough to maintain shadows throughout the days, so the lingering summer warmth quickly departed. It took longer for everything to dry now that there was moisture in the air. Dew and mist in the mornings dampened everyone's clothing, and Annalla changed back into her still-damp clothing when it appeared there might be a return of the rainy weather.

Larron pretended not to notice at night when his people on either side of Annalla spread their cloaks a little extra, exposing more of themselves to help her remain a bit less damp. It was useless in the earlier deluge, but worked well enough with the lighter falls.

Patchy rain clouds dotting the skies did more than dampen them with periodic heavier rains, and the constant moisture was just enough to keep their footing precarious and their pace slow. Fortunately, he was correct that they were not restricted to the slowest pace they were forced to keep in the massive storm.

As they plodded along, they began to miss even the dehydrated green color of the dead forest left behind. Now, they were constantly inundated with grey. Stone, sky; it was everywhere they looked. They had to be satisfied with the brief glimpses of blue overhead when the overcast deigned to part.

Slower winds held off the next storm until late on the thirteenth day of their trek through The Claws. A moderate rain fell, and the wind lacked the strength of the first storm, but their clothing and hair were clinging and dripping where exposed, and Annalla was yet again drenched from head to toe.

Larron hoped Palan returned soon with word of a likely campsite, but he was already late. If they came across a suitable place before his return, he would call a halt for the night and let Palan backtrack further to them. However, he suspected his delay was due to no suitable location having yet presented itself.

"Palan is late," he called back, always cautious in times such as these. "Stay alert, and I want quiet until he arrives."

Unfortunately, the darkness only deepened, and there was still no place they passed even remotely suitable or stable enough to stop upon.

Up and down, they had been on a continuous slope

one direction or the other since before mid-day. A slope made up of loose stone they and the horses sank into with each step. It was as much work as wading through snow or water, having to pull their feet out of the ankle-deep gravel.

At the moment, they were headed back down, and Larron hoped they would find Palan waiting on enough solid ground at the bottom to stop for the night. They would be racing true darkness to reach even that far.

Noise from behind him in the line broke into his thoughts of shelter, as it was uncommon for his party to break discipline.

He peered around Dusk to find Annalla stopped near the end of the line. She stood there, completely frozen and staring forward, and he could not interpret the expression on her face. The noise he heard was Thanon trying to gain her attention from behind to get her moving again.

"Annalla, why have you stopped?" he called back to her with just enough volume she might hear him.

She held up a hand to stop further questions and peered into the growing shadows before them. The worried look on her face was enough to have them brandishing weapons. With a frustrated shake of her head, she finally responded to him, but quietly through a relay.

"I thought I heard something ahead."

"Palan is due back," Bealaras offered between them.

"It's this damned rain! I don't know. Maybe."

Hearing that tone and those words from Bealaras's mouth was odd, but he felt her frustration even through the relay buffer.

"Everyone on alert until Palan returns," he passed along.

It was an unnecessary warning, as they would already be prepared for an attack without his order. With an uneasy feeling, they started moving again.

Larron was sharply reminded that he would have expected Palan's return before now. The hour was late enough, and with the arrival of the rain, he would have turned back early.

Palan was experienced enough that even with rough terrain to cover, he would have accounted for the extra time needed. Every step without sign of him pushed unease further toward dread, but a safe camping location was still necessary, and he would know that as their scout.

Another noise brought him to a halt, and he looked back to its source. Thanon set an arrow at the ready and was in the process of taking cover, while Annalla scrambled dangerously over the loose rocks past Geelomin and Bealaras, who were doing the same.

"Attack!"

He pulled out his own bow, reaching for an arrow, even as he started to ask for specifics. Annalla suddenly lunged across the short distance remaining between them. As she made contact, he heard the unmistakable sound of an arrow sinking into flesh and cracking bone.

He had a wild thought that Thanon shot at her in his defense when she attacked him, but it did not fit the circumstances. Her unexpected assault as he peered elsewhere left him without time to brace himself, and Larron fell backward to the ground with her landing on top of him.

The fall jammed jagged rocks into his back and knocked the breath from his lungs. It was then he heard the harsh hissing-snarl that was distinctly Gilar paired with the singing of bowstrings from both sides.

Still gasping to regain his breath, he and Annalla rose to their feet and supported each other as they sought shelter from the incoming missiles. The horses had panicked and scattered at the first sound of gilar, leaving the elves even more exposed.

The two of them took a position behind Larron's fallen packhorse even as arrows thunked into the body, and he finally readied an arrow to the bow in his hand. She looked around the body of the horse while he was arming and took count of their enemy.

"Three archers. Two on the right, the first is on a close ledge fifty feet up." Without doubt or hesitation, he rose, sighted, and released at the enemy archer, quickly ducking back down before the arrow hit home.

There were few vulnerable places on a gilar's hide, and at that distance, only the best archers had a chance of taking one out. Modesty aside, right now he was grateful well-trained elves could claim to be some of the best.

"Second is back further, maybe twelve feet, and kneeling at the top of the small cliff, seventy feet." As he rose and let his arrow fly, his peripheral vision caught approaching movement on the ground.

"Last archer is on the left, ten feet closer than the second, just below the top, seventy-five feet. Loosen your blade. Ten come on foot."

Laron rose to fire at the last archer. The arrow flew from his string, and he saw Annalla vault the dead horse and charge the leading gilar.

There was still time before they reached him. He knocked another arrow to continue his ranged attacks for as long as possible now that their support was—hopefully— taken out of the picture.

Before he could fire into them, Annalla reached the gilar front line. The leading gilar positioned his sword as if to thrust straight into her, but it was predictable and obvious, so she slid down on the loose rocks under its blade at the last moment.

With her body on the ground, sliding into position under the gilar's out-thrust arms, Annalla swung her legs up, knocking into its hands. She hit with enough force to loosen the blade from its grip, and her movement continued over until she was on her feet in front of the surprised and furious gilar.

Her entire maneuver had taken no longer to perform than it had for him to reload his bow and fire again. Sighting his next arrow, he saw she had gained the blade forced from the gilar's hands. As his arrow sang toward another target, she took the gilar's head with one fluid strike.

It was in that movement he noticed the dark shaft of a gilar arrow protruding from her forearm. There was a barely discernible slowing of her movements on that weakened side. The size of the gilar blade was too much for her injured arm, and she was barely compensating for it.

Unfortunately, he could not aid her any longer. Three stopped to attack her, but five charged around her and headed straight for him.

These were not trakins. They would not ignore the threat of his arrows to mob a weaker target, allowing him to pick them off one by one. Loose footing slowed their ascent, but not much. He reduced the number of attackers to four with one final arrow before they were upon him.

Two gilar slashed at him as he dropped his bow and drew his sword. It was brought up in time to deflect their attack and gain better positioning. He could no longer see how the others fared. All his attention was on his own fight.

With the first two attackers off balance, he spun to meet the blade of the third and ducked under the deadly arm spines of the fourth. It was a delicate dance, spinning and ducking and thrusting to meet or avoid blade and spine, all the while, working to land a blow of his own on one of his attackers. Any misstep or miscalculation would be fatal.

A sudden slip on the loose footing proved the truth of that thought, as one of the gilar stumbled and gave an opening for which he had been in desperate need. He cut deep into its torso, slashing flesh and bone, while shifting through the same movement to meet the oncoming blade of another. With a hiss of pain, it fell to the ground, immediately forgotten, and the fight continued against three without interruption.

It was grace against savagery, skill against force, though finding that initial advantage had taken too long. Night descended rapidly, giving more of the advantage to the night-sighted gilar, and he was tiring. His reactions slowed.

Three became two, and two became one. His blade was deep in the chest of the third to die, but his final opponent raised its battle-axe and the downward arc had already begun. He would never free his blade in time to defend or move to avoid the blow.

His nature would not allow him to simply give up. He forced away his weariness and reached desperately for the impossible, to bring his sword up to parry.

Time slowed, the moment extended, as if vivid paintings were strung together for him to view. Halfway through the arc, the axe paused then faltered. The blade angled slightly and the gilar tilted sideways on the slope. One of its legs fell away and dark blood poured from the stump. Behind where it stood a moment before, Annalla reversed her grip and thrust the blade in her hands through a groove in its armor and up into its chest.

Breathing heavily, she pointed back up the path. "There are more."

She was already moving past him, with as much

speed as the shifting rocks underfoot would allow.

"Take this."

He tossed her his sword, lighter and more suited to her stature and one functional arm. Larron retrieved his bow, thankfully still intact, from where he dropped it. The gilar archers had not taken out any of his people before they eliminated them.

The three elves were grouped behind him, facing another unit of attackers. They must have circled around, cutting off any escape from the ambush. That also explained why Thanon had not shot at any of the archers, even though he already had his bow in hand when the attack began.

It was a well-planned ambush, and it would have worked perfectly if they had not stopped upon the slope, and if an impatient archer had not suspected they knew and let his arrow fly.

Larron calmly aimed and picked off the gilar attacking his people. Annalla cleaved into the gilar, showing no concern as his arrows flew past her.

With the unexpected counterattack, the elves gained momentum despite the gilar's superior numbers. Only eight remained when he and Annalla joined the second fight, and they did not hold out long against four with blades and arrows flying in from a distance.

It ended as quickly as it had begun. The clash of steel rang out over the barren rocks for less than a half hour, but only the steady patter of rain broke the stillness around them now. As the tension of battle settled, many looked up and let the rain wash the blood from them.

Larron steadied himself and cut through the quiet in the most confident and commanding voice he could manage.

"Injuries?"

"Thanon has a deep cut on his arm from a gilar arm-spine. Bealaras, a gash on his head. His is not serious, but we need to stop the bleeding," Geelomin's response was nearly immediate. "Are you alright, Commander? That first arrow was meant for you. We saw you fall and thought you were dead."

He and his horses were likely the first targets. Their bodies would serve to block the easier escape down the hill and into better cover. As Geelomin spoke, he took stock of his own condition, noting that the falling axe had sliced through the leg of his pants, but it was not bleeding much.

"I suffered a scrape to the leg, but nothing serious. Annalla took the arrow meant for me. Geelomin, help me gather the remaining horses and supplies below. The rest of you, help each other down there, and do what you can to stop the bleeding. We will treat your injuries as soon as we find the medical supplies."

They heard Geelomin give a whistle. It was one way to summon the horses, but it did not always work when they were spooked from blood and death.

Without riders, the horses would seek self-preservation around the gilar unless their lead-reins were drawn tight. With riders, they could be formidable allies in mounted combat.

After a few moments, both Moonshine and Storm, the packhorse usually trailing behind Thanon, came trotting into view. Dusk peered out from rocks down the slope a moment later.

Annalla was already halfway there. She must have begun moving off as soon as the last gilar was killed, because she was much further down the slope than the rest of them.

"Geelomin, do not go far in your search for the other horses. They will return if they are able. We will search again in the morning if necessary. There are enough bandages in

Storm's bags, so I will see to the injuries now."

Geelomin nodded in acknowledgment of the change in orders, and walked off.

CHAPTER TWELVE

The base of the hill opened into a little flat area. It was still covered with scattered rocks, but she started sweeping a space clear with her foot after she collected and drew Dusk over with her to one side.

She felt numb. It was probably shock from the combination of the attack and her injury. Though the pain was distant, she felt hollow. Annalla knew there was something she was forgetting, but her brain could not make the necessary connection to understand what that might be.

She watched as Bealaras and Thanon leaned on each other as they walked into the clearing. Larron followed them, leading Moonshine and Storm. He pointed the two elves over toward where Annalla stood.

She chose a spot where the cliff wall pressed in to form a divot. While they walked over, Larron set the horses up where she had left Dusk quickly and efficiently.

A bundle, likely a medicinal kit, was in his hands as he walked over from the horses to join them. Annalla saw him quickly check and clean his own wound before making the rounds, looking over each of them in turn.

He pointed to her and then Bealaras. "The two of you

should have a seat. Stay together for warmth and let me know if either of you starts slurring your words or falling asleep. Bealaras, hold this against your head. Thanon, we will sit over here."

Thanon held the wound in his arm, but blood dripped steadily to the ground as he joined Larron where the waning light still reached against the opposite cliff face.

"How is your head?" Annalla asked as they both watched Larron work, sitting together with their backs against the rock wall.

She felt more than heard Bealaras's sigh. "It stings, but I believe it is a small cut. Unlike Thanon's arm."

"Do you think he will be able to use it again?"

"Commander Larron is one of the best medics we have." He nudged her with his shoulder and they both winced in pain. "Sorry. I meant that I think Larron will have him sewn up nicely. It will take time to heal, but he will get better, just like your wings."

"That is good." Annalla said somewhat distractedly.

"How are you feeling?"

Annalla cradled her arm, trying to block out the pain. She knew they were supposed to keep each other talking to watch for shock or head trauma or such. She was a little shaky right now but trying to remain calm, and she was not sure how to answer his question.

"My arm hurts really bad," she said when she settled on an answer.

"I am trying not to look at it," Bealaras admitted. "You saved Larron's life; taking that arrow instead of him."

She sighed. "Yeah. I should have yelled at him to get down like I told the rest of you. Instead, I was an idiot."

Both of them slowly turned their heads until their eyes met. They smiled and started to laugh, but it turned into a simultaneous groan when the action jostled their injuries.

"That was painful," Bealaras said when they settled again. "I have to say, I do not know what to continue talking about."

"Hmm. Do I still look good enough to paint?" she asked sarcastically, both of them still avoiding the truth neither of them wished to face.

He kept this smile from turning into a painful laugh. "At this moment? I could probably convey drama with the image, but I think I would rather draw the end of the battle. Larron's sword in one hand, the other still pierced with the weapon that wounded you. Fierce retribution upon your face…"

"Okay, stop," she interrupted him there. "You can't expect me to believe you talk like that. Even about painting. That last line is over the top, even for you."

Bealaras's smile was sad. "I may be exaggerating, but you are fierce in battle."

There were tears in her eyes. One fell down her cheek as she tried to blink them away and rubbed her chest with her good hand. "It *hurts*."

"So much," he said and ignored the physical pain he caused them both to wrap his arm around her shoulder. Both of them cried over their loss.

They said little more—only checking in periodically to make sure the other was not sleeping—until Larron and Thanon joined them. Larron peered at both of their injuries again but seemed dissatisfied with something.

"I am going to need a fire tonight. The rain is sparse, so I should be able to have it going quick enough. Will you two be alright while I start one?"

"You want to light a fire?" her voice sounded thick to her ears.

"If there were other gilar close, I believe they would have joined in the fight. I am also hoping the walls around us in this location will hide the light well enough. It is going to be necessary to see your injuries properly enough to work on, and to sanitize what I use from the kit."

"Oh," she said smartly. *That makes sense.* "That is why we brought a little wood with us."

"Yes."

He looked her over again and leaned over to peer closer into her eyes.

She knew she was not bad enough to worry him. It seemed he recognized that as well when he nodded, handed both her and Bealaras one of the pain leaves to chew on, and left to start the fire.

Each pack horse had a bundle with one or two fire logs and some kindling. Each bundle would not last long, but they needed to spread it out in case any of the horses fell. And now some of them have.

As Larron worked, Geelomin returned, leading Fleet and Holly, who both carried more packs lashed to their backs. Annalla heard him say that those two horses were fine and ask about status, then he quickly hobbled the horses and took over feeding the spark Larron started so he was free to collect his next charge.

Larron helped Bealaras to stand and they walked a few steps to the growing fire. Thanon was already sleeping, likely from whatever medicine he was given, but Annalla scooted gently toward him to share warmth.

"It stings, but I think it is a surface wound." Bealaras told Larron as the latter pushed back hair and angled his head to look at the wound in the light.

"I believe you are correct. The bleeding has already stopped, but I want to clean it again and properly bandage it."

He reached into the kit at his side.

"I would like to help with the camp. I am well enough to do so, and I will be less help with Annalla's arm."

Larron paused, then nodded as he continued. "Nothing too strenuous, and work slowly. If you feel tired, especially if you feel dizzy, you stop and let me know immediately."

Annalla did not even realize she had drifted off into a pained fog until someone touched her arm. The increased pain sent her mind back to the fight, and she lashed out instinctively with her leg. Fortunately, Larron was beside her and not in front of her.

He placed a hand on her shoulder trying to have her relax. She looked around to find the sun was gone, and the stars hidden behind the clouds, so she could not tell how long she had been out of it. Geelomin and Bealaras were near the horses. It looked like they were still working to unload supplies and harnesses. Thanon continued sleeping undisturbed on her other side.

Larron reached for her arm again. "I should see to this now."

She nodded, and he supported her arm and helped her stand so they could relocate closer to the fire.

His eyes scanned and his fingers probed to see what damage the arrow caused. It had entered at an angle, with most of the arrowhead striking the bone in her left forearm supporting the smaller fingers. The bone cracked with the impact, but it reduced the force of the arrow. Most of the arrowhead protruded from the other side of her arm, but it had not gone clean through. Her arm was also beginning to swell around the injury on both sides.

"I need to push this through. Their arrows often have barbs near the head to do more damage when pulled out.

Drink this." He handed her a small metal cup with steaming liquid.

"I am already drowsy. Will this put me under? Are you sure that's a good idea?"

He sighed. "Why can you not simply do as you are told?"

"Paranoia. You were the one to point out that I like control."

"This is going to hurt you. Drink."

"Because it felt so good on the way in?" She sighed, knowing she was just delaying the pain to come. "Fine."

As she took the cup, he called Geelomin over. The liquid was just cool enough to drink, so she downed it quickly. He positioned her arm so he could cut through the shaft against a rock as gently as possible. Geelomin joined them, and handed them each some thick cloth, hers to bite down on and Larron's to pad against the cut end of the shaft.

Getting on his knees behind her to support her back, Geelomin reached over and grabbed her arm to take over supporting it. His frame went hard around her, bracing against the movement, and Larron pushed. She whimpered into the thick cloth and fought back the threatening tears as Larron worked the arrow through the other side of her arm.

When enough of it was through, he quickly moved to her other side and finished pulling it out. Her stifled cries were ignored as Larron manipulated her arm, placed the splint, and finally bandaged her arm.

She was sweating and exhausted before he was done, and Geelomin had nail marks in his arm from where her other hand dug into him. As Larron moved on to the treatment portion of her torture, Geelomin wrapped one arm around her in a supportive embrace and leaned his head against hers, murmuring words that were likely encouragement. She could not recall anything he had said. Once it was finished, all three breathed a sigh, and Geelomin patted her shoulder as he rose. "Good work."

Larron paused at her side as if deciding something. "You saved my life. You probably saved all our lives. We—"

"Are even," she interrupted, hurting from the knowledge of what tonight's ambush meant. "I only wish it could have been more...sooner."

He bowed his head but moved to help her rise. "You should rest. We will search for Palan in the morning. Good night, Annalla."

He walked away once she was settled again, leaving Annalla alone.

There had been so many of them. Annalla thought they would never survive. Outnumbered, what was it...five to one?

It brought back the old nightmare. Annalla had been afraid the indistinct memory of her father's death would have made her freeze, made her hesitate. She didn't, no hesitation. They escaped when they should have died, but if they faced another attack of this force, the outcome would not be in their favor. Loss of another scout was a possibility, and two of them had injuries restricting their ability to fight.

Her forearm was broken, and the muscle of Thanon's arm was cut through based on what she saw of it. Neither of them would prove accurate with a bow, or probably even be able to draw one. They would be handicapped with a blade. That left three with unhindered fighting ability.

If only she had been able to hear further ahead, but with the sound of hooves and rainfall on the stone around her, it drowned out and camouflaged the distant sounds until too late. Even now, she strained to hear beyond the still-falling rain. Her fear of missing another sound of attack kept sleep from taking her again.

However, the medicine that put a fog between her and the pain won out. Sleep took her quietly, but it was restless and did not hold her for as long as she needed. She woke the following morning feeling anything but refreshed, and still bruised and broken.

It was a subdued group rising in the continuing drizzle and preparing to move out of camp. Annalla would have almost preferred a heavy rain to be falling on them. The light fall was more like a thick mist coating them than anything more significant.

The moisture wrapped around and clung to everything in a thin film, making her feel dirty, despite the fact it was only water.

Maybe it was simply that she killed people this time instead of animals. Maybe she felt guilty for not warning them sooner. Maybe she had come to like these people, and now one of them was most likely dead. Her father's death was still only a nightmare, this was memory.

They lost four of the horses in the attack—five if Palan's Kelley was among the lost—so they were down to five remaining. Supplies would be carried behind riders, since there were no longer any horses for baggage alone.

To make sure they had enough to last them through The Claws, they would not be riding at all until the food store began to run low again. Larron and Geelomin double checked they collected all they could off the dead animals while the others ate.

No one said anything. She would see someone think about starting a conversation, even take a breath to speak, but sorrow clouded their eyes and the words would not come. It was the same for her. She wanted to go back in time. Maybe they could do something different and it would change things.

It was not long into the day's travel before they found what was left of Palan and Kelley. If the gilar had not needed to set their ambush, they would probably have been carried away as food and nothing would have been left for them to find.

"His death was quick. This was done after he was gone," Larron said, kneeling next to the mutilated body of their friend. His face was stone. "A funeral pyre is too risky, and there is no suitable ground for a burial in the earth. We will give him a burial within the rocks."

Annalla looked around, lost, and another tear escaped.

"The smaller slope we passed just before this should work." Geelomin's voice was rough, and he swallowed thickly, but everyone nodded in agreement.

They laid Palan to rest at the base of the small slope. It was all they could do to ensure his body would not be disturbed by any other foul creatures roaming The Claws. He was wrapped and bound in cloth, and they tied off a rope so Geelomin and Larron could safely descend to lay his body out properly, his horse next to him.

Larron would not allow the injured to risk the descent, so the three of them kept watch from above as Palan was covered with rocks by hand. Once he was concealed to their satisfaction, they climbed back to the top and began as much of a rockslide as they could. It was far from ideal, but better than leaving his body as they found it. The five companions stood at the top when it was done, the dust starting to settle.

"Be at peace, my friend," Geelomin said next to her, and Annalla felt tears continue to sting her eyes.

Bealaras stared at the spot numbly, and Thanon

hugged himself against the hurt inside. Both cried with her. Larron whispered something too low for even her to hear, kneeling at the edge. He rose and signaled it was time to go.

With their respects paid to their fallen companion, they could not linger. All the supplies Palan carried were laid aside while they cared for his body. Items were distributed among the remaining horses, but Larron approached her with a final bundle in hand. She saw a couple nods from others as he passed, obviously knowing his intention, and approving.

"Take these," he said as he handed her Palan's weapons, wrapped in Palan's cloak.

Her first reaction was to open her mouth in protest. She had wanted weapons and a cloak of her own, but these were not hers. These belonged to a friend, and she did not want her wishing for *things* to be why he died.

Would he still be alive if I had not wanted? Would I have been able to prevent this?

Annalla knew the answers were 'no,' that there was nothing she could have done to stop what happened, nor did she contribute to his death. But her heart hurt, and guilt tugged at it for her failure.

Remembering the true reason they were available gave her pause. Gilar were here, in this same pass they traveled. The enemy was no longer to the distant south, but right in front of them.

They were on alert when Palan was late, but more of the elves would have died without her help. This was not about her and what she wanted. It was about having someone to step into Palan's place. To have his sword, even if they could no longer have him with them to wield it.

She took a deep breath, and her determined gaze met his. Those green eyes were hard as steel over the pain and left no room for argument. She would give him none.

With a nod, she took the weapons. His sword went at her side, and she maneuvered the straps of the quiver and his bow at her back into a position that would not interfere with her wings. The torn cloak settled over all. His weapons would continue to fight for his people, she would see to that.

"We move out. Geelomin is scouting. Annalla, take point. It might eliminate some of the noise from the horses if you are in front of them."

They were on their way again. By Larron's earlier estimate they had up to eight days of travel remaining through The Claws. Annalla focused all her senses on their surroundings, hoping caution would prove unnecessary, and that they would make it those eight days without losing anyone else.

***

The loss of Palan remained an open wound for Annalla. It was an open wound for all of them. Little beyond basic orders and necessary communication was said between the travelers, each left to their own grief.

Larron continued as though nothing had happened, nothing had changed beyond a shifting of responsibilities. At least he tried, he spoke less, joked less, just like the rest.

She knew that for him, the friend was subdued in preference to the commander. Commander Larron had a duty to the survivors and a mission to fulfill for his people. It only helped him so much though, and she suspected it was only on the surface.

The other elves had more varied reactions to the loss of their friend and companion. Geelomin became—though she had not thought it possible—even more reserved than before. His conversation went from little to none, helped by the fact he was now their primary scout and absent most of the day.

She saw him sitting off to the side of the camp at night, staring off into the darkness. What went through his mind every night? Guilt? Anger? Fear? Simple vigilance?

Bealaras and Thanon were less evasive with their thoughts and emotions. Neither had known him well before this mission, but they had centuries of random encounters to recall. They would cry and laugh and try to remember his life rather than his death in the days following the attack, but especially the night of the burial.

"Do you remember the time he was stuck in that tree?"

Bealaras let out a watery laugh. "Yes, I heard the stories brought back about it. He took that odd, angled jump up to a higher branch and could not remember the path to come back down. He remained on watch the rest of the night because he could not wake the next person in the rotation."

"And fell asleep in his saddle the next day, wandering until we caught up with Kelley and found her munching happily away."

"Ha! I did not hear that part. He must have pushed to keep it quiet."

Geelomin came over to join the three of them where they sat close together. "Palanthuiel had a rare talent with a bow, but he was forever distracted in training."

"You taught him?" Annalla asked.

"I tried. One time he brought a small knife with him to the practice session so he could carve designs into the bow 'whilst waiting his turn,' he claimed."

"I did not know he carved." Bealaras noted.

Geelomin sighed. "He did not, at least not well. It was, according to him, a way to prevent boredom while listening to us lecture."

"I can't imagine you being boring, Geelomin."
Annalla smiled at him.

Geelomin gave her a responding smile. "He did not
think so either after another Blademaster put an arrow in
front of his whittling nose."

Everyone laughed again, and they wiped tears from
their eyes. Most were still sorrowful, but a few came from
laughter. They talked about Palan for hours those first few
nights, eventually everyone joining in with stories. It helped
a little; started the healing.

"He volunteered for this mission," Larron said when
she approached him alone later one night. "He had traveled
to The Palonian before and knew the way. It was long ago,
but no one else with us has made the trip before other than
me."

She slid her arm around his waist in a side hug.
"That's why he scouted for us. He was the best choice."

Larron shifted to pull her into a full hug and rested his
cheek on her head. He swallowed thickly, and she heard tears
in his voice. "That does not make the loss easier. I used him
to warn us. Sending him ahead would flush out enemies, and
doing so placed the greatest risk upon his life."

"No, him being the right choice does not make it
easier. But this mission will succeed, and he will have
contributed to that. They can't take that away from him. You
said he volunteered, so he knew exactly what you were doing
and exactly what was at risk. You should not take that
bravery from him either."

She felt him take a deep breath against her. "I am glad
he met you. I know seeing fairy wings brought wonder to his
life, and he considered you a friend. It is something."

He did not pull away, so they stood there like that for

a while, but she knew he needed sleep. She lifted her head and gently pushed him toward his bedroll. "Go rest, Larron. I have this watch."

She was not sure he slept, that any of them slept much the first night. All were bleary eyed the next day, but the late nights helped more than they harmed, as there was a sense of renewed purpose in the morning and as they were on the move again. Annalla took point and watched for any marks left on stones by Geelomin during his passing before them.

"The camp Geelomin reported is up ahead. Want me to check it out first?"

"Yes, we will wait here."

She handed over Moonshine's reins and moved silently up and right.

It was early afternoon on the day following the burial, and Geelomin reported finding the gilar camp upon his return last night. He found it empty, and a marker today indicated the assessment remained unchanged, but they would take no chances.

If the gilar had been traveling in the same direction along the pass, they would have had warning of their presence before the encounter. The elves could camp somewhere at night and leave it the next morning without a trace of anyone having been there. Gilar, it seemed, were either not capable of the same stealth, or simply did not care if their passing were known.

Both fires were long gone cold, and flies buzzed around the entire area, drawn by the stench of decay. Annalla tugged down the sleeve of her oversized shirt and covered her nose as she peeked into the camp.

It was a relatively wide space between two walls, curving at the further end around the wall to the left. Off to one side was a pile of soggy excrement. Light rain had not washed it away, only softened it, so it started spreading over the flat ground.

Annalla had to fight not to retch, first at the sight, then again at the smell when she was no longer far enough upwind. There was no evidence any enemy remained, but she pressed forward to look around the next corner.

The sight that met her angered as much as it sickened her. Even gilar held to the adage 'don't shit where you eat,' it seemed, because here was their food supply. All of it coated in some thin, filmy resin, probably for preservation. Despite the coating, there was no mistaking the limbs and torsos of people. Another pile sat further back full of bones with obvious teeth marks.

This would have been their fate if they lost that battle. Some might have been taken alive as prisoners, but only so they could be killed to eat later.

What would they have fed the prisoners? Annalla thought in horror as she looked at the body parts.

She had to take a deep breath to steady herself, immediately regretting it and starting to cough when the reeking fumes overwhelmed her lungs.

The smell and morbid thought had her retching this time, and she bent over against the opposite wall before starting to stumble back. It was a moment before she regained composure enough to reach the place she could signal the others forward.

"They were traveling light," was Larron's only comment upon seeing the body parts.

Thanon looked at him in surprise. "Light? There have to be nearly five people there."

"One gilar would eagerly consume one person about every five days. There were more than twenty in the group that attacked us, and they would be held to nearly the same pace as us through this pass. This was hard rationing for the crossing."

"We were lucky," said Annalla.

Her thoughts were under enough control this time to restrict her reactions. She could now see Larron's logic and agreed with his assessment, and with what it likely meant.

"That they were rationing?" Thanon asked in a voice pitched from holding his nose.

"That we made it into the pass at all," Annalla answered. "With this kind of rationing, they had to be expecting supplies at the other end, which means they had reinforcements planned at the other end of the pass where we entered. A week later, and we might not have made it even this far."

As Larron's nod confirmed her logic, Thanon and Bealaras looked at each other with wide eyes before grimly pulling their mounts forward. She pushed ahead to take the lead, and heard Larron fall in at the rear of the line as they left the grim camp behind.

CHAPTER THIRTEEN

They passed eight more camps like that one, though no others with any of the gilars' 'food,' over the next six days. Twice they were forced to camp in the same locations the gilar had due to the terrain offering no other suitable locations. No one slept easy on those nights as they huddled as far from the refuse mounds as possible.

Larron was grateful for any rain that came before those days, as it meant more of the foul remains were washed away before they arrived.

Judging by the spacing of the camps, they were making better time than the gilar had from the other direction, but they also had the horses to carry their supplies. No evidence of a permanent base in this pass of the Claws was found—not that it was a likely location for such a thing—and their suspicion of an unfortunate, random event gained more confirmation every day. It only proved the need for constant vigilance, an attack could come without any signs or warning.

Or almost *without any warning,* he thought to himself with a grim smile, remembering Annalla managing enough of an alert to keep the rest of them alive.

Larron looked toward the sun shining in the sky again and felt himself intentionally breathe out a little of the constant tension. He longed for the feel of a thriving, healthy Woodland.

That was not the usual way of his travels. More often, it was the rigidity of the Woodland, or any place he stayed overlong, feeling stifling and driving him to leave for something different. People, places, and even landscapes were always changing out in the rest of the world. Few were as careful with their changes as the elves, so they were not always changed for the better, but it was never as bad as this.

Now, everywhere, people were living in fear. On the roads, in their homes, it did not matter. His home was not immune to the effects of war, but the degradation they saw in the forest was only a small example of what was happening elsewhere. It was worse to the south.

He knew they were fortunate their destination did not lie in that direction. Larron wanted something safe and a land that was not dying around them. Kahnlair was a poison leaching into the world from every direction and leaving destruction in its wake. People, land, animals—nothing was safe or spared.

A fist in the air put an end to his wandering thoughts. Without even thinking about it, he told Dusk to stand and had an arrow at the ready in a moment. Bealaras would have his out as well, while the injuries of the other two kept them limited to blades. All scattered and hid. No one doubted Annalla heard something ahead, even though it would need to be much closer for them to make out.

It was too soon for Geelomin's return unless he had something to report. Even then, they would not relax until they could be certain it was him.

Time crept forward. Annalla did not move forward to

investigate, so she must think the noise indicated something near enough and minor enough to wait, but that did not make the time pass any more quickly.

Few people of any race would spot the four of them scattered and hiding among the rocks. Though they could do nothing about the horses except order them to flee. They wanted, *needed*, to be out of this place with all their remaining animals, so that was not an option unless Annalla was hearing another troop of Gilar approach.

Larron was beginning to wonder if he should order her ahead to search around when Geelomin came around a bend in the path ahead. Their scout pulled up and took in the abandoned horses with a quick glance. Without hesitation, he motioned the sign for 'all clear' and continued toward them.

He was back early, but whatever the reason, it was not to warn them of an attack. Swords were sheathed, bowstrings relaxed, and they emerged from their sheltered sightlines. Geelomin paid no special attention to their movements, but Larron smiled at the memory of the awe some had when elves seemed to materialize out of the ground. It took effort, but he often found himself doing so on his travels. He enjoyed being able to build and encourage the *mystery* of the elves.

"Report?" Larron asked without greeting.

"Commander, we will leave The Claws before the day is done," Geelomin said with more emotion than he usually showed.

He could feel the pressure ease from the entire party at those words. "How long would you estimate?"

"Not more than an hour from here the pass ends. It is without an exit, but I already found a path up this slope. I returned to lead you to where the path begins, as it is best accessed before the dead end." He sighed and added, "We will finally quit these dreadful rocks."

"I would assume that means the horses can traverse this path?"

He nodded with a wry smile. "The footing is marginally better than the entrance, and no worse than we have faced since then."

Larron allowed himself a moment to share their relief and smiled. "Lead on, Lieutenant."

All of them had grown accustomed to the sheer drops and loose footing over the last two weeks. Even the horses appeared more sure of their movements. When they stopped at the bottom of the hill and looked up, no one even blinked. They simply started checking supply ties one last time.

"We can do this," Thanon said with a dismissive air. "Did you get a look at the other side?"

Geelomin nodded from the front. "This is the worst we will face. It is still steep on the other side, especially at the top, but the slope appears relatively secure."

"Our greatest risk will be exposure on the descent," Larron reminded them. "Geelomin will scan for enemies at the top. If there are any, we will need to descend this side rapidly and hope we can set up an ambush should they head this direction. If it is clear, we will proceed as quickly as safety allows and move to cover."

Geelomin started up as soon as he was ready, and they each followed as they finished their checks. Larron waited until the end. He would be last this time. Annalla gave him a look, but he simply raised an unamused eyebrow and waited. She thought about arguing, or making some point—he could see it in her eyes—but decided to instead roll her eyes and smirk at him before heading up after Thanon.

Their loyal horses pressed up the hill with them. They were leaner than before The Claws. The oats had to be rationed and were going stale. The grasses they had collected were starting to mold of late, so some had to be tossed when there were suitable locations to do so.

Many nights they slept without cover, some nights they slept with the supplies still strapped to their backs. Their coats were wet and tangled from the elements despite the frequent brushing. Shoes had been replaced, but only when absolutely necessary, and their legs were cut from wading through deep gravel. Some of their herd had died and were no longer with them. Yet they still followed, still pushed on.

Larron watched ahead as Geelomin's head turned, scanning the land below and around them as far as his eyes could discern. One pass across, one pass back. He nodded to himself and proceeded, disappearing over to the other side with Fleet right behind him.

Each person did another quick scan at the top before they too, disappeared from his sight. Bealaras, who now led Storm. Thanon, Holly and Annalla, Moonshine. Finally, he reached the top and scanned below. Forest and patches of open land stretched below his elevated perch, and all of his people were safely making their way down the slope. While there might be people within the trees who could still spot them, no threats were visible to him. He also saw that Geelomin spoke true when he said this side would be much easier to descend.

It looked like a large portion of the rock wall broke off within the last decade, crashing down and sliding to settle on the south end of the slope. That might be the reason the gilar had been in this pass. With the impassable portion of this wall having fallen, it was much more accessible from this end than it had been in the past.

Previously, they would have had an extended search for a traversable exit. The change in the rock wall made this passage a more viable option. Larron would also not dwell on whether this would have changed his decision of their route. Decisions were made with the information available, there was no changing them with hindsight. Though not whole, their party made it through, so it was a correct decision.

This crossing was much less eventful, with no landslide with which to contend. The horses were eager to reach the bottom and the grass they could smell since the morning. Gradually, the slope declined, the gravel lessened, and the footing became sturdier. They could extend the leads for grazing and were finally able to look around.

It was as though waking from a nightmare with the stark contrast between the two landscapes moving them from one world to another. The Claws had been grey, bleak, and lifeless. Looking out from the base of the range, autumn was on full display. Greens, reds, and golds. Even the soft rain falling enhanced the surrounding life as it fell softly upon leaf and grass.

At the base of the cliff, tall grasses and wildflowers spread north and south with a few trees dotted through the open landscape between the rock at their backs and the forest to the east. The heavier flowers bowed over with the weight of the rain water pulling at the thick blooms. Areas beneath the trees were similarly weighted down with wet leaves collecting on the ground and turning brown. Leaves still in the process of abscission upon the branches ran the range of colors and added to the palette provided by the wildflowers.

No one spoke for some time. Larron's eyes were wide, soaking up the sights before him even as they continued to walk toward the tree cover. His breath caught in his throat with the overwhelming joy of it.

It was likely none of them had known just how deeply recent events had touched them and how little they had allowed themselves to feel as they slowly sank their emotions into the desolation around them. Now it all rushed back and the elves' innate connection to life within the earth threatened to engulf them.

They thrived off the life in the land as much as it did from them, and they had been suffering from the lack. Unshed tears moistened their eyes before they blinked them back and regained a hold on their composure. Escape from The Claws gave new life to the group as they pushed ahead, putting distance between themselves and that dead landscape full of ill memories.

"No fire tonight, but allow the horses to stay on longer leads," Larron said when they found an adequate spot to camp. "We should also dig a hole in which to bury the food and fodder in our packs that has started to turn."

"Do you think it will be safe to have a fire tomorrow to resupply?" Geelomin asked him. "We know there are gilar on this side of The Claws."

"We have little choice. If you find an area surrounded by dense cover in your scouting tomorrow, we should stop there. No matter how far along you are, start back immediately to lead us there. That will offer us the best protection."

There was one small shovel for digging their latrine, so he grabbed it and started working while the others unloaded the horses and gave them each a good brushing and checked all their hooves again. Rather than a standard trench, this time he dug deep and wide, and when he hopped out, they carried over the cut grass and some of their food that started to mold due to the rain. He threw dirt in periodically to fill some of the space the grass left, and they stomped it flat after it was full.

Larron then used the remaining dirt, starting on one

side and moving across, to scatter in the area and hide their digging and passage as much as possible. Some leaves were thrown to fall as they would beneath the branches to further obscure their presence, and the rain would remove the final traces.

"How much food do we have after this?"

"About two days. We could stretch that to six if we ate all of the bread," Thanon answered, as he was the one handing out rations tonight.

Larron shook his head. "No. Keep that to a minimum. Tomorrow we will pair up while Geelomin searches for a secure location where we can have a fire. Each pair will cover north or south of our direction to hunt and forage whatever we can find. Allow the horses to graze often, and one of the pair is always on watch, not helping with forage.

"Bealaras and Thanon, you will take the north side. Annalla, you are with me to the south. Keep your bearings and return to the path an hour before midday and drop markers. We will likely remain at the next campsite longer than usual to prepare. Questions?"

No one had any before they began to bed down for the night. The horses crowded beneath one tree and their bedrolls cuddled together beneath another. Yes, they were sleeping on the ground, and rain penetrated the remaining leaf cover. But compared to stone or gravel for bedding, and no protection from the rain, it was luxury. Larron was not sure of the others, but when his watch was done, he slept soundly that night.

The following morning, they smoothly packed and rode out on their assignments.

"I must admit, I expected some objection or question from you last night," Larron stated quietly.

As he was looking over, he caught her shrug.

"I had questions, but figured I could ask them today since I would be coming with you anyway."

"Such as?"

Annalla gestured in a generally eastward direction. "What if Geelomin finds a camp immediately and we pass it before we are back on the path? Wouldn't the markers not work?"

"Standard protocol is to drop markers every twenty minutes. If you are on a path without markers for more than a half hour, you are likely beyond the rest of your party and you backtrack, removing your markers as you return."

"And Geelomin should be furthest out or have a camp set up and markers out to notify the rest of us as we backtrack."

"Exactly."

"But we could be too far north or south and miss the markers."

He shook his head. "Less likely. You saw us take bearings before we left. Even should the path he needs to take divert, he would return to place another marker. It is not foolproof, especially in unfamiliar territory, but at worst we lose a day reconnoitering at last night's campsite."

She looked thoughtful, but he could tell she would prefer something more guaranteed or less likely to be discovered. However, a party needed to communicate and regroup. They could not pass as invisibly as one alone might.

They both scanned the area for a short time before he asked, "Anything else you wanted to know?"

"That was all." She paused. "You know I can't help you hunt still, right?"

He looked at her splinted arm and said dryly, "I am aware. I am uninjured, which is why you are with me. Thanon and Bealaras are both healed enough to use all their weapons."

She made a sound he could not interpret.

"You disagree?"

"Thanon's arm is still pretty bad. You think it is healed enough?"

Larron gave her a grim look. "There is a fair chance that if he is forced to fight, he could do irreparable damage to the arm. However, he can draw the bow if necessary. I have warned him of this, and he will be on watch, not hunting."

Another unintelligible sound came from her.

"You still disagree?"

"Nope." She popped the end of the word.

He waited, but she said no more.

"It feels as though there is more to that statement." After a slight hesitation, unsure of the answer, he asked the question that mattered to him. "You would prefer to partner with one of the others?"

"Yes." She sighed, and he felt his heart constrict at her direct answer. "You and I are the best fighters. It's a *waste* to have us together, but right now I *am* the weakest link. It's very irritating and makes me feel partially useless and partially restless."

That was not the response he expected, and it had him jerking his emotions under control. "You believe we are the best fighters?"

She just turned her head and looked at him in a way that said he was an idiot for asking, rolled her eyes, and kept riding. It made him laugh to himself and, if he was being honest, preen a little.

Annalla respected strength and ability, and she acknowledged his abilities.

I sound like a juvenile in my own head, he scolded and scanned the forest again.

A short time later she pointed to the left, and he could see a couple squirrels rooting around in the dirt. He took one, the other ran, but they discovered that the tree the squirrels were under was a walnut tree. Setting the horses to graze, he dealt with the squirrel first while she stood sentry.

"I could collect some of the nuts. I would still hear something coming," she complained as he worked.

His lips turned up, but he kept his voice unamused. "You are unlikely to hear vampires if they see you first. And I am not going to ignore my own orders and set a bad example."

"A bad example for who?"

"Whom," he corrected absently. "For you; a bad example for you."

"Hmm." The emotion she could convey with a sound astounded him. This one was grumpy, amused, bored, and noncommittal all at once.

"Larron, the others told me the war is not going well for the Derou, or anyone really. Now there are gilar between one Woodland and another, on land that belongs to the elves. What are you hoping to accomplish with your mission?"

He washed up, grabbed a bag, and started collecting any nuts the local wildlife had not yet taken.

Her eyes bugged. "You cannot seriously expect me to keep watching!"

"I have two good arms, so I absolutely can." He smiled, then set to work before answering her other questions. "The Palonian Woodland hosts the northern war council. It is where reserves are trained for the war, where serious injuries are rehabilitated, and it helps coordinate supplies being sent to those in the south where the fighting started. Refugees were relocated with the assistance of the northern war council in a way that would not overtax resources and still allow support to the war effort.

"While the southern council determines tactics for the war and the disposition of our troops, the northern council is the resource and support hub. It is from where we received our updates before we lost communication. We were holding our own, but that is no longer true. We need help."

"If the gilar are this far north…"

"I know." He interrupted her, knowing that it could mean nothing good. "My orders were to find help, no matter what I needed to offer on behalf of my people. The council is the best hope of speaking with our allies."

She turned silent for a while, and he continued collecting whole nuts in the bag. He needed to reach The Palonian for help, or everything that was 'The Derou' would fall. The elves and the Woodland itself.

"What if the counsel can't, or won't, help?" Annalla asked into the silence. It was a question he had asked himself, a question he had asked Prince Erro before he left.

"Then I move on to the next."

He could feel her looking at him, weighing his words and intent as if he had spoken more aloud than he intended. "I will go with you. I will help."

There was a weight behind that promise as he met her eyes. Something beyond either of them was in those words. He knew that weight, as he spoke with it when he represented his people. A powerful mage spoke with such authority in their path of learning, and an essential spoke with it in their concentration. It was a power that went beyond the person and represented what they could command.

Larron took a breath and nodded, unsure of exactly what he was agreeing to with the movement. It was very possible he was reading more into this moment than was there. He often heard more than her words when she spoke, saw more in her gestures than she expressed. So, maybe he was hearing more in this promise as well. Perhaps it was the strength of her conviction alone. Either way, he would take the support, and he would accept her sword at his side.

CHAPTER FOURTEEN

For those first few days in the forest, they took it easy on the horses, allowing them to regain some of the weight they had lost while at the same time hunting and gathering to replenish their own supplies. The area was sparsely treed, but the grass was tall, and some locations offered enough protection to risk a fire.

They would need to take larger prey to warrant a stop long enough to smoke-dry more reserve meat. Until then, they would continue the daily trapping and hunting. Each day added a little to their reserves, though, and Larron wanted to push at a faster pace again.

"We are fortunate the game is not as scarce as it was in the eastern forest," Thanon said as he roasted the breakfast rabbit.

Annalla cocked her head. "You mean the trakin forest to the west?"

"Yes." He shrugged. "It is east of The Derou."

"Our entire journey is east of The Derou," Bealaras teased him, laughing at his own joke.

She shook her head at their banter. "Does the forest have an actual name?"

More shrugging showed him no one else knew, so he was the one to respond. "There were some human villages along the river we crossed. Most thought the forest to be part of The Derou. Further south it is simply considered unclaimed wilderness without a name. The human kingdom has declared it elven land that humans have passage through but cannot claim. Most call it the Elven Forest."

"Larron, join us." Annalla patted the stump next to her when she looked at him, then continued the conversation. "What is this forest called then?"

He moved to stand next to her but looked out at the landscape surrounding them rather than sitting. A hand grabbing his and giving a gentle tug had him looking down and taking a seat in response.

"This is also called the Elven Forest by humans who live on this side of The Claws."

"Why do elves name the mountains but not the forests?" she asked him, and thanked Thanon as he passed out food.

As she released his hand to take the plate, he realized he had still been holding on. He ignored Thanon's smirk and answered her.

"The Woodlands grow and contract their influence around the Heartwood over time, so the forests of the world are all, on some level, part of the Woodlands. Each Heartwood is given a name, and the Woodland boundaries as we call them are defined by the active influence at any point in time."

Her forehead wrinkled. "I'm still not sure that makes sense."

"It is an old habit, and most elves stay in their Heartwood. The forests have never needed names, so we do not name them," he simplified.

Annalla shook her head again. "This is going to get confusing. I haven't decided on this one yet, but that other forest is now Trakin Forest for our reference. If you can get it to catch on with the rest of the elves, even better."

"I wish you luck with that," Bealaras commented without committing to any such thing as he began to clean up.

"The quiet here is unsettling after the attack." She commented quietly to Larron when they were done and cleaning up.

"We do not know where they came from or why they were on this side of the pass, so it is difficult to assess the level of risk."

Her rinsing paused. "But you have a guess."

"The main pass is south of the one we took. I suspect the gilar group was travelling from the fighting in the south toward The Derou to join the fight there. They likely had orders to scout this side of The Claws along the way to the pass but missed the main pass entrance. With the changes to the rock wall where we exited, they could have mistaken the area. It would explain their light rations and presence with no evidence of greater gilar activity in the area."

"That would mean the threat is...not as bad as it could have been."

"Huh," he let out a breath. "It is a fair way to summarize. I do want us to begin making additional progress each day though. We will set camp early in the evening and break camp later in the mornings to forage, but nothing during the day unless we come across an obvious windfall."

"How long until we reach The Palonian?"

They packed their final supplies and mounted with the others. "At the current pace? More than two weeks. With the increase, I believe we should arrive in approximately thirteen days."

Thanon rubbed his hands together, the arm healing well, as he fell in behind Annalla in line. "Two weeks. I can taste the pie already."

"Speaking of food, Thanon," Annalla turned her attention to him, "will you teach me how to set your snare?"

"Of course. I will show you tonight."

Their conversation faded as Larron waited to fall in at the end of the line, and he continued weighing the risks. This leg should be safer, but he knew not to trust old expectations. And yet, each day forward was relaxed and quiet. Geelomin found nothing, no sign of gilar or other forces, and they hunted and gathered at least enough each day to get them through to the next. If Larron's math was correct, with another four days having passed, they should be approaching the north end of the swamp before long.

"It smells as though we are nearing the fen." Thanon confirmed his assessment late the next day as they finished setting camp for the night.

He was likely commenting on a moist odor of mild decay coming in with the shifting wind. Thanon sat preparing snares, while Bealaras brought in wood for the breakfast fire and Larron finished the two-handed tasks with the horses. Geelomin was just returned and tending his own mount.

"And we will be passing through this bog?" Annalla asked with a wrinkled nose, not attempting to hide her preference against such a course.

She only spared a moment for the comment, though, before returning her focus to the snare in her hands. As promised, Thanon had tried to teach her how to make one. It probably would have worked well enough if she had full use of both arms, but the splint and sling he insisted she wear continued to hamper her movement. This resulted in a great deal of concentration needed, a lot of effort, and one or two very poorly constructed snares each night. Thanon thought this was fantastic and smiled like an overindulgent parent every time she handed him one.

"Ha!" Larron smiled largely at her disgruntled comment and finished checking the last hoof. "No, fortunately we will be able to go around this time. It will add about a day's travel looping north, but trying to cross through it would add much more since the rains have started."

Bealaras had finished his task and started to hand out evening rations. "How large is it?"

Everyone looked to Larron as he joined them.

"No more than five leagues at its widest," he answered. "We will be crossing around the northern edge, but it stretches south and east for a distance yet. This one, we call it the Naurice wetland,"

"You named the wetland but not the forest?" Annalla muttered.

"Named so by the humans when they began to explore it," he continued with a pointed look. "It becomes rather passable in the summer. There are still areas where mud will swallow your boots, but firm and dry paths are more common.

"With the dry summer we had, it would have been faster to travel through this section rather than around before the rains came. The same cannot be said of the Carsanje wetland in the south. Part of the Yaziren River branches off and feeds directly into that area. It is about three times the size of the Naurice and remains a flooded quagmire the entire year. The only way through is using the shallow, light-weight boats made by those who live along its borders."

"Sounds appealing," Annalla said with no little sarcasm.

"I am sure I do not do it justice. It has a certain appeal. There is a thriving, dense collection of plant and animal life both above and below the water."

"You have been there?"

"A few times. It is one of those places that is so remote and isolated, you could almost describe being there as an experience taking you back to nature in a profound way."

"You certainly have a unique perspective of a smelly, insect ridden swamp land."

"Perhaps I will be able to show it to you someday. That is likely the only way I could share the experience I am poorly implying."

"I am going to reluctantly decline that offer, Larron," Thanon put in. "If we have time to rest again, I will surely never want to leave the Derou again. I will leave the swamp wandering to you travelers and be perfectly happy in my quiet woods."

"Well, if my memory is not back by then, you probably *will* find yourself with a traveling companion. It might save me from another round of amnesia and fighting enormous, insatiable bugs."

"You would be more than welcome," he heard himself say. Larron felt the unspoken surprise of the other elves. They knew travelers were usually solitary by nature.

"Annalla, mosquitos might not be enormous, but they are certainly insatiable bugs," Thanon warned her patiently and smiled. "Be careful what you allow Larron to talk you into doing."

"I'm sure I could handle a few mosquitos," she said to a round of laughter even as her attempt at a knot fell apart again in her hands.

***

She could not handle a few mosquitos! Or maybe she could handle a few, but this was not a few. Maybe a few hundred, but *definitely* not just a few.

"I thought we were going around the swamp," Annalla complained as she slapped at her neck again and growled.

"We are." Larron was second in line, just behind her, to help guide them. "This is only the northern edge of it. The mosquitos are worse than usual, and you appear to attract them more than anyone I have seen before."

The smell was not bad, more of an earthy aroma you grew accustomed to quickly. The dense foliage of trees draped with moss provided greater cover, while the damp earth did not slow them overmuch. Sometimes the horses walked through ankle deep water, but it came and went, and they could find solid places to sleep nearby easily enough.

There were three main drawbacks she found so far. First, they needed to ration. Foraging was more time consuming here, so they did not do much of it. Larron did not want to cut their supply too close yet, in case there was another delay, so he had them limiting their food intake while crossing through the boggier area.

Second, at night, they slept on ground they almost sank into. The damp seeped up from the ground and leached much of the heat from their bodies even through their cloaks and blankets. They cuddled up at night like they had in The Claws to keep warm, but it was far from comfortable. Fortunately, they might not even spend one more night in the damp land if they made good time.

Finally, there were the bugs.

Bugs were the biggest problem. The little, biting insects were only half deterred by more special goo the elves brought with them. They focused their attacks on her rather than the elves, and she was itchy in places no bug should have been able to reach.

Annalla squeezed her hands into tight fists, ignoring the pain it caused in her arm, to refrain from scratching at some of the bites. She rotated her neck and pulled the cloak tighter in a futile attempt to keep the vermin out.

"I'm going to use up that sting-goop of yours," she said as Moonshine stepped onto dry ground again from the hand or so of water trudged through for the last quarter hour.

She heard Thanon chuckle and knew he was going to say something snarky to get himself in trouble again. "Commander, you should make sure she is administering it correctly."

"Thanon…" Larron started to scold, but Holly reared up under Thanon at that moment and cried out in pain and fear as her rider was thrown into the shallow water.

Thanon rolled through the water, taking the brunt of the fall smoothly even as he sliced out with his knife at something. "Snake."

Larron quickly dismounted and handed his reins to Annalla. "Bring Holly up here, try to calm her. Where is the snake?"

The horse was limping and tossing her head even as she did her best to follow Thanon's lead through the pain. With his blade still out in his other hand, Thanon flipped half the snake toward Larron even as he made calming noises and Annalla arrived to help after hitching the horses to a branch.

"What is it?" Bealaras asked, bringing up the rear of the party.

It was an unassuming looking snake, not too large, black, with a lighter color head. She heard him respond to Bealaras, but not to the question asked. "You have the anesthetic in your pack?"

"Yes," he said, while Larron only looked toward where she and Thanon stood coaxing Holly forward. "I will get it out."

Even by the time they made it the few steps to dry footing, Holly was staggering, sweating, and breathing heavily.

"Try to have her lie down." He took a vial from Bealaras but waited to approach until the two of them had talked Holly into settling.

Unstopping the vial, Larron opened it and allowed two drops to enter the small puncture wound on the horse's front leg. Over a handful of minutes, with all four of them petting her, she gradually became calm, and eventually fell unconscious.

"What in all hells happened?" Annalla asked him and pointed to the swelling spreading around the wound. "A snake bite did this?"

He nodded and looked at the half of the dead snake Thanon had killed. Larron looked lost behind his mask as he stared at it. "A water snake found in the Carsanje Wetland. It should not be here. They cannot survive this far north, and we are nowhere near a location that could resemble its southern habitat."

"How is it here then?"

She saw he had no answer to Thanon's question. There was another question she thought she already knew the answer to. "Will she survive?"

His lips pursed, and he hesitated. "Horses do not do well with these bites, and water snakes are already highly dangerous. We have no remedy for this with us, and what I gave her was simply a distillation of the trakin anesthetic. Either her heart will give out before it wears off, or she might survive the venom."

"And if she survives, will she recover?" she looked at him.

Larron sighed, and she wished she would have withheld the question. "Unlikely. This will kill her, now or later. Bealaras, stay clear of fallen trees and other such hiding places. Move ahead and see if you can bring Geelomin back. We will try to set up camp for the night here."

He nodded and rode forward, while the three of them removed equipment from Holly and searched for enough solid ground for a rough campsite. They checked on her often as they worked, taking turns stroking and talking to her despite the fact she did not wake.

"She's gone," Annalla said less than an hour later.

She was crying again and had to swallow thickly around the lump in her throat. As she petted Holly, Annalla had felt the horse's heart stutter, and her last breath leave until she lay motionless.

"It was just a snake," Thanon whispered, kneeling, and putting a hand on Holly's neck. "I did not even see it until it struck."

Larron placed a hand on Thanon's shoulder and Annalla grabbed his other hand.

"There is nothing you could have done, Thanon. There is no viable path for such an animal to relocate here. We had no way to know we needed to watch for them. This location would have been completely dry two months ago."

Thanon nodded as he continued to cry, but whether it was agreement or acceptance, she could not tell. "She was a good horse."

They remained like that for a time, holding a short vigil for another lost friend. Annalla looked over at Larron eventually and cleared her throat. "We should move on," she said to him, wiping her eyes.

"What?"

"She is right, Thanon." Larron squeezed the hand on Thanon's shoulder. "This is a poor place for us to linger, and we did all we could for Holly."

There was a moment he fought with himself before he looked around at where they were and finally agreed with a nod.

"We need to redistribute the supplies. You will ride with Annalla."

Another nod. Thanon removed Holly's harness so that it would not be left to betray them. Larron and Annalla worked to pack everything back on Dusk and Moonshine. When they mounted up, she took care to stay clear of potential snake hiding places. The shallow water held a much greater menace to it than before. The ripples on the surface as they passed through all held hidden danger in her mind.

It was a couple hours later when she heard horses approaching from ahead, and she signaled to Larron. They hid until Bealaras and Geelomin came into view, and Larron called out to them.

"We should spread out the supplies, but I think that would be best done in the morning. Have you passed a fair place to camp tonight?"

Geelomin nodded, noting Thanon and Annalla riding together with a resigned look. "Not too far. Bealaras and I marked it on the way back."

"Lead on. We can decide more once there."

The echo of sorrow followed them through the trees and water. She knew they would say more goodbyes tonight, and they would continue to carry sorrow with them even as they carried on.

***

Annalla relinquished control of Moonshine to Thanon the second morning, and she rode behind him now. As the two lightest people in the group, Larron ordered them to ride together as they moved on. She was the one who told him to take the reins because she wanted to try out her wings.

She had begun exercising them during breaks as they healed. Now she continued the exercise as they rode for a couple days, stretching and building strength. Annalla thought she should be able to fly for short periods. Her wings were stronger and healthier than ever.

Maneuvering around on the horse, she brought her feet up and crouched on Moonshine's rump with her hands on Thanon's shoulders.

"What are you doing?" he asked, at the same time Larron called her name from behind. Larron's tone clearly said, *What do you think you are doing? Sit back down on that horse right now so you do not re-break your arm.* She just as clearly ignored the unspoken order.

"Don't worry," she said to them both. "I'm going to try flying."

"And you believe jumping from the back of a moving horse while still healing a broken arm is the best option?" Thanon's laughter at Larron's implacable tone was felt more than heard, and she flicked him on his ear as he snorted.

"I'm not jumping off a horse. I'm going to see if I can float along *behind* a horse. And I know how to fall properly."

"Your arm is still broken. Knowing how to fall properly does not change that fact."

She turned to glare at him. "Thank you, Mother. I had completely forgotten."

He held his hands up in a manner that said he was not

pleased with her decision but was resigned to it. "I simply ask that you take care."

"Meh, meh, meh, meh." She muttered under her breath when she turned forward again, and Thanon was silently shaking with his mirth.

"Stop laughing," Annalla hissed at him as she tried to suppress her own grin.

"You know if you injure yourself, he will tie you to the horse again. I will then be forced to ride with Bealaras," he teased.

He might try, anyway, she thought, but kept her response to herself.

Annalla opened her wings and focused on feeling what they could tell her about the air or flying or anything that might help. She needed to learn this. Something inside her remained terrified she would never do more than glide uncontrollably.

Immediately, she felt lighter, but that always happened, and she had never simply started floating or hovering off the ground. Movement had to be a requirement, but how much and how often was the question, and she did not want to go zooming off randomly.

"Perhaps you need to flap your wings."

With a sighing growl, she slowly turned her head to look back at Larron again. The man was actually smirking at her! Making light of something that could be a very serious deficiency in her like it was no concern at all.

"Commander, I am not usually one to offer relationship advice."

"That is a lie." Thanon chimed in as Bealaras spoke.

"However, I feel in this instance I should recommend that you stop...trying to help." Bealaras offered politically while skillfully ignoring the commentary.

This time, Thanon's laughter was not silent or contained, and she wobbled in her hold on him as he bent forward holding his stomach.

Annalla took a deep breath and tried to ignore the good-natured teasing. An embarrassed blush rose in her face as she gently moved her wings. There was a tiny lurch in her gut, and she released her hold on Thanon as she rose to float in the air. Her eyes widened and her heart sped up at the wonder of it.

Fairy, it seemed, did not fly, so much as their wings allowed them to move through the air as they wished. Her wings moved slowly back and forth with the same small, gentle movements, and she drifted away from Thanon. Or rather, he and Moonshine moved away from where she hovered.

"So, you do fly."

She turned less than gracefully to find Larron had ridden up beside her, smiling like he had known all this time. An echoing smile lit up her face. "I can hover. Let's see about flying."

Her turn back was a bit smoother, but when she leaned forward to try to move in that direction, nothing happened. Leaning and stretching her legs back, then forward, also did nothing other than having her legs begin swinging.

Bealaras passed her by, but she could see Larron waiting off to the side out of the corner of her eye. Probably still smiling, even more amused now, but she was not going to look, as she tried reaching her arms forward this time.

Maybe if I move like I'm walking on the air it will work off the intent, she thought, and decided to give it a try.

Annalla was certain she accomplished nothing more than looking ridiculous.

"Despite the helpful relationship advice from my soldiers advising me otherwise... Might I offer some perspective?"

Biting her tongue, she turned back toward Larron very calmly.

At least I'm getting better at turning, she thought as she waited, with what was a remarkable amount of patience, for him to continue. A student waiting for correction.

"I have observed your wings move when you turn, but you have only tried to use your body in your attempts at forward motion." His eyes moved over her wings.

"How have I been moving my wings to turn?" she was honestly curious now about what he had noticed.

"Watch the bottom edges. You have been doing it faster, so you are definitely feeling what you do on some level."

As she turned forward again, she watched, and she knew. "It's like a boat in water!" she said excitedly. "Which makes absolutely no sense because I'm not moving air around and air is not holding me up like a boat and water, but it *is* like a boat."

"I am afraid I did not follow that at all, but I am assuming by your tone you have discovered the trick of it?" he asked with a chuckle.

Instead of answering, she narrowed her eyes ahead, curved both wings the same direction, and drifted forward. Annalla felt herself giggle and grin. A little more curve, and a little more speed, and she was slowly catching up to Bealaras.

Her flight was completely silent, so long as she did not jostle any branches or leave with her passing. There was no flapping like a bird or butterfly when she was not hovering; she moved her wings in a way that would take her in the direction she wanted to go. The trick was more in the subtlety required, and she was still trying to work out those subtleties to figure out how to go around Bealaras to reach Thanon again. She slowed to give herself more time and did some experimenting.

How is it I can perform a complicated sword dance flawlessly, but complex maneuvers in the air are still a trial and learning process? It made no sense, when she should have had her wings long before she could have ever held a sword.

The things I know, or what is coming back to me, are in no logical order I can follow. Or, perhaps, it's not the order that's confusing, but the level of knowledge instead. I am remembering things as they become necessary, so that is the order. Fighting when that was required, limited wilderness skills when I needed to find food or water or shelter, drifting when I took to the air for the first time.

Flying still feels like I am trying to carve with an axe rather than a carving knife. I have the blunt skill it took to keep myself off that cliff, but I have to learn the softer touch of the slighter movements. Why is it different this time?

It was frustrating. She had never *expected* to have the same level of skill in everything, but it did not mean she would not have *preferred* skills all came to her with ease.

By the time she made it back up to Thanon, she asked him to stop while she got back on behind him. The landing was not elegant, but she at least made it onto the horse instead of falling to the ground. Later that day, she made another flight, but kept it short so she would not overtax muscles unused to exercise.

Her back was only a little achy the next day, so Larron approved slightly longer exercise durations. The approval was issued with another stern warning to be careful of her arm. On the third day of flying, she was ready to try maneuvering faster, so she did not ask for permission. She gradually built-up speed and weaved between horses and trees.

Each day they travelled after leaving the swamp, Annalla noticed the elves seemed more eager. They had quickened their pace and, though it seemed near impossible, their vigilance for signs of others also heightened. Both could be taken as signs of anticipating an attack, but they were not looking for the enemy.

After months of traveling with them, she could distinguish the difference between concern and anticipation. No one had updated her on how much further they still had to travel, but with each passing mile she became more certain they were close to reaching the Palonian Woodland. Their excitement became contagious, and Annalla could not help but become caught up by it. Her enthusiasm was more tempered, though, as her nerves resurfaced.

"Oh, no! No, no, no!" Annalla said as she was pulled from her musings.

In her budding confidence, she took a corner too close and overcorrected. Her left wing tucked in. She angled to the right a bit too much, and ended up smacking directly into the trunk of a tree just past the gap for which she had been aiming. The speed she hit at was not great, but the automatic protection of her face with her arms earned her a searing reminder one of them was broken.

"Are you alright?" Thanon reached her first, backtracking from where he was in the lead.

She held her arm to her chest and grimaced. "I'll live."

"Good." He was laughing at her again, starting to wipe at his eyes watering in his mirth. "Because that was funny. You just ran into a tree. Did you two see her run into that tree?"

Larron hopped down, and she saw Bealaras trying very diligently not to join Thanon in laughing, but so close to failing. "Let me see the arm."

"I don't think I did any more damage." She held out her arm regardless for him to prod the still sensitive break area and probably provide a different searing reminder of her injury.

"How is the tree?" He looked up from her arm over her shoulder.

Annalla blinked at him in confusion, looked back at the tree, then back to him and opened her mouth a few times. It took a few tries, faced with his serious expression, before she sputtered actual words.

"You did not just ask me if I damaged *the tree.*"

"It did look rather humorous." He started chuckling along with Thanon, and then Bealaras could no longer help joining in.

"Like someone running on ice. Woah, woah, woah," Thanon's arms flailed about and he tilted to the side like someone trying not to fall, "and not getting anywhere."

She tried not to laugh with them, but there were tears in their eyes from laughing so hard, and Thanon and Bealaras kept miming more exaggerated demonstrations. By the time they were done, they were leaning on trees and horses and shoulders while holding their stomachs. Then someone would look at someone else, and they would start up all over again.

"You are all impossible to live with." She smiled at them as Thanon helped her up and back on the horse with him after they finally regained some semblance of control. "What if I had been injured?"

He looked at her and said nothing.

"Fine," she relented. "You all checked first. I'm just looking for something to complain about."

"And embarrassed," Thanon said smugly.

She sighed theatrically. "Impossible."

He laughed and grinned at her, as she knew he would, and they returned to the direction following Geelomin's path in companionable silence.

"I am happy we found you, Annalla. I think you are one of my best friends." He spoke after a while. The happy elf abandoned his common teasing tone, so she knew he was serious.

"Me too, Thanon." She squeezed his arm and hesitated for only a moment before continuing quietly. "May I ask you a personal elf question? As a friend."

"Sure. I will not share it."

His answer was immediate and earnest, but she hesitated again, thinking about how to ask her question without further embarrassing herself. "Outside of the bond, do elves have relationships?"

"Oooh! You do like him." He looked over his shoulder and smiled as he teased her, but he kept his voice down.

Annalla froze and backtracked. "I don't know what you mean. I'm just...curious...in general."

"That was very convincing." His voice dripped with sarcasm.

She sighed. "I don't know, Thanon. This whole situation is complicated, and I'm not even a whole person. Plus, there's a war going on and people are getting hurt and dying. Things don't need to get *more* complicated. Part of me just...wonders."

"First, you are a whole person. You possess a

personality far too strong to be anything except a whole person. You will never convince me otherwise. Remembering more about your past will only add to it, but I refuse to believe you would become a *different* person."

Smiling, she huffed out a laugh. "Thanks, I think."

"Second, life and living cannot stop because of war, even if it might hurt more or sooner for some in such a time. What are we fighting for if we let war become all that we are? Third, relationships do not necessarily complicate *things*. Sometimes they clarify a situation for the people involved."

"Or make things very awkward," she added with a wry note. "I don't know that I'm ready for potentially awkward."

"I promise I will tell no one else."

"Thank you, Thanon."

"I do *not* promise I will not harass you endlessly." She groaned in response to his words and thumped her forehead on the back of his shoulder as he continued. "I will also generously answer your initial question."

"Such a benevolent friend. I don't think I remember my initial question though." She murmured into his back.

"Fortunately for you, I am, and I do." He nudged her. "Yes, elves do form relationships outside of life bonds. Some friends offer the physical comfort of a lover. Some loving relationships last a day, a decade, a lifetime. The bond is physical, relationships are emotional."

"But the bond could break a relationship? Pull someone out of one?"

"Annalla, we do not lightly enter relationships waiting for something better to come along and be handed to us. Every relationship, no matter the duration, has meaning and connection. Most often, the bond forms around and builds upon existing relationships. I will not say it has never been otherwise, but I have never heard of a bond forming where it would break a strong relationship."

"Which indicates some intelligence to it. What if he is meant for someone else?"

He took a moment, and she knew he was giving her question the thought it deserved.

"I do not believe the bond is *fate* exactly. There is some level of intelligence, or complex factors that appear to be intelligence, to it. I believe those factors filter out most aspects that would push one to reject the bond, as it can only be made once. Maturity is an example, as I have never heard of a bond forming in an elf under five hundred years of age. I believe the emotions of a strong, existing relationship are a similar factor.

"I have been in long-term relationships, and we loved each other and still do. Those relationships changed as we did, and we turned down different paths. One of my loves is now bonded, but that bond formed well after we took our divergent paths. They have chosen the bond and to walk that path together."

Thanon looked back to catch her staring off to the side in thought.

"I am telling you to stop focusing on life bonds. Live your life and love with everything you have. Anything less is a disservice to yourself and whoever you bring into your life."

She smiled at him and hugged him from behind. "You are a good friend."

Patting her hand, he grinned. "I know."

CHAPTER FIFTEEN

The river that fed the marsh had many crossings as it drained and spread out to fill the wetlands to the south before reforming into the Yaziren River. East of the river, Larron had told them, the forest covered a strip of hilly land before flattening again. They were not even a full day into the hills before their growing excitement changed back to concern when Geelomin returned from scouting early.

"Trouble?" Larron asked, seeing the worried look on his face.

They were in another downpour, and not even Annalla heard his return over the driving rain. He had used the soft, damp earth to quiet his passage, emerging in front of them without warning, and without his horse. It had been a tense moment as blades were drawn and the group formed up against an attack that never came. All of which took place in the time it took Geelomin to sign 'all clear.'

"There is an encampment of human men ahead of us. They rode as a sentry party, so I left Fleet off to the north where there was no evidence of activity and followed for a short time. This party met no others and circled back north. I returned directly to find you ahead of where this patrol ran."

"Do you believe they might range this far?" Larron asked.

His response held no hesitation. "Unlikely. Their path looked well worn, but this location is closer than I would be comfortable remaining in for an extended period."

Larron nodded. "Retrieve Fleet. Rendezvous at our previous campsite, we will need additional scouting to determine what situation we are facing."

The three elves took turns walking at the back of the group, erasing hoofprints coming and going as they passed and attempting to hide any horse manure. Annalla would have helped, but her healing arm would have made her too slow at it to be effective, so she rode Moonshine alone back to last night's campsite.

Their progress was slow, covering up for three horses, and Geelomin arrived only shortly after they did. They huddled beneath a large tree to talk, but with the leaves all fallen, it was much less protection from the rain than before.

"It is only a day to the Woodland border from where I saw them. Correct?" Geelomin asked.

"Approximately, yes," Larron responded. "We need more information about their disposition. Without knowing why they have been allowed to remain, we should attempt to prevent our presence from being noticed and avoid confrontation.

"Geelomin, Thanon, Bealaras, the three of you will fan out to reconnoiter the areas past the hills north, east, and south. Coordinate your efforts to cover the greatest area most efficiently but return here in two days. If you find anything Annalla's hearing could help with, return early and we will reassess. Your goal is first to identify if they are allies. If they are not or it is undetermined, then your secondary goal is to seek out a path around them."

Those three gathered supplies in packs and quickly headed out, starting together discussing who would go where, as they moved out of hearing range. She and Larron set to unloading everything else and setting up a better campsite. They would be here longer than any location yet on their journey.

"We ate the last crumbs of the bread yesterday. I still can't hunt, but I can fish, and we can probably smoke it at night to time the last of the smoke with the morning fog we get here."

"Good idea. We will need to ensure the wind is not blowing east, so the smell does not alert them, but it is more likely to push down over the water from here. There are going to be more of the mushrooms we have been finding around as well. I will search for more to supplement our stores and see if I can take a bird or two."

"You don't think they are friendly," Annalla stated about the humans, reading Larron's grim expression.

"I have no doubt elves would partner with humans to defend a Woodland, but if you are partnering, elves are the better sentries and patrols, especially in a forest."

"I have to admit, I'm a little glad for the delay."

Larron stopped what he was doing and looked over at her with genuine confusion. "How do you mean?"

She finished wiping down the last horse and felt her shoulders sag. "You are all getting so excited, but I feel more...apprehensive. The journey is coming to an end, but I like travelling with you. Obviously not the danger, but...the people."

He made his way over, tilted his head forward and smiled. "I thought you promised to come with me after."

"Yes." She smiled back, but it was short-lived in the face of her worries and fears. "Think about it, Larron. You believe I'm half elf. If I had even visited a Woodland once in my life, would you have been surprised at my very existence when we met? I violate one of the fundamental truths of elven life—that you cannot create children with someone from another race—yet you didn't even know it had happened. I know I've never set foot within one of the Woodlands."

"And that matters?" He put his hands on her shoulders, rubbing her arms to offer comfort, and angling his head to catch her eyes. "They are tied to us no matter where we are born or raised."

"You cannot say for certain it's the same for *what* we are born. You have no more idea of the effect my diluted blood will have on that connection than I do, and you have no guarantee how the *people* will react either. My own people could think of me as a mistake, or an abomination!"

He quickly pulled her into a firm hug, the action as though he were trying to shield from such thoughts. "No. I understand from where your concern comes, but no. Your blood is not diluted for being mixed-race. You are not a mistake, abomination, nor any other word rattling around in that mind of yours."

Annalla breathed in the scent of damp leather and Larron. Relaxing a little, she uncrossed her arms and returned the hug.

"I'm a little terrified," she said against his shoulder.

He moved his hand to cradle her head against him. "You hide it well."

She could hear his heart beating steadily against her ear, and hers started to settle.

"You know your father loved you. You know we all care about you. Yes, even Geelomin." She laughed, as she knew he intended. "Either it will not matter, or they will not matter. I do not believe you will need it, but you will have my support."

She closed her eyes and held on, and he let her. Eventually, she stepped back and looked around at all they still had to do.

He touched her cheek, bringing her eyes back to him. "None of that now. We have time."

Taking her hand, he drew her down to lean against him as he sat at the base of the tree. They had plenty of time, and over the next day they spoke of many things as they set up camp, took turns on watch, gathered supplies, and made other such preparations for the group to proceed forward again when everyone returned. She learned he had a brother and nephew back in the Derou, and they usually took care of his small home while he was away.

"It is only Erro this time, though." He said as they prepared meat and fish for the fire they would have tonight, and she heard a catch to his voice.

"The war?"

He nodded, and she cleaned off her hands and was the one to hug him this time. "He was reported captured, not killed."

"How long ago?"

"It happened early this spring. Some years the gilar ease off, some they press upon us harder." She felt him sigh. "This is one of the bad years."

"How is your nephew doing? Especially with you leaving on this mission?"

Larron smiled absently as he thought of him. "He told me to go, told me The Derou needed me more than he did. He would focus on finding his father and defending our home, and I would bring back help."

"Smart child."

"Ha! I would wager he has seen more years than you have."

She gave him an eye. "He is your nephew. Are you trying to say you don't still see him as a child most of the time?"

"Hmm." He looked away and scratched at his ear without answering.

"See! You—" She cut off and looked into the woods, stepping away and taking up her sword. "Someone is coming."

They melted into the reeds on opposite sides with weapons drawn, watching in the direction she pointed. It was not long before Bealaras appeared in camp, clearly having walked openly and not trying to hide his approach. He gave the 'all clear,' and they emerged to greet him before he reported.

"I would like Annalla to help me listen in on a small group of humans to the south. It is my belief they are not with the sentries but are hiding from them. I would like confirmation so we can take action if it is warranted." He started drawing in the mud. "They wear this symbol, which I believe is the human's royal seal."

Larron leaned over his drawing. "A fair representation of it, yes. How far?"

"They are beyond the sentry perimeter, so I believe we can be there and back before tomorrow first watch. Midnight would be the latest."

"What royal seal is this?" She asked them.

"The human kingdom of Ceru."

"I would be listening to try to confirm this?"

He nodded. "Pack and go. I will handle everything here. If you can confirm it, try to make contact, Bealaras. They should trust an elf, and Ceru are allies as of our last reports."

Bealaras acknowledged the order. Annalla hesitated next to him, not knowing what to say after the recent easy camaraderie. "I... We'll be back."

***

The two of them ran for a couple hours before stopping under some brush to sleep. It was well hidden, so they curled up together and decided not to set a watch.

Sleeping through the night enabled them to rise again early and start off in the same ground-eating stride. Annalla was not in the same running shape as Bealaras, but she compensated some by switching to flying when her legs tired. Even with that help, she asked for a break to catch her breath when he said they were getting close.

"They have someone on watch," he started to summarize for her. "I came close enough to see, but not close enough for me to hear their words. This group appears to be more alert and capable than the patrols we scouted, so I did not want to take the risk when you might gain more information from a safe distance. We will go slower from here, and I will allow you to take the lead position when we are close to where their watch might notice us."

From that point on, they moved silently from point to point, scanning the area each time before moving again. Each move became shorter as they went, and soon enough, Bealaras tapped her shoulder and pointed in their next direction, indicating she should go first.

Annalla then took them forward, listening intently for any voices or movement. The first sounds she heard though, were from a different direction. She motioned to Bealaras, and they took up hidden positions to wait for the person to pass.

As he did, they could make out the form of one individual briefly through the trees coming from the northeast and heading toward the camp location Bealaras indicated. As Bealaras's had at their camp, the man's steps became less stealthy as he approached, likely to alert those within to his imminent arrival.

After waiting for him to move out of range, they followed as quietly as possible until Annalla could hear voices relatively clearly, though the people speaking were not visible from this position.

"...neither organized nor disciplined, even though they are numerous in at least two base camps. We can map the paths and slip through."

It sounded like someone was pacing slowly, like you would in thought rather than agitation. Either that person or another spoke softer than the first man. *"I'm more... elves would react to us 'sneaking' into their Woodland. We can get past the incompetent siege, but..."*

"You believe the elves would attack us, Sir?" This voice sounded worn out, like whoever it belonged to had faced one too many troubles in a row.

"A group of humans sneaking in? I'd say it is a valid concern," a fourth, gruff voice commented.

The pacing stopped. *"We will need to move north and hope to find a large enough gap in these exiles to walk in openly."*

"Your Highness, we could try to return home and report this situation." That was from the gruff voice again.

"We lost half our number getting here. No. Unless you know of a safer route, the elves are our best chance, and we may still find the answers we need."

Annalla turned to Bealaras to whisper in his ear,

missing further discussion by the humans. "I have heard four distinct voices, though I cannot confirm their number. One of them referred to another as 'Your Highness.' They speak of the patrolling humans as enemies and the elves as allies and have stated they lost half their group coming here. I do not know from where, they referred to it only as 'home.'"

"The human king has a number of sons," he whispered, but did not need to press as close as she, so they did not need to shift position.

"They want to enter the Woodland, but they are afraid sneaking past the other humans will provoke the elves to attack them."

Bealaras was silent for a minute, and she allowed him time to think, listening again to the humans.

"...north. Do you think you ... positions in ... to lead us safely around tomorrow?"

"Yes, Sir. Their perimeter has not changed, so we will only need to swing wide and we can avoid them. I have not scouted beyond a day in that direction, though."

There was a delay, and Bealaras leaned forward again as someone started to reply. "I believe this is enough confirmation and I should risk contacting them. Thoughts?"

"I agree. I believe their plan was to head north tomorrow based on what I just heard," she added. "Do you want me to hide for now, or join you?"

"Hide. If I use the word 'unquestionable' it will indicate they are a threat. If that happens, try to cause a distraction before you run and meet me where we slept last night. Report back to Larron alone if I am not there by nightfall."

She nodded and gave him a hard, quick hug. "Don't die."

As she snuck off to the right, she heard him move

forward and call out. *"Hello the camp!"*

Swords were drawn as the humans could be heard spreading out to flank the newcomer.

"We greet you, traveler, and ask to whom we speak." The presumed human prince asked as his men continued moving.

"I am the elf Bealaras of The Derou hoping I greet an ally."

There was a pause, and she could imagine the man weighing his options and responsibilities.

"The situation we find here at The Palonian is unexpected and unsettling. Would you consent to entering our camp with one of my men behind you? I will remain unarmed."

Could Bealaras escape one man close to him? He could probably disappear into the forest if left free, but she was less confident with one ready to strike. She settled quietly into place beside some noisy brush, where she still could see nothing, prepared to scream for help and run. Her heart was in her throat as her friend put himself at risk.

"I am armed and will remain so, but I will consent to your man behind me."

People moved, all of them slowly, but it sounded like they held to his word and only one closed in behind the lone elf. It felt like they were taking forever, and Annalla held her breath to hear every step.

"Stand down. Oh, thank the gods. Stand down, men."

She let out the breath at the obvious relief in the voice that came with seeing Bealaras spoke true.

"Please, be welcome in our camp."

"I would be interested to know your purpose here."

"Supplies have not been arriving in the south. I am Prince Tyrus of Ceru, and my father sent me to speak with

the northern council to discover the reason and coordinate a solution. " He paused and considered his next words, *"The forces ringing the Woodland are not ours, I swear to that. Can you help us enter?"*

"Do you have proof of your position?"

"I have my signet ring, but such things can be stolen, and tales spun. If you have means to defend us, I will order a relinquishment of our arms until satisfactory confirmation can be made."

Annalla heard instant unhappy muttering at that promise, but no one spoke against him.

"That will be up to my Commander. Will you consent to packing and joining our camp?"

"We will," was his quick reply.

"Very good. I will speak to my companion now." A pause, perhaps waiting for a nod of approval. *"Annalla, please report to the Commander. I will be guiding Prince Tyrus of Ceru, and his company of seven, to our camp with a likely arrival late tomorrow morning."*

She left without revealing herself, just in case, and headed back. Bealaras believed them, so did she, and she hoped they were both right.

Annalla tried to keep to the pace the two of them had set, as it would see her back to camp by dinner time, and maybe she would enjoy some fresh cooked food again. However, she was heaving for breath as she slowed outside of camp well past the dinner hour and made her way in the dark.

It was deserted, of course. Even elves would have heard her panting a mile away, but she breathlessly signaled all clear and bent over in an awkward walk trying to cool down and regain her breath.

"We thought you chased by gilar with all the noise,"

Geelomin stated arrogantly, but she saw the humor in his eyes. There was concern there as well when Bealaras did not join her.

"Bealaras was fine when I left him," she managed while still gasping, but she waited until her lungs no longer burned before continuing.

"He said to report that he was bringing Prince Tyrus of Ceru, and his company of seven, here, probably in the late morning. It was a longer run than I have trained for," Annalla said as she still fanned her face.

"I do not know Tyrus personally, but I know that is the name of the youngest prince," Larron confirmed for them. "It would seem Bealaras thought them honest?"

"We both did from what I overheard, and when he went into their camp. I did not hear any concern in his voice, nor did he use our code to indicate trouble." She shook her head and thought about the relief she heard. "It sounds like Prince Tyrus lost men getting here and is desperate to enter the Woodland. He offered to give up their weapons, which his men were not too happy about. And, you will have to ask Bealaras to confirm, but it sounded like he wanted to hug him when Bealaras turned out to be an elf like he claimed."

That earned and amused smile as they imagined the scene, but even with the smile, Larron pushed for more. "Can you confirm the number of men?"

She shook her head. "I only heard five. Four distinct voices and another murmur that sounded different."

Annalla nearly laughed as all three elves crossed their arms and chewed their lips in thought at the same time. Instead, she left them to their thinking and went to the small fire looking for the food they probably saved for her and Bealaras.

Mmm, seasoned fish. She started eating as they turned

toward where she sat and slowly followed, still thinking.

Geelomin spoke first. "Taking all their weapons wastes resources if we believe they are allies."

"If," Thanon emphasized.

"Yes, if. And eight is more than I like in this situation." He was doing the same math she did, and they simply had more fighters.

It was not as bad as they faced against the gilar in the mountains, but if they were enemies, they might be able to call on the patrols to assist them.

"We will take the weapons of Prince Tyrus only, and he will ride next to me. It sends a message of trust, but a clear threat as well," Larron stated.

"Based on what you observed, do you believe they would be held hostage to his safety, Annalla?" Geelomin turned to her.

"Yes. It was limited observation, but before they knew someone was watching, there was clear deference to his orders, and there was respectful concern in their distress at his proposal to disarm themselves. I believe they are what they claim, so if I'm wrong about the one…"

Larron waved off her shrug. "I agree with your interpretation of what you have described. We head in tomorrow as planned. If this group is false, it will allow them less time to plan while we are on the move. You said they would arrive in the morning?"

"Yes, I would expect Bealaras to push them to meet that timetable and that they are spending the night relatively close because they agreed to pack and join us when he asked earlier today. They would have not run the entire way and likely stopped at a reasonable hour for the horses, but close enough."

It then hit her that he mentioned heading in tomorrow

'as planned.' She raised her head and asked, "You found a way through the patrols already?"

Geelomin snorted in derision, but not at her. "This group is disorganized and ill-trained."

"Heh, one of the humans said something similar," she commented even as Geelomin continued.

"The main camp sends out periodic patrols, like the initial one I followed. I do not believe they are searching for hiding individuals attempting to leave the Woodland by stealth. Their behavior is not intent enough for anything of that nature.

"They passed by at least twice at night but did not even attempt to investigate more obvious hiding places. It is my belief they are in place to watch for larger groups and engage them, trapping the main force of the Palonian within the Woodland, or severely cutting their numbers should they attempt to break free.

"The patrols appear made up of the least experienced and motivated of the camp. If they are lost, it is no great setback, and if they do not return from a patrol it serves as an indication that a force may have overcome them in an attempt to leave. Any individuals falling into their path would be a minor bonus.

"The next day, a group came from a different direction. The men acted in the same manner as those from the first encampment; searching, or scanning passively, but not thoroughly. I followed them to another camp and found it positioned north and east of the first, comparable in size and number. The encampments are easily avoided, and, with caution, we should be able to avoid detection by the patrols. Their rounds follow a simple pattern."

Thanon nodded at Geelomin's summary. "I found much the same. There are two smaller encampments to the southeast, about a fourth fewer in number by our estimates, but the patrols I observed followed the same, easily followed patterns he described.

"My main concern is not for our safety in seeking a way past them, but why the Palonian elves have allowed such token forces to remain at their borders. A large confrontation might cost the Palonian some of their people, and I do not mean they should waste lives, but these men are lax in their vigilance and would not be difficult to catch unaware."

"It is a question I would like to know the answer to myself," Larron shook his head as he spoke, "but we will know nothing until we enter the Woodland. We will angle to the north. No distant scout. We stay together from here, including the Ceru humans. In the places where we would be nearer the paths of the patrols, we will travel by foot and Annalla will range ahead." He looked at her. "It may provide us with additional warning if you are not surrounded by our sounds."

Geelomin caught her attention. "By following the patrols to investigate, we have not scouted the entire distance between here and the Woodland. Once we reach that farthest point, I do not know patrol rotations, so you might want to push further ahead of us."

Annalla nodded at him and spoke to both of them. "Understood. How do we handle the humans in the morning?"

"Geelomin will meet them outside the camp and collect Tyrus's weapons, then I will let them know the plan and we leave. I want us ready to move early so they are not waiting on us to pack." He swallowed and looked at each of them in turn. "We are almost there."

She saw the longing on the faces of her friends at that statement and hoped she would be as happy as they to enter the Palonian.

***

Morning saw all of them more than ready to resume their travels, including the horses who gave off a restless energy as their backs were loaded. It was likely they were just responding to their riders' enthusiasm, as Larron said, none of the four had travelled this way before.

They finished packing early, so Geelomin and Larron joined her for her morning exercise at the sword dances, selecting a more challenging version today that only favored the one arm. Her spirits were light with the accelerated pace today.

As she heard horses in the distance, she judged their timing—she was much better at distance now—and led toward the cooldown.

"They are getting close."

Geelomin wiped his face and put his tunic back on along with his sword. He raised an eyebrow at her, and Annalla pointed to confirm the direction before he melted into the foliage.

She smiled a little sadly at how well she knew them all now, how well they could communicate and knew each other. It would all change soon. Her discussions with Larron had helped in that she knew he would not abandon her, but she was less certain about the timing of those promises. A lot changed quickly in a war.

"State your business." Geelomin called out from somewhere off to the south, and Annalla listened in to the exchange.

"Lieutenant, I would like to make the introduction of Prince Tyrus of Ceru to our Commander Larron."

It was an acceptable code phrase from Bealaras. *"In good faith, we ask Prince Tyrus to relinquish his weapons and leave his safety in the keeping of his men."*

"I don't see how—" That was gruff-voice again.

"Of course." The prince cut off his man.

"Please follow me." Geelomin said after a minute of quiet rustling, and the horses were moving again.

Eight men came into their small camp leading their mounts. All of them appeared around thirty, give or take a decade, their leader was a broad-shouldered man with olive skin, dark hair, and tilted steel-grey eyes that scanned the elves.

"Prince Tyrus, you have the look of your father. I am Commander Larron of the Derou elves, and I had the opportunity to visit Ceru about fifty years ago." Larron bowed his head in greeting.

"Commander, it's good to see friendly faces again." The relief she heard in his voice was just as apparent in his expressive face. "I'm afraid our journey has been more challenging than anticipated when we set out from Ceru."

"We have suffered losses as well." All were silent for a moment, remembering those no longer with them.

"My men and I would be grateful for an introduction to The Palonian Woodland. We would have snuck past the interlopers, but we did not want to seem...intrusive."

Larron briefly outlined their plan. "Thanon and Annalla will lead on point. Bealaras and Geelomin will be our rear guard, which will leave me free to ride with you and your men in the middle."

"I place my men at your command. What are your orders if we are seen?"

"While riding, we turn and ride out through the closest side, whether that be toward or away from the

Woodland. Follow my lead, as I will know which that is. We will fire at them while leaving, but escape is the priority.

"Discovery will be more likely when we are walking if we are unable to hide the horses from a patrol. Should that happen, you and your men will stay with me. Fire upon those that discover us. If an alarm is raised before we eliminate them, the nine of us will mount and retreat toward the Woodland border while my people cover and follow."

"What of the human woman?" Tyrus asked, confused, though she could see his eyes scanning their party and comparing the count of names given.

"Annalla is one of my people."

By the confusion on their faces, she could assume human women did not often take up arms as often as elven women. Now was also not the time to confuse them further with the truth of her heritage.

Tyrus did not miss a step and instead smiled charmingly at her. "There is a story there, I am sure, my lady." He ended with a wink.

Annalla's back straightened and she blinked, caught off guard by this behavior. Tyrus noticed, and his charming smile tilted slightly and became roguish.

Larron casually paced between them, and she heard Thanon snort as he poked her in the back as Larron spoke again. "Our plan is to head out now if you have no objections."

The prince turned his attention back to Larron, the polite smile back in place, and held his hands out. "Lead on, Commander."

"My Lady. Wink." Thanon said in a laughing whisper to her when they were mounted and leading the procession, one of Tyrus's men at their back.

Annalla could feel herself blushing. "We are heading

into enemy territory, this is hardly the time for jokes, Thanon."

He was unrelenting. "We have at least a half hour before the buffer zone. There is plenty of time for me to note how our dear Commander was *not* okay with the human's shameless flirting."

She knew her blush was growing brighter. The back of her neck was probably glowing. Letting out a deep breath, she groaned quietly. "Have I mentioned how impossible you are to deal with?"

His laugh was silent, but she felt it. "You have not mentioned it for days now. I have clearly been remiss of late in my duties as your best friend."

"Hmm, I will be sure to mention it daily from now on."

"Only if I earn it. Otherwise, I will have to do something so extreme you come up with a new term for my behavior."

They were both laughing silently now, trying to hold a dignified posture while continuing to lead the way. It would be about an hour more of cautious riding before Thanon expected them to dismount due to the outermost patrols. Over that time, they traded a few good-natured barbs that trailed off the further they went as they watched and listened to the woods around them. When the time came, Thanon turned toward the rest of the group and spoke in a tone that should not carry far.

"We should continue on foot from here. The patrols do not cross, but they are not far enough apart for us to ride again until we are within the Woodland."

Thanon tied off Moonshine to follow Bealaras and Storm, and the two of them pushed ahead; him to lead the way, and her to listen.

As they needed to remain visible enough to follow, they would push ahead hidden by the brush, then step back to be seen before melting forward again. It was easier for Annalla to push aside the common forest sounds and those of her companions if she remained stationary, so she made their pace much more varied than those following. Many times, Thanon moved back to step out while she remained listening until his return.

Through an entire day and into a second, they maintained this scattered pace, moving slower with the challenge of moving a group with the needed level of stealth rather than one alone. Only one scare so far, where a patrol came near enough for Annalla to call a halt. She heard them ahead and to the right of where she and Bealaras stood, gave the signal to 'stop and hide' from the top of the next rise, then dropped to the underbrush.

The small group passed close enough to the two of them for the ripe scent of unwashed bodies to clog their noses, but they concealed themselves well and gave enough warning for those following to have the horses lay down and hold still.

With the midday stop of this second day, they came to the end of where Thanon had been able to scout, and their progress slowed further. Rather than leading, Thanon searched out signs of additional patrol routes, while Annalla continued to listen for approach.

For all their caution, it was pitifully simple to evade and avoid the men. Often, they were chatting away and telling ribald jokes so loudly she heard them far enough away to simply point her group around a different rise in the land. They did not even need to stop and hide. That evening however, the rain returned in force and it became significantly more difficult to distinguish sounds. They were hoping to push through the night to reach the Woodland border rather than sleeping out again.

Annalla stopped and shook her head in frustration, reminded of the gilar attack that heralded Palan's death, the rain fell off the hood of Palan's cloak before she threw it back to listen intently. Her hair instantly soaked, and water trickled down her neck.

"Anything?" Thanon asked as she looked around.

She started to deny it, but stopped and strained. "Maybe, but there is too much interference. Wait here, when the others are in sight, have them stop and hide. Just in case. I want to look around."

With his confirmation, Annalla started up over a slope, crouching down at a near crawl as she moved. Light flashed, and thunder clapped in the distance. Two men crested a small hill, voices still muffled by cloak and rain, but no longer by land and distance. She dropped to a crawl and started creeping back to warn Thanon and the others, they could still back away from a patrol in time.

"I don't know why we have to keep checking the stupid traps. Does he think we are going to catch ourselves an elf out here? They are animals, but they aren't dumb," one of the two said, laughing at his own horrible joke.

What traps? she thought, even as she continued to work her way carefully away.

"Spread out!" A barked order, and she looked back to see the first two followed by eighteen more. This was clearly not a simple patrol. "The sooner we check 'em, the sooner we are back at camp!"

The order had been shouted.

Even Thanon had to have heard that, she thought to herself.

At first, she was relieved they would already be

looking for places to hide, but when the cry of a man in pain reached her from the direction of her own party, she wondered where those traps were laid. Half the heads perked up, even though the cry was cut short and quickly muffled to even her ears. Weapons were drawn as the men regrouped under their leader's commands.

They would flee toward the Woodland, with Geelomin, Bealaras, and Thanon giving cover if an alarm sounded, but first try to pick them off. That was the plan, depending on who was injured, but they would make sure that person was brought along as long as they were still alive.

That meant taking them out was the first priority, trying to prevent any alarm. She could not fight all of them, though, so she would need to take some by surprise when most were already over the hill in sight of the elven bows.

Annalla backed under a thick bush and held her breath as the group passed her by. With the last of them beyond her position, she moved out and up behind the trailing few like a shadow in the night. The first man cried out as she stabbed him from behind, and those not yet over the hill turned and saw her with the dead man sliding off her sword even as a horn was blown. They were discovered.

CHAPTER SIXTEEN

Thanon was alone when he came into sight again, which was not unusual, but he motioned for them to find an adequate place to halt. It was caution, not yet alarm based on his indications, so they halted before an area with thick brush to settle the horses behind at need. Larron knew the risk was higher with the coming of the rain. His plan placed a great deal of responsibility on Annalla's shoulders, but she was the only one with the required skill and ability.

Thanon's head whipped around to face the rise off to the right. They all heard the voice at nearly the same moment. It was not nearly loud enough to make out any words, but Larron thought the speaker to be male.

He did not even need to issue the order to hide. Everyone started to lead the animals off into the brush immediately. Larron heard a thick *chink* sound with a meaty *thunk*, and one of the men cried out involuntarily.

"Law!" Tyrus hissed and leaped to cover Lawrence's pained screams. He looked down at the man. "Is that a gods forsaken bear trap?"

"Mount up," Larron ordered the men. "Eliminate them before they raise an alarm if you are able." He knelt next to Lawrence across from Tyrus to help.

Bealaras charged forward with Moonshine trailing, while the humans and Geelomin crowded around on their horses with weapons drawn. Tyrus stepped on a lever of the trap as Larron did the same on the opposite side, and they each grabbed an edge and started to push it apart. Lawrence bit his hand and let out a muffled, pained cry as his leg was jostled.

Bowstrings sang, men cried out, and a horn blew as they strained against the trap, fighting for every inch. The trap had rusted, causing build-up to clog the mechanisms. There was no telling how long it had been left out here.

"Pull your foot out, Law. Now!" Tyrus gritted out.

The soldier lifted his leg as ordered, using both hands when his leg alone would not seem to follow his commands.

Tyrus saw it clear and looked at Larron. "On three. One...two...three!"

They released at the same time and the trap snapped shut between them, jumping against Larron's leg, and likely leaving a bruise. He helped Lawrence onto one leg as Tyrus called Harndorn, his second in command, over with his horse. The three of them heaved the injured man up behind Harndorn and tied off the extra mount. Larron had to hope he would remain conscious enough to hold on for the ride to come.

Larron mounted Dusk and took stock of everyone. Thanon and Bealaras were providing cover fire closer to the men charging over the hill with swords and axes in hand, steadily backing away even as the humans closed in on them. Geelomin and the humans were still with Tyrus and him. They fired arrows as well, but rain and distance made them less accurate. He looked at his Lieutenant, who was watching for the moment he would order Bealaras and Thanon to the next fallback position.

"Annalla?" He asked, hoping for some sign of her.

Geelomin shrugged and shook his head. He had not seen the missing member of their party and fully expected Larron to follow his own orders. "Go. We will cover you."

His face was hard. That horn meant reinforcements were likely. They did not know how near that might be, and they could not remain. He turned Dusk's head, barely restraining the vicious yank he wanted to give in his anger. The animal did not deserve his wrath.

Larron called for the humans to follow and charged forward past the fight. They rode hard toward the Woodland for a short time, but he shifted to an easier trot well before the horses became winded. It was still a fast pace, and he could only hope they found no additional traps as they rode.

Another horn sounded to the rear, but it was far enough back that he called a halt near midnight and dismounted. Lawrence was slumped over, held up only by Harndorn's awkward, and slipping, hold on his jerkin. Tyrus was at his side in a moment, and they worked together to lower the injured man to the ground.

"He is likely in shock from the pain and blood loss. I need to stop the bleeding, and we need to keep him warm. Can you grab blankets?" He retrieved the med kit from his pack as Tyrus collected blankets.

"Take care of the horses but be ready to move out quickly." Tyrus was giving orders to his men even as he grabbed blankets from each of them. "Someone also needs to keep watch for Larron's people. And by all the gods, carefully check this area for bear traps before we step on another one."

"We're on it, Sir."

Geelomin would likely curse him as a fool for leaving

himself exposed to seven strangers with weapons, allowing his only hostage to move about freely and issuing orders, trusting them to take care of everything, but he was focused on the injury. Besides, if they wanted an excuse to make noise to draw the other humans down upon them, there were easier ways to do so than having one of your people step on a bear trap.

A bear trap! he cursed mentally. *What were they hoping to catch with a bear trap?*

He was thinking of the elven scouts that would have been walking through the forest scouting the group, who would not have missed seeing the thing. Maybe it was larger parties or distant messengers they were targeting. Clearly, being forced to hide mounts made larger parties more susceptible, as theirs just disastrously demonstrated.

Cutting open the torn leg of the pants, he looked at the wound as Tyrus spread blankets over Lawrence and then held one above to keep the rain off. It was finally starting to ease.

The wound was not too bad. Likely fractured, and the skin torn where the trap's teeth dug in, but even in his shock at the injury, the man had not tried to yank his leg out. He dug out the appropriate leaf and stuffed it under the man's tongue to hopefully help prevent infection.

"I will need you to hold him down while I clean the wound, in case he wakes during the process."

Tyrus knelt to put the last blanket around his man, then straddled his waist so his knees held down Lawrence's arms and his hands on his shoulders. He peered back at Larron and nodded.

"This is a painful process, so I hope he remains unconscious. I have given him some general-purpose medication, but that trap was severely rusted. He will need a

Healer or more specialized medicines than I carry."

"I imagine the Woodland will have such things?" Tyrus asked over his shoulder.

"Yes. Your man should recover fine," he said as he set to cleaning out the particles embedded in his flesh. When that grisly task was done, he went about setting, bracing, and binding the leg, very similarly to how they had worked on Annalla's forearm.

"You may release your hold. Try to prevent him from spitting out the leaf when he wakes up. He will need to be kept warm, but watched for extreme shifts in his temperature as well as vomiting or other discharges." Larron said to Tyrus as he started rubbing the man's arms and other leg to generate warmth and ensure blood flow. The prince wrinkled his nose, but nodded in understanding.

Someone called out, and he heard Bealaras answer. Larron looked up at Tyrus. "Can you take this over and then make sure he is wrapped up for now?"

Another nod, then Tyrus started copying the movements. "Thanks. I've got Law, go see about your people."

Larron did not wait longer and left him to watch the injured man while he quickly approached the only elf to yet rejoin them.

"Commander." Bealaras dismounted and another man—*Franklin?* he thought absently—seamlessly took his horse for him, walking it over to where all their mounts were grouped as he continued speaking. "We split up to add confusion to our trail. The humans did not have horses, and even the reinforcements we saw were poorly coordinated. I believe we will be able to remain ahead of them."

"Did you see Annalla?" he asked, hoping for some indication she found a place to hide.

Bealaras did not have the answer he wanted. "No, but Geelomin was going to circle around to where he thought he heard combat behind their line. He ordered me to report to you. How can I help here?"

He shoved his concern for all his unaccounted-for people to the side and looked about their rest area. Tyrus's group had the situation well in hand. One man was making what looked like a final circuit at a wide range around the camp. The branch poking the ground before him indicated he was hunting for traps. The rest of the men had settled the horses with a quick brushing around their tack and allowed a small area to graze or rest, and they were now busy quietly checking and preparing weapons. One would wander over periodically to check on their wounded comrade.

"Pass out food to everyone and have some easy to hand for the others when they rejoin us. I need to check on Lawrence's condition, but I want us to be moving again within a half hour. We do not need to run the horses, but we should keep moving."

"I think we are beyond their lines now."

"As do I, and with the Woodland close, I do not believe they will pursue much further." He gave a comforting pat to Bealaras's shoulder as the elf walked away, then turned back to his patient.

"Your people?" Tyrus asked him when he returned, and his concern did not appear feigned.

He leaned over to check life signs. "They are reported to have split up before heading this direction to reconnoiter with us."

"If any of the horses hit another trap…" He spoke the known concern aloud, then paused and shook his head. "You already know that. Sorry. If they did get them to split their forces, that would improve the chances even if a horse went down."

"Yes." He was being short and knew Tyrus was trying to be optimistic, but Thanon was better at it.

"Are we waiting for them?"

Larron shook his head and sighed, the only emotion he allowed to show. "No. The Woodland border is close. That is our best chance of safety and aid should we need it." He paused as Lawrence stirred. "He is waking."

Tyrus shifted his attention back and leaned forward. "Law. You back with us?"

"Hmm. Thirsty." He moved his tongue around. "My leg hurts."

"Just a swallow for now." Larron said as Tyrus grabbed for the nearest water skin. "Try to suck on the leaf, as it will help with your healing and with the pain."

"Law, we are going to need to ride again soon." Tyrus said as he helped his man take a drink.

He grimaced and coughed. "My leg still hurts, Sir. I don't know that I can ride."

"That's okay, you will ride with Harndorn again." Tyrus quickly spoke again before the man could start talking about valiantly being left behind, sword in hand.

Taking one of the blankets, Larron rolled it up and shifted positions. "We are going to take this slow to start. Tyrus and I are going to help you ease up a bit and lean against this blanket. If you can handle that for a few minutes, we will try sitting you up."

His color was better, and he looked more aware with each passing moment. By the time they had him sitting, he looked impatient, but scared when he looked at the bandaged leg.

He swallowed thickly and looked at Larron, steeling himself. "Will I lose the leg?"

Smiling at his courage, Larron set his mind at ease. "No. Barring any additional unfortunate accidents, or acts of sheer stupidity on your part, your leg will heal."

With that promise, he could see the impatience overcoming the fear, and he sighed when Larron firmly told him not to move when they heard someone else arrive. "If you are not dizzy in another minute or two, Tyrus can help you to stand. We will be leaving soon."

He looked over to see Tyrus nod that he would watch the eager, but still injured, man and left them again.

"Commander." Thanon called out as Larron joined his two elves where they had met.

"Pursuit?"

"None that I could see."

"What happened?" he asked his scout.

Thanon shook his head and pursed his lips. His frustration, and a sense of failure, was clear to read.

"Annalla heard something but could not make it out clearly with the rain. She wanted to check on it to be safe, so she headed over that little hill. She ordered me to tell you all to hide in case it was a patrol, which you saw and began to execute. I heard an order given to spread out and check something, I think he said 'traps.' There was a scream from back with your group as I moved to hide myself, so I instead took up position to cover your escape. Annalla was still on the other side of the rise when everything happened."

"One of Tyrus's men stepped on a bear trap."

"A bear trap? What were they hoping to catch with those?"

He shrugged at Thanon's question and continued. "That must be the traps they were talking about. It looked like this group included more people than the small patrols we had been seeing. We stood little chance of preventing at least one of them from raising an alarm."

"At least three times as many, likely more." Thanon agreed. "I heard fighting from the other side of the hill before Geelomin ordered our retreat, so I think Annalla pulled the back of the group off us. That is one reason Geelomin decided to circle around."

"Will you be able to ride again soon?" He asked Thanon, who nodded, so Larron did not need to split the party further again. "Bealaras has food prepared. We should plan to move again when we maneuver Lawrence back onto a horse."

Law was already on his feet when Larron turned back around. He was clearly in pain and a little pale, but he was steadier on one foot with a hand on Tyrus's shoulder. Riding was still going to hurt, but they could proceed at a slower pace now that both Thanon and Bealaras reported no pursuit.

Tyrus called Harndorn to bring his horse over, and they helped Lawrence off the ground, supporting his knee until he could use his good leg to lift the injured leg over. He was breathing hard, sweat beading on his forehead from the effort, his eyes closed as he leaned forward to regain control.

"Still with us, Law?"

"Yes, Sir." he gritted out, face still squeezed taut. "Damn that hurts."

Harndorn patted the young man's good leg and took his foot out of the stirrup. "Alright, son. Let me up there and we will try to take it easy on you."

They set off at an easy walk, heading as straight for the Woodland as Larron could figure, with Thanon out front and Bealaras bringing up the rear. He hoped that with the elves spread out and clearly in charge, any scouts would not attack the humans among them. Tyrus was still unarmed, as Geelomin carried his weapons. Even if he had wanted to return the weapons at this point, he could not.

Nearly two hours later he felt them cross the border. The land reached up to envelop his senses as the feeling of being Home settled. They might not be safe, but they were certainly safer. The eleven of them here were safer.

"Another half hour, Thanon, then we rest," he called ahead. They would rest, and they would see if their friends caught up, or if they needed to investigate possibilities for a rescue.

***

"Well, crap," Annalla said to herself as she faced nine men ready to avenge their dead companion. That was more than she wanted to pull back from the group heading toward her companions.

"Get him!" One of them yelled, and they charged at the same time she turned and ran away to the southeast.

She was lucky they did not think to use their bows before chasing after her. With how close they started to her, there was a fair chance they would hit her even with the rain and her being a moving target. Someone stumbled behind, but she did not dare to look and risk tripping over something on the forest floor herself.

She was grateful for the recent days of running with Bealaras. It taught her how to push through when her lungs were straining. About a mile later, an arrow zipped by in front of her face and it surprised her enough to make her stagger for a few paces before she caught her feet and sped up again.

"Double crap," Annalla breathed out. That had not come from behind her.

A quick peek to the right showed her a second,

smaller group—possibly another scouting group—armed and already helping their pursuing companions. Her course altered further east, and she weaved between trees to dodge the arrows. It was something her pursuers would not have to do, so they were going to gain ground. Ducking around a large tree, she grabbed at it and lurched to a stop behind its cover, turning to peek back around behind her.

They had spread out as they followed, some running faster than others. She could wait and try to take out those in the lead, but that would mean the archers would have time to close some of the distance they lost every time they stopped to fire, and maybe those trailing would remember they also had bows.

Pushing off the tree, she started running again, deciding it was not yet time to make a stand. It would be soon, though. At least a few of them were in better running shape with longer legs than she, as they were gaining even as she felt the toll the sprint was taking. However, the new bowmen would need to start running if they wanted to keep her in range.

Another mile and her lungs were on fire, her throat was thick, and she had a stitch in her side. Her legs and feet, and even her backside, were feeling a little numb and more than a little pain as they protested the extended sprint.

She was becoming slower, despite her efforts, but maybe they were, too. They had to be even more spread out now, with fewer within bow range as the lazier ones had to drop out of the chase. If she did not turn and fight now, she might be in no condition to fight at all. Laying her sight on another larger tree ahead, she angled toward it and readied herself to stop on the opposite side and prepare to engage.

It came fast, and she stumbled at the sudden stop, her legs not immediately understanding the command, but moved into place while hoping it was enough movement to keep her muscles from cramping.

The first man to come around was, unfortunately, neither dumb nor inexperienced. He noticed she had stopped and, instead of following her directly by cutting close to the trunk, he circled wide and ordered the man behind him to circle the opposite side.

Annalla held her sword ready, her back toward the tree and eyes unfocused trying to watch both at the same time. They were well coordinated, and still fast even after the long run. Every time she brought her sword to block one, the other man struck at her. Instead of fully blocking and countering to create an opening, she had to swipe the blows aside as she dodged and danced around.

Her weak legs and injured arm cost her. Annalla was too slow twisting to the right as she batted away an overhand strike. The weak arm gave too much against the pressure, and her opponent's sword slid along her upper arm drawing a long gash in its wake. The hit made her too slow dodging out of the way of the second man's strike. His sword sliced along the top of her thigh, leaving another bleeding wound in its wake.

She hissed at the pain, but both felt like surface injuries. Her muscles still worked. The dance continued, though she was tiring faster than they.

Finally, a lucky parry follow-through slid her sword along the forearm of her first attacker and he stepped back a moment to regroup. It allowed her to kick out at the second man before they were both back on her, hopefully bruising his knee and slowing him.

They were not as talented as she, but with two of them, and her being injured, they were better together than she was today. A nick on the side of her hand. A tiny cut just below her eye. A small slice on her injured forearm. Annalla knew others had to be getting close. There would be no capture. These two knew they had to fully press for a killing blow—not hesitating to take her prisoner—if they were going to win.

Annalla pushed aside the looming certainty of death and all thoughts of other potential enemies. Her mind had no time for attention on anything but the two men and where their swords were headed. Suddenly, the first man stopped cold in the middle of an attack. She used the moment to slice her sword along the throat of the unprepared second opponent as he moved to execute his half of a no longer coordinated attack.

Blood sprayed over her as he dropped his sword and clutched his throat. He was already dead. So was the first, Annalla discovered, as she turned back toward him only to find him facedown with an arrow in his back.

"Annalla!"

She looked to the north and saw Geelomin firing back at other men who had chased after her. Without hesitation, she ran for him. He kneed Fleet around, guiding him with legs alone, and fired one last time before reaching a hand down to her. Grabbing it with her good arm, she jumped, and they swung her up behind him even as he kicked the horse forward. As she wrapped her arms around his waist to keep from falling off as they galloped off, an arrow sunk deep into her thigh. She cried out and groaned in pain.

"Are you hit?"

"I'll live. Go!"

That was all the assurance he needed. Geelomin urged Fleet faster through the rain and over the rolling landscape. She grunted with every jump but held on as they headed due east. Fleet was breathing hard when Geelomin finally slowed them to a walk.

"We are going to need to walk her for a time or she will end up lame."

Annalla grit her teeth. "I don't know that I can walk."

He started to twist in the saddle to look at her and immediately saw the arrow shaft. "I am not a medic, but let me look at this."

Annalla grabbed his hand to swing down from the horse's back, but she could not get her legs under her and immediately fell on her butt when she let go of his hand. He quickly followed her off the horse, but with much more grace in his dismount. His eyes widened when he looked down at her.

"You are covered in blood! How injured are you?"

She laid back and simply breathed. "I have no idea, but most of the blood is probably not mine. You can walk Fleet for a bit first and then we can torture me with another arrow removal."

That startled a laugh out of him. He nodded and walked Fleet in circles to cool the horse down before returning and frowning down at her.

"Maybe we should cut the shaft and leave it for Larron," he said with his face scrunched in uncertainty.

"Do you have any bandages? If we cut it, we can wrap them around it for stability, and I probably need the other leg and this arm wrapped, too."

Annalla nearly passed out when they broke the arrow shaft in half, then had to breathe deeply to keep from vomiting as the pain made her feel ill. She rallied and was able to help him wrap her other injuries. Everything just went over her clothes, neither one of them was a skilled enough medic to warrant trying to disrobe her around the arrow they had already decided to leave. They were both bloody and tired when they finished. Geelomin handed her some of the dried meat and water from his pack. He gave her a few moments to sit there and nibble.

"We are not too far from where the fight happened. Are you going to be okay to ride?"

She was tired. Everything hurt, and she wanted to curl up under a tree with a blanket and sleep for a full day. Then she would wake up to find she was magically healed and in a nice, soft, dry, warm bed somewhere safe. That is what she wanted.

Geelomin looked concerned, like he was considering other options available, when she did not immediately respond to his question.

"If Fleet can carry me, I can ride," she assured him. He helped her back onto the horse, and started walking northeast with the lead line in hand.

"You led them away," he spoke some time later.

"That was the goal. I pulled more of them than I expected, though, and those two were good. They would have had me if you had not come along. Thank you for saving me."

He shrugged off her gratitude as though it were not necessary.

"How did you find me?" she asked him.

"I circled around to the south after we covered the group's retreat and saw people running. They had no reason to flee from us, so I guessed they were following you." He glanced back and smirked. "You look awful."

The comment surprised her, and she could not help but laugh. "I'm okay with looking awful. I thought I was dead, so I'll live with awful."

He glanced back again and his lip kicked up in disdain. "Our bandages are also terrible. Larron is going to lecture me—again—on how I should train up my first aid skills when he sees this."

"In that case, I will not admit to helping. I will already be getting a lecture from him on running off for this incident." They shared another grin before she sobered. "How are we going to find the others?"

Geelomin did not seem concerned about that part. "Larron would have most likely run straight for the border. I am planning to cut back toward that path and then do the same. Keep your ears out for anyone. Thanon and Bealaras peeled off in other directions. If they were pursued, we might find enemies before us as well."

"Got it. At least the rain is lighter now."

"I am pleased as well."

They had worked Fleet roughly in the initial escape, so they alternated between Geelomin riding behind her and walking ahead, allowing a brief rest after midnight. She knew the moment they crossed the border into the Woodland. It was a feeling all at once more alive and powerful, but at the same time wearier and more fragile.

Accompanying that first step across was an almost audible click, a key turning, a bolt falling into place. A thrilling tingle coursed along her skin, while a sense of connection took root in every fiber of her body. Annalla's eyes widened, and she could feel the entire Woodland. Its myriad of life, its currents, became visible, tangible; both.

It was like flying, like being in the air. The connection, the currents. They felt nothing alike, but at the core of the two connections, she knew they were of the same source. Annalla was still for a while, oblivious to the movement around her, and for a brief moment, oblivious to the aches and pains. Geelomin looked back at her and smiled in understanding even as he continued pulling them forward.

CHAPTER SEVENTEEN

Tyrus looked around as the main party caught up to Thanon, and they halted in the middle of the forest around mid-morning. "Why have we stopped?"

Before he finished the sentence, three elves appeared around them with arrows nocked. Their clothing was the same Larron and his elves wore, though in a slightly more vibrant color matching the evergreen forest around them. All three were lighter in their physical characteristics than Larron's party, with their faces smudged to better blend with the shadows of the forest in which they would hide.

The one to the left had light brown hair, and his skin held a yellow undertone. Larron could tell the other two had stained their hair as well as their faces to better scout unseen. The one with reddish skin had strands of light blond hair shimmering in the twists of his braids, while the palest among them hid hair of vibrant red. All were tones much more common to the fair Palonian.

"State your name, and purpose for bringing outsiders into the Palonian Woodland," the pale one on their right ordered.

Fortunately, the outsiders with him remained calm

and did not attempt to reach for weapons. He had done what he could to appear as guides rather than hostages, and Tyrus was an intelligent leader who understood his intent.

"I am Commander Larron of the Derou Woodland, and we bring word from Prince Erro to the Palonian King."

"Larron!" one of them exclaimed at the introduction. "We have not heard from the Derou in so long, we feared the worst."

"As have we, Captain. Now I see The Palonian is also besieged."

"A persistent nuisance recently added to our troubles," he agreed. "As you mention, Commander, we have had enemy humans in the surrounding forest for some time now. I am afraid I must ask after your companions here before we proceed."

"Of course, this is Prince Tyrus of Ceru and his guards. He carries the royal seal, and I can attest that this man looks very much like King Garrett, whom I have had the pleasure of meeting. We met their party outside the ring of enemies. Having the same goal, we joined forces to enter The Palonian."

"Welcome, Prince Tyrus. I would presume you are both here to speak with the council?"

They both inclined their heads.

"I am Captain Evarlund. We will send a runner ahead to announce you. Tonight, you may stay with us at our guard post, as it is too far to travel to the heartwood now."

"I thank you for your hospitality," Tyrus responded with sincerity.

The captain nodded and extended an arm, another scout appeared with perfect timing leading a horse behind. "If you will follow me, we may proceed."

Larron nodded his thanks. "We have companions who

may have been captured by those surrounding the Woodland.
Are there any available who can help?"

"It saddens me to hear this, Commander," Evarlund
said, but he gave Larron some hope. "We do regularly scout
their encampments, so we can discuss the location they went
missing and dispatch scouts to the most likely camps. If your
people are alive, we will endeavor to rescue them."

"One of Tyrus's men will also require additional
medical attention. I did what I could in the field, but the
injury was inflicted by a rusted bear trap. I did not have the
specific treatment with me."

"We will ensure he is seen to. Our post is well
stocked and staffed."

There was nothing more he could ask at the moment,
so Larron said his thanks and allowed Tyrus to move up
between them to converse with the captain as they all fell in
with the scout leader. Two other elves followed at the back of
their party on additional horses pulled in from some hidden
location, while the others who had emerged melted back into
the forest.

The pace set was slow, serving to both allow guests to
not feel rushed as well as allowing plenty of time for word of
their arrival to reach the ears needing to hear of it. As such, it
was easy for the scouts to catch up to them, as one did, not a
half-hour later.

"Captain, more approach, heading this way and
following their trail."

Larron's head raised at the words. "How many? They
may be those missing from my party."

The scout looked at his captain for approval, as he
should, before answering. "Two riding, Commander. One
does appear to be an elf. The other is injured…there are
many bandages."

Captain Evarlund motioned his people back into the forest, and they disappeared to guard in case these were not Larron's missing people.

Waiting was interminable, and he hated being at the front, where they would be the last to see who was arriving.

"Geelomin!" Thanon finally called out, and Larron's head stretched as he stood in the saddle to see Geelomin's small wave of greeting.

Larron grinned, dismounted, and started to quickly walk to them through the horses and riders crowding the path. His smile grew when Geelomin turned Fleet to the side to help Annalla, in her still ill-fitting clothes, dismount from behind him, but it instantly fled in the face of concern. She was caked in blood and covered in bandages, and when her feet touched the ground, she was limping.

"Annalla!" He rushed forward, stopping in front of her and cataloging the injuries.

"Most of the blood is not mine," she sounded exhausted and wrinkled her nose, which was clearly the only thing not injured from what he could see. "We were not sure of the best way to remove the arrow, so it's still there. Are we staying here tonight?"

"How much of the blood is yours?" Her last comment sounded off to his ears, and some of the bandages were soaking through.

Geelomin was still at her side, holding her waist. "I believe riding kept reopening some of her injuries and may have dug the arrow in further. We thought it best to see her to a medic rather than do more damage removing it ourselves, but I am no longer certain that was the correct decision."

"We have an infirmary at the guard post."

"Thank you, Captain. How far would it be?"

"Less than an hour's ride."

She looked so tired. He was not sure waiting would be wise, especially with Geelomin's growing concern with that course thus far.

"Annalla?"

"Will there be hot water I can clean up with? I can make it, Larron. Let's go." She slurred her words, and he shook his head.

Larron looked at Evarlund. "Captain, I believe the arrow should be removed before we move her again. Are you willing to wait while I do so?"

"Of course, Commander, what do you need from us?"

"Nothing at the moment, thank you," he said as an unnaturally subdued Thanon brought him his field kit. "Geelomin, help her sit off to the side here. Annalla, I am going to remove the arrow. The rest can wait, but we must see to that now."

She looked at him as he knelt at her side, but was not focusing well. She reached a shaky hand out to brush his cheek.

Good enough, he thought and cut open the bandages and her pant leg.

"You ripped Palan's pants," Annalla muttered, and he heard tears in her voice.

Blood soaked the cloth. The movement of riding seemed to have stirred the arrow in her thigh, causing more damage with the movement. He would need to remove it by feel and possibly cut it out to ensure a smooth extraction without unnecessary additional damage.

"We could use the trakin distillation," Larron said aloud, not liking the idea for some reason, but this was going to hurt, possibly more than the last arrow removal.

"No." Thanon was adamant. "You know you cannot take that amount of control from her. Throw her back into the trakin attack."

"You want to remove that without it?" Someone incredulously asked behind them, and he knew they had an audience.

Larron gave some of the pain-numbing herb to Thanon. "Have her chew on this somehow."

He reached back into the kit for the tiny knife included for this purpose, a small flask of highly concentrated alcohol, and some prepared bandages.

"Hold her so she does not stab me." He said aloud, and three elves chuckled knowingly as they grabbed limbs tightly. Their audience probably thought they were out of their minds.

He grabbed her face and forced her to look at him. "Annalla, I am going to remove the arrow now. Do try not to kill me."

She blinked slowly a few times, and he let go, placing a leather bracer between her teeth. With efficient movements, he rinsed the blade and grabbed for the small portion of the arrow shaft still visible. He pulled on it gently, trying to discern how the head was positioned. Her eyes went wide, she strained against the restraining hands, and a snarling growl came from her as she bit into the leather. When he thought he knew the positioning, he let go and looked up briefly. She was alert now.

Annalla looked angry. He really hoped it was not aimed at him. Her eyes closed briefly, then she refocused on him and nodded once, pursing her lips around the leather. Without waiting for more, he probed her swollen flesh with the side of the blade to find the entrance. Larron ignored her pained breathing and moans as he pushed, pulled, and cut. She was no longer thrashing against them, so Geelomin could assist, and he handed Larron items as asked, even wiped his brow at one point, though he did not notice at the time. Finally…finally, the delicate work was done and the arrowhead came free.

He could do a better job of closing it after cleaning the wound in safer conditions, so he caused her one more sharp pain as he lashed a bandage tightly against the wound and tied it off. They were both sweating when he was done, and tears streaked through the blood on her face.

She spit out the leather, panting. "One of you…can take the next arrow." Her head rolled to rest against Thanon's as he held her and cried while laughing.

Thanon kissed her temple. "Only a little further and you can sleep, love," he whispered before rising and leaving them, even as Geelomin packed the supplies.

"Can you stand?" Larron asked her.

Annalla looked a little drunk as she turned to him. "If you mean, can I rise to my feet and remain upon them? No."

He laughed at her answer. "We will help you."

Thanon returned, bringing Dusk, and he mounted first before Geelomin handed her up to him.

He looked around for the captain, to indicate they were ready to go, and found the entire party other than his group staring at them.

"Captain," he said with dignity, "I believe we are now ready to continue."

He felt Annalla laugh more than he heard it as the elves and humans scrambled to mount and form up again. As they headed out, he fell in toward the front, but again allowed Tyrus to ride with the captain.

"What other injuries do you have?"

Annalla slouched back against his chest. "Many sword cuts, but most fairly shallow. The arrow hit happened as Geelomin was rescuing me. It was probably better this way than if it had hit Fleet instead. I'm not sure we would have made it, and he came all that way for me." She was quickly fading. "Will you wake me?"

"Yes, sleep. I will not let you fall."

Her head relaxed back, resting against his cheek, and he closed his eyes. Breathing deep, he squeezed his hands on the reins to stop their shaking. The scout captain was watching him when he opened his eyes again.

"Captain, please, tell me about this siege. Do they have so many they can ring the entire Woodland?"

"Fortunately, no, but they guard the main thoroughfares and make our coordination efforts significantly more challenging. We have sent word out, but we fear many have been caught unaware upon the road here before word could reach them."

Tyrus spoke up on his other side. "The river road north was beset with enemies as well. There must be a stronghold Kahnlair has established in the east."

"I am afraid the Derou have been cut off for years, so I would know nothing of this."

"It will be good to hear if the council has any additional information."

He was beginning to wonder if they would have information or simply more bad news for him and his people.

***

"We will continue at dawn."

Annalla felt a shake and heard voices dimly through the mist of her thoughts. She shook her head to clear the fog. Her injuries still hurt, and she ached everywhere.

"Quarters will have been prepared for you tonight, but I am afraid we do not have enough rooms to spare for you to each have your own." The scout captain stopped and dismounted, handing his horse over to those waiting for them by a small stable.

As others followed his lead, Annalla realized she was lounging against Larron, his arms curved around her holding the reins and holding her up. Trying to sit up straighter strained her thigh injuries, and even as she ground her teeth against it to try again, he was pulling gently on her arm.

"Relax a moment longer," he whispered in her ear as the captain continued, and she leaned back again.

"Supper has not yet commenced, but we can prepare a small meal if you would prefer that over waiting. We have one room available if you would care to use it, Your Highness."

"I am grateful for your generosity, but I would prefer to remain with my men until we have a chance to introduce ourselves to your king," Tyrus responded first. "There is also no need to tax your kitchen. We will be pleased to eat with the rest of your people."

"I believe you said there was an infirmary?" Larron had remained mounted. "We should see Annalla and Lawrence there first."

Tyrus agreed, "Yes. Harndorn, will you assist him to the infirmary?"

"Of course, if you will follow me. You may remain mounted until we arrive there," Captain Evarlund was offering even as Harndorn nodded.

Four of them rode after the walking elf, but it was not too far. The closer they got to it, the more Annalla could smell food cooking. She felt Larron hand her the reins and realized she had closed her eyes again. He held her arms to support her as he scooted back in the saddle, then he helped her reposition so it was easier for her to remain seated upright on her own.

As he got down, she leaned forward slightly to take the strain off her thigh again. Larron turned to her with his arms out. For a moment she blinked in confusion as he wiggled his fingers in a 'come here' gesture.

I'm so tired, she thought as she caught on to his intent, then placed her hands on his shoulders and let him ease her weight down, sliding off Dusk's back.

Rather than carrying her, he held her against his side and helped her limp to a door held open for them, leading to a clean room with six beds to the right and a screened-off area to the left.

"I'm way too dirty for those beds." She stopped in her tracks. Moving was waking her up further, and she was not comfortable stepping further into the sterile room in her current state.

The captain laughed, but it was amused rather than mocking. "The shower is behind the screens, and the water should be warm from the cook fires. Do you need me to send in an assistant or healer?"

"If you could please send a healer in to check the wound on Lawrence's leg it would be appreciated, as would any spare clothing you have that might fit Annalla."

He efficiently looked her up and down at Larron's request. "I believe one of our medics is around the same size. I will ask her."

"Thank you," Larron said, and the elf turned to leave. "Lawrence, please have a seat on one of the beds. Annalla, I believe you will need to disrobe to provide access to all your wounds based on bandage placement. Which also means we will need to remove those soiled bandages first."

She looked at the bandages and all the cuts and tears in her clothing. Even the thought of trying to take her pants off made her lightheaded, so she was not certain she could accomplish that goal.

"Yes. I think that is for the best, but I will need to cut them off. At least the pants anyway." Her hand was reaching for a knife as she sighed.

"Wait, they will have something better here to accomplish that." Harndorn was helping Law onto one of the beds as Larron eased her to lean against a wall and went to a table full of supplies.

"Get out of here, Har, you will just be in the way when the medic arrives," Lawrence said to the other man.

"Haha, alright." He turned to Larron. "Let us know if you need anything else, Commander. We are most grateful for your assistance."

Larron was holding scissors as he nodded, and Harndorn left. She thought about the scissors for a moment and what needed to be done. "Help me get behind the screen. I can probably do most of it myself."

He half carried her hobbling over to the shower area, where she found two sections, one with a seat and handles beneath a faucet. That is where Larron guided her and helped her sit down.

"Soap, but do not scrub any injuries." He set the scissors on the seat beside her and held up a little bar. "I will place a dry towel on the screen here, so you can wrap up when you are done. Do not dry off though. I will help with that, as I want to make sure you do not make something worse by rubbing it, and we may need to clean some of the wounds further. Toss the dirty clothing over there. Just pile it up. It is probably good for nothing other than rags at this point, but the guards here will determine what to do with it."

"Okay."

Hesitating, he stepped closer to hold her arm and

lowered his voice so Law would not hear. "Are you certain you do not need assistance?"

Annalla touched his face, where a bloody streak remained. "You should wash this off your face unless you're hoping to look frightening," she said distractedly. Annalla shook her head and remembered his question. "Nothing is beyond reach here. I should be fine, but I will let you know. My wings... Don't let anyone else back either."

His hand gripped hers, and his lips pressed briefly against her forehead. "Alright. I will be just on the other side of the screen."

She would not need help getting her shirt over her wings this time, but she had to keep them low enough not to be seen over the top of the screen, where she was sure the top of her head would show if she were standing. Rubbing her face, Annalla felt blood and grime flake off against her hands.

Gross, she thought as she started to unwrap one of the easier-to-reach bandages. Some of the knots were too difficult to undo with one hand, some too tight even with two, so she simply cut through. A couple of her injuries started bleeding again, including the arrow wound on her leg, but neither were gushing so she continued.

When all the gauzy material was gone, she started removing her clothing. First went her shirt. She peeled it off and away from her injuries, hissing when she tugged on where the cloth edge had become wedged slightly in a cut. Larron shifted on the other side of the screen at her sound of pain, but he made no comment.

Instead of messing with the pants, she cut from the waist down each leg past her knees, then let them slip down to her feet. They were borrowed pants, and already too large for her, so they slid easily to pool upon the floor. Using the handles installed for just this purpose, she eased herself onto the seat, and picked the pants up with the rest of her clothes to toss them to the side.

Another person entered the infirmary at that moment and started to talk to Larron first, then Law about how his leg was feeling.

He must have been the person to cry out when they were surprised by that group of men.

She focused on getting clean, trusting Larron to keep everyone on that side of the barrier. The water was only moderately warm, but it was clean, and she scrubbed at the blood on her face and body and tried to rinse it off her wings as well. When she was done, she did her best to lift her butt off the seat to get that rinsed before stopping the water and reaching for the towel dangling to the side. Deciding she did not have the energy to rise, she wrapped herself up and called out, "Larron, come check how well I cleaned these cuts so I can dry off."

She heard him move, and he arrived with another towel and a smaller cloth, which was set aside as he knelt before her. His hands and face were washed clean, and she watched as he diligently inspected every cut he could see. "Did I miss any?"

Annalla shook her head.

"I would like you to stand while I wash out a couple more spots if you are capable."

He was asking if she could stay standing for a time.

"Help me up," she said.

Larron grabbed her elbow and pulled her to her feet. She leaned her weight on her better leg and used the sturdy screen for support as he took the hose and more diligently washed her wings and rinsed the still bleeding cuts as she held the towel around her. With gentle hands, he used the second towel to pat her dry then helped her into the clothing he had brought. It turned out to be a loose chemise that fell to mid-thigh. She could hide most of her wings beneath it if she was careful.

"Something to offer modesty while allowing access to your wounds. Mara brought a change of clothing for you to use after we have your injuries bandaged properly."

Annalla made her way to the other side of the screen, Larron still taking most of her weight, and was brought to one of the unoccupied beds in the room. The new elf, Mara, was wrapping Lawrence's leg, so they were probably done with him. She wore a grey version of the scout uniforms that was a bit looser and without the leather armor over it. Unlike the scouts, her golden-blond hair was gleaming, and she wore it pulled back in one, no-nonsense braid running down her back.

Larron met her eyes. "You are going to need stitches. I can use the trakin sedative this time if you are willing."

"Just a painkiller. I don't want a trakin knockout again."

"We are equipped with a localized anesthetic," the medic offered. Her eyes widened a fraction when she looked over and saw Annalla's injuries now fully exposed, but she recovered quickly. "The field medic did well with this man's wound, so I am almost done here and can assist."

Larron reclaimed her attention. "Annalla? I will defer to your wishes, but this is a good suggestion."

"I trust you." He looked at her in a way reminding her she had just refused one treatment suggestion. "I do. You would not have used the trakin stuff anyway."

"Where do you store it?" he asked Mara, ignoring the last remark.

"Top shelf of that cupboard there."

It did not make her completely numb, so she still felt the pinching of the needle, but it was so much less than the earlier emergency arrow removal. He and Mara worked efficiently, and soon enough, she was bandaged up and Larron was helping her into a new set of borrowed clothes. The pants were a little tight around the hips and her more muscular thighs, while a little long in the legs. The shirt fit better. It would have been loose on Mara, but it had short sleeves that did not pinch tight enough to be restrictive.

"This person is clearly skinnier and taller than me," she muttered with her hands on Larron's shoulders as he knelt before her to roll up the pant legs and put on her new, also borrowed, boots.

"I am, indeed. Those are mine. I am Mara, by the way," the medic said from where she was finishing cleaning up and checked on a sleeping Lawrence. He had taken the trakin knock-out serum. "Sorry I did not introduce myself earlier."

"Thank you for the clothes. These are definitely a better fit than my last set."

Larron helped her to her feet again.

Mara smiled. "Of course. I am pleased I could help. I was told that when we were done, if you were not staying here overnight, I should lead you to the spare room."

"A moment to grab her equipment," Larron said and led her back around the screen. He handed her a cloak and her weapons before moving behind her and deftly cutting two holes in the new shirt. "How are you feeling?"

She pushed her wings out, only tearing the holes a little more in the process, and wrapped them around herself. "Better. Thank you. I guess I will not be returning these to her, at least not the shirt... And I thought you or Tyrus was getting the room."

He smiled at her. "I will replace them if needed, but I am sure King Oromaer will do so himself. As for the room, Geelomin decided the most injured should have it. He expected you would not remain in the infirmary."

Annalla was the one to raise an eyebrow this time. "Geelomin decided?"

"I am not one to argue with my Lieutenant. Especially not when I place him in charge while I am busy elsewhere."

She made an aborted movement forward. "I can walk on the leg, right?"

"Slowly, with small steps, yes. You are going to feel very tired before we make it to your room."

"Ha," she breathed. "I'm already tired, so let's get this over with."

It took her…a long time to make the trip. Step by tiny step she walked with Larron harrumph-ing at her, and her leg protesting, whenever she started moving faster. Annalla held onto his arm the entire time and leaned on it more as they progressed. Mara was their ever-patient guide, strolling along as though on a leisurely walk through a park.

"You must do this a lot," Annalla noted.

Mara smiled serenely. "Many a stubborn warrior has made this walk, and I guide them all."

Larron actually snorted at that, but she was more dignified.

"I am honored to now be among their number." She grinned over at him.

The room they showed her to when they finally arrived was sparse, with only a small bed, table, and chair to furnish it, but she had never known anything other than hard earth beneath her and trees or rocks around her when she slept. This was luxury for her, literally without compare.

Almost as soon as she sat on the bed after her nurse-guides left there was a knock at her door, and she had to call for a moment to regain her feet and hobble back over. When she opened it, her mouth immediately began to water, and her stomach cried out as her eyes locked onto the plate held before her.

"May I?" The hands holding the tray tipped forward, indicating toward the room.

She looked up, noticing for the first time the elf holding the plate. He looked much like the other elves she had thus far encountered; slender, strong, and gracefully beautiful. Both his hair and eyes were a dark brown, with paler skin than all in *her* group except Annalla herself. With a nod toward the room behind her he smiled and raised an eyebrow to emphasize his question again.

"Oh...Yes. Thank you," she replied awkwardly and moved aside to allow him in.

He went about his task quickly, efficiently, and without further conversation. The tray with the plate and a steaming cup she had not noticed initially was set at one end of the small table. With another smile and nod, the door closed, and he was gone.

Annalla didn't hesitate to pull up the chair and set into the feast before her. It was not hot, they had said her healing detour made them a bit late for supper, but it was still warm from the lingering heat of the cooking fires. There was seasoned venison—the seasoning was something other than half its weight in salt to preserve it—and the first fresh bread she could remember eating. Oh, the taste of bread with butter melted on her tongue.

This was certainly a fresh batch cooked especially for her. It could not possibly be this good otherwise. Flavorful squash and fresh apples rounded out her plate, and all was accompanied by a hot cup of a bittersweet liquid with such a relaxing effect that she wondered if they had conferred with her medic. The effect was certainly compounding the impact of the painkillers.

Each bite was savored, each sip relished with a smile on her face. Annalla finished every bite without trouble, and, for the first time she could remember, she was not hungry at all. Thinking back on her first meal with Larron, she thought she had eaten her fill, but this...was bliss. It was a surprising sensation to no longer have her gut gnawing at her.

Her throat choked up and she fought back tears at the sudden relief. This was safety. Despite all her aches and pains, this was a security found nowhere else. When she regained control of her emotions, a sudden exhaustion struck her so much more deeply than before. She moved over to the bed and threw back the blanket on it. Her body sank into the mattress as she lay down and the pillow cradled her head as she pulled the blanket tight. Food, drink, and comfort gave sleep aid, and it took her quickly and completely that night.

CHAPTER EIGHTEEN

Another horse had been offered for Thanon, so Annalla was back on Moonshine alone. Larron was not sure of her leg, and he missed holding her, but he knew she would not want to be seen as less, no matter his wishes for her health and his own comfort. Law was also stubbornly back on his horse. That one was plain stupid, but Tyrus had whispered to him that he would make sure he was off it for plenty of time after they arrived at the Heartwood.

Dedicated soldiers made some of the worst patients, but they both made it through the last day without complaining, and—more importantly—they allowed him to check the injuries when they stopped for the night. Larron was certain his ultimatum of being drawn on a travois behind their horse instead if they did not was the deciding factor in that regard.

"We should reach the Heartwood before mid-morning, Your Highness," one of their guides called out to the group.

"Will we be going straight to see King Oromaer?" Tyrus asked him.

The elf looked over and tipped his head. "Yes. Those

are our instructions."

"You all look so excited," Annalla said to his people around her. "I thought only Larron and Palan had been here before."

"That is true," Thanon said. "But any Woodland feels like coming home in some ways."

Bealaras breathed deep and spread his arms wide. "You can feel the life here, and the Heartwood is more profound, even if this is not our home Woodland."

The Palonian was the most likely to be *her* home Woodland based on her father's hair and complexion.

Larron spoke over her thoughts, "Crossing the border into your home Woodland is…staggering."

Annalla looked over at him. "And when you leave?"

He thought of the ache in his heart at the first step out every time he traveled. "It hurts."

"So why do you go?"

"Some experiences are worth the pain." His heart raced at a spike of fear he could not place. "I am able to travel the world, see it change and meet new people, and I can always return home. The pain is not physical, nor permanent. It is more like saying farewell to a close friend for a while. You miss them, but they will be in your life again."

"This is not The Derou, but I feel as though I am able to once again relax," Bealaras said. "It feels safe and serene here. I could paint again," he finished with wonder.

Thanon laughed. "You never stopped talking about painting all the way here, so do not begin lying about limitations now."

"Will all of you be talking to the council?"

"I hope not!" Both of them exclaimed at the same time, making her laugh at their vehemence.

"We should all have some well-earned free time." Geelomin looked like he was close to breaking control and rolling his eyes at the pair. "Annalla, they will have the other weapons here. You should dance swords with Larron after you are healed."

Larron's head snapped around, frustrated that his Lieutenant would suggest something so dangerous. Maybe she would not know the dance to which he was referring. It was too risky when performed true to form.

He was still staring daggers at his Lieutenant when she responded with a wistful smile. "I'm close, but not there yet."

"Very close based upon the fight I saw. Those men were highly skilled, and you would have defeated them if not for your injury."

"Thank you. Maybe you and I can cross blades as well." She smiled at him in an exaggerated fashion. "What about you, Thanon, what are you going to do here?"

"Explore for a while. Palan said you can always find interesting new hobbies that way, and part of me wants to do something for him; something he wanted to do himself."

He went on to talk about their lost friend and what he had planned to see. Larron—all of them—wished Palan could have made it here to do these things himself. Perhaps Larron would explore a little as well when he had the time, in honor of Palan.

They would find answers here and hope for The Derou. Their people would not be left to die. He had to believe that.

***

They were about to come to the completion of their mission

begun months ago. Annalla felt little of that anticipation, but her senses were hit again upon entering the Heartwood. All the sensations flooding into her were compounded and enhanced here, to the point of becoming intoxicating if one were not aware of the connection and could not acclimate to its presence. Though, she did not think she would describe the sensation as "staggering."

As they were led through the Heartwood, people waved greetings, but no one stopped them to talk, and they were ushered into the King's presence without delay, which would have surprised her without Tyrus's presence.

All her nerves from before the talk with Larron came flooding back as they strode through the simple, though large, dwelling. She would be outcast, hated, feared, or worse. They surely could not want mixed blood, and they had to hate the fairy for hiding away while they fought evil creatures like the gilar in a war lasting decades. Here she was to ruin their deeply held beliefs while at the same time mocking them for not having better defenses.

Annalla nearly jumped when Larron grabbed her hand. He knew. He knew she was panicking, but the gesture of support had her breathing again. With a squeeze and a smile, he moved to the fore again as they approached the end of a hallway and the doors opened.

King Oromaer looked much the same as other elves, with the same timeless and beautiful features, though, if she was any judge of elven age, his eyes showed greater years than most.

Well, most of those I have run into, anyway, she thought.

His hair was golden, and he had bright blue eyes. Without the circlet on his forehead, he could have been any other elf. He reminded her of her father. The only aspect to mar his elven perfection was the strain showing on his face. The same weariness and worry clouded the features of all they had met so far, but his face lit up with something like relief and joy when he saw Larron.

Another elf walked forward and bowed, the eight men and Larron's party all followed suit, with Tyrus and Larron at the head of their party.

Rising from the bow, an attendant stepped forward. "Your Majesty, King Oromaer, may I present Prince Tyrus of Ceru and Prince Larron of the Derou Woodland."

The air left her lungs, and her mind went numb.

Prince? They had lied *to her. All of them. For months.* It was a blow to the gut and embarrassing to be so fooled. She thought they came to trust her and see her as one of them, but that was clearly untrue. She was as much an outsider as she had feared.

Annalla swallowed back her hurt as Oromaer came forward and embraced Larron as he might his own son.

"Larron, my friend, I almost did not recognize you. It is good to see you still with us. When we lost touch with The Derou, we feared the worst."

"You as well Oromaer, though I wish our reunion were not brought about by such dire times." A brief, yet grim, silence of understanding and agreement met his words before the king replied.

"I have been told your journey here is one that deserves telling, but I think that might be something the northern war council may need to hear. Yes?" At Larron's affirming nod, he turned to Tyrus. "Prince, it is an honor to have you here with us."

"The honor is mine, Your Majesty. I bring news from my father for the council as well."

"We will have time to hear all. For now, please

introduce me to those who have risked so much to bring you both here."

She liked this king, who thought about the regular soldiers. He greeted each of Tyrus's men as they were introduced and asked a question or two. Annalla pretended to pay attention while she worked to not cry and get control of her breathing. Her hand was grabbed again, and Larron's face was there before her. The honest apology and concern in his eyes did not help her roiling emotions.

"We will talk. I promise."

It did not matter. She tamped down the emotions and walled off the reasons for them. They were still with her and would still support her. The situation was simply different than she had thought. She still had friends. Taking her hand back, she smiled. "I'm good."

He frowned at her but continued, "I would like to tell those here about you now."

"And who are your companions, Larron?" Oromaer asked, reaching them before she could respond, so he introduced the others first.

Was she ready to be known? Was she ready for the response? Annalla would probably never be prepared for a negative response and waiting would only make things worse. Her heart raced, but at this moment she had her friends with her, and one of them a prince of elves. That had to count for more. Annalla nodded at him when he came back to her side, her jaw clenched with nerves.

"This is Annalla. We met her early in our journey from The Derou. She has fought valiantly and helped us greatly along the way. Oromaer, she is an elf, though, we do not know of which Woodland."

The king looked confused but responded directly to her rather than questioning Larron. "Annalla, forgive me as I say you do not have the look of an elf. Maybe elven features, but…"

She moved her hair behind her ears to reveal the tips—which Bealaras assured her were very much elf in shape—and braced herself. "Your Majesty, no forgiveness needed. I'm only half-elf."

"What?" he whispered, looking from her to Larron and back with a shake of his head. "How is this possible?"

The moment was broken when she heard Thanon snort and mutter, "Wait for the other half."

"What do you mean by that, Thanon?" he had not been quiet enough, it seemed. Annalla struggled not to laugh herself when the king's attention turned back to him.

"Uh…" Her friend blushed.

"And half-fairy," Larron finished for them.

The King and all Tyrus's men looked at Larron in confused disbelief. Some laughed at what they thought was a joke. She was finding their reactions humorous enough to push some of her own hurt and confusion aside.

"Surprise!" Came her quiet, nervous exclamation.

They still just looked at her. Thanon snorted again— he was close to cracking up with her. She glanced over at him, and he grinned at her as he winked. "Annalla, wings."

"Oh, right."

Lifting her arms from her sides, she smoothly unwrapped her wings from her body and snapped them open. There was no glitter or music at the presentation, but she did like their colors. Those in the room found themselves staring at the shape of enormous, person-sized butterfly wings.

While the guards behind her were shown a pattern of rich forest greens with veins of earthy brown running through, Oromaer was treated to the sight of a range of sky blues with veins of white and grey. The colors seemed to shift and blend before their eyes as the light in the room played off of and through them with a life all their own.

Into the silence, she heard a door open behind Oromaer across the room and footsteps approach. A voice followed in short order.

"Majesty, the rooms are being prepared, and the healer mage will... My lord, it's a fairy..." The newcomer breathed the words out.

It seemed to jar the king out of his stunned silence. "I must say, Annalla, I am literally at a loss for words."

"Yes, it is a lot to take in, I'm sure."

"They are." He looked up from her face again with an expression of awe. "Your wings are beautiful."

She swallowed at his implied acceptance and whispered, "Thank you."

"Larron said you do not know your Woodland?"

Shaking her head. "No, Sir. I was injured and have very little memory of my life before, including my parents. I think my father looked much like you, but I do not think I have the connection Larron described to The Palonian, but maybe that is because I am only half-elf."

"Ah, well, I am sorry you were injured. Perhaps the healers can help with the memory loss as well. The Palonian have several travelers with similar features to my own. I will see if there are any images I can dig up, and we can talk more. Until then, welcome to the Palonian, elf-fairy Annalla."

"Thank you," she said again, letting herself relax enough to give a tentative smile.

"For now," he spoke to all, "I believe Rolandor was about to let us know that a healer mage has been requested to meet you all at the baths. If you have no objections, we will have your belongings transferred to a common room near the quarters that have been prepared for you. Larron, if you would join me for a visit after your people are seen to, I would very much like to hear of your family. Again, I welcome you all to the safety of The Palonian."

"Of course, Oromaer. I will see you then."

They all turned and followed another attendant down the hall.

"It is all going to work out now," Bealaras said.

The council they needed help from was still here and active, so they would find the help they needed. Annalla was still adjusting to Larron's revelation, but despite the deception, they had supported her and Oromaer welcomed her as an elf. At the moment, she felt lighter than air and smiled at Bealaras in turn. "Yes, I think it is."

EPILOGUE

Larron joined Oromaer and his bonded, Lady Arbellie, for dinner that evening. Oromaer announced a feast the next day, to celebrate a visit from their allies from Ceru and the Derou elves, but tonight was just for them. Larron had fostered here, with these two, for a fair portion of his youth. They were as much family to him as his flesh and blood.

"My people told me you brought word from Prince Erro." Oromaer said after those helping to deliver the simple meal on the table left. "What of your brother?"

Closing his eyes, Larron took a breath. "Zeris was taken in an attack in the spring. Erro rules in his name, but I do not know for how long that is reasonable."

Arbellie covered his hand with hers. "Do you think there is no hope?"

"I wish to hope until that hope is proven false."

"Your people will stand with Erro, prince or king. The title matters not."

Larron smiled at that. "They will, indeed. No more talk of war tonight though…if we can help it. We have enough sorrows without them encroaching upon reunions."

"Very well." She got a mischievous glint in her eye.

"So, are you and Lady Lydiya still on friendly terms whenever you stop your wandering?"

"We… I…" *Walked into that one,* Larron scolded himself.

He had forgotten this motherly elf liked to see people paired while they waited for the life bond to come, and she thought of him as family enough to poke into his romantic life as often as she could.

"She was needed at the family home a few years into the war. We had seen each other infrequently of late. Sorry to disappoint, Majesty."

Arbellie smiled at him. "Leadership can be difficult without someone to talk to, relax with, and share the burden."

"Erro and I share the burden. I worry more for him now with his father missing."

"Yes, you would. Does he have no one in his life either, then?"

He could not help but laugh now and would shamelessly divert her attention. "You are impossible. I have to wonder if you have played matchmaker for your son as you try to so often with my family."

"He takes after me," she said with amused pride. "*He* did not need any help making acquaintances. I do have a number of friends who would be delighted for another introduction now that you have returned to visit us, Larron."

"Ah, my dear," Oromaer patted her hand and matched her smile. "I believe you might be too late with this one. He does not need help making acquaintances either."

"Oh? Do tell! What did I miss today at your introduction?"

Oromaer looked at him and raised an eyebrow.

"I am afraid you have me at a loss," Larron told Oromaer with feigned ignorance.

His friend laughed at him and shook his head. "Then out of concern for another elf, I will ask. What are your intentions toward your fairy?"

"Hmm, you sound so concerned." His voice was wry.

Arbellie's smile was gentle now. "You did not deny it, Larron. She means something to you."

He looked at them both, then down at his plate, his lips twitching in either a smile or grimace. They would understand, and maybe they could offer some advice or insight.

"More than something," Arbellie said intuitively into the silence.

"She is mine."

Oromaer looked thoughtful, while Arbellie nodded. He spoke, "You are bonded."

The words Larron had been afraid to say aloud himself, or even think. He rubbed his chest. "I can feel it settling in. It is difficult to describe, but I know."

"How do you feel about this?"

"Exhilarated...and terrified. What if she does not feel the bond?"

Arbellie tilted her head and spoke dryly, staring him down, "You could ask her."

"Are you in love with her?" Oromaer asked instead. When he looked at his friend in confusion, he continued, "They are not the same thing, Larron. You know this."

"Falling," he sighed and admitted, letting his head fall into his hands. "Definitely falling."

"Then are you more afraid she will not feel the bond, or that she will not love you?"

Larron peeked an eye over at him. "Both?"

"Larron, you should know the bond does not make you fall in love with someone. Its presence indicates compatibility, but you must work for a relationship as much as anyone else. A life bond magnifies things, makes some level of understanding easier, and knocks you over the head with an obvious path, but you still need to travel that path. She can still walk that path with you, with or without a bond."

"She could leave that path, though."

"As could you," Arbellie scolded. "A bond does not make you incapable of arousal for others, Larron, simply as infertile as you have always been, and fertility has never been a primary requirement for elven relationships."

"That statement, from you, Arbellie, makes me extremely uncomfortable."

"Ha!" she and Oromaer laughed. "That makes it no less true. I do not want to hear of you thinking less of her in all of this for lacking a bond."

"I would never think less of her." He thought of the strong, independent, troublesome fairy in his life. "No matter what, I would never think less of her."

Oromaer's smile remained, and his voice took on a conspiratorial tone, "She is also an incredibly young adult. The bond is much more gradual for the very young."

"Maybe." Larron closed his eyes. "Maybe."

*** ﹅

Marto sat in the common dining hall and answered yet another question about the visitors.

"Yes, guests from Ceru and The Derou," he said to one person.

"No, there was no information about any news or information they brought with them. The council would meet as scheduled, so it was not urgent," was his response to another.

He was only eighteen, but no one thought twice any longer about coming to him for such information. No one wondered why he was on the council instead of one of his peers. The truth of it was, he had no peers in his specialization. Marto was the first combat mage to complete his studies after the group of students and elders with which he traveled arrived at The Palonian Woodland. His mentor, Mage Heather, had been in her final years when Kahnlair attacked the southern mage academy, and he was the only graduated combat mage when she passed three years ago.

That left him as the only potential combat mage available. While he would have been content to leave the council position to one of the senior magai, Mage Gregry led the magai who currently lived in The Palonian, and no one argued with him when he said, "A war council should include a combat mage." So that left him as the council's magai representative, and he reported out to the magai leaders, gaining their approval when necessary.

"Hi, Marto."

"Hey, Kels," he said to Kelsey as she sat down across from him.

Kelsey was still a student, but she was close to finishing her required studies and would be a second combat mage. She was two years older than him, but she shifted magic concentrations from architect to combat after first-year training and had to repeat it in the combat concentration. Marto had also studied fiercely and graduated four years early.

Kelsey's black hair with tight natural curls was pulled back into a poufy tail at the moment, and her dark eyes stared at him waiting for him to spill all his secrets. "So? Have you met our guests yet?"

Marto shook his head. "No, not until the council meeting, I think."

"Do you know who they are?"

"Kels, you have a better line on gossip than I do. There has been no official word, so you would know better than me at this point."

She groaned. "We need a mission. At the least, we should attack the humans trapping us here."

"Boredom is no reason to be hasty," Marto scolded. "I agree with the council that it would be premature to attack the camps at this time."

"You sound like the one who trained as an architect with all of your words of caution, patience, and planning."

Marto shook his head and sighed. "I wish you would apply some of that training yourself. An incautious combat mage will burn bright and die fast. We have lost enough of us already."

His parents had lived in one of the human settlements near the capital of Ceru when the attacks came. They wanted to be close to him while he was in schooling, so they moved south with him. It was a decision that cost them their lives. Marto's father was the combat mage of the two of them, his mother an artist mage, but he knew she would have stood by his side, doing what she could to help anyone escape the slaughter.

Kelsey reached across to squeeze his hand.

"I promise I'm not reckless in combat." She grinned at him. "You know my teacher would never allow me to get away with such behavior. I'm still just angry that the magai leaders rejected your proposal for the fairy expedition. Magai know the power and detail of an artist's renderings. They are acting like outsiders."

Artist magai were known for the detail and accuracy

in their stories. The visual and audible creations were stunning and life-like enough to be mistaken for real until one tried to interact with them. His mother's family was known for a particular tale about an encounter with a fairy many generations ago. Even some elves who had seen the fairy before they disappeared had been impressed with the images included.

With the war continuing down a path leading to victory for Kahnlair, the year before, Marto had proposed an expedition based on his mother's story to seek out the fairy and enlist their aid. It was soundly rejected. They were not desperate enough.

"That was not even a full year ago. I will bring it up again after you graduate. That will provide additional leverage with one of their objections removed."

Kelsey rolled her eyes. "I see what you did there."

Marto laughed with her. While his intent had been to hint that she should take her studies more seriously, he also hoped her graduation would help his argument for the expedition. His mother shared the story with him so often as a child. He knew the fairy still existed, and he would prove it to everyone by finding them.

THANK YOU!

Thank you for starting this journey with Annalla and Larron! I hope you enjoyed the book and are looking forward to the next installment to see where events take them.

How has the war impacted the rest of Elaria? Will they get the help they need?

What does Annalla discover about herself and the fairy race?

Does Larron tell her about the life bond? How does Annalla feel?

Book 2, *Hidden Sanctuary*, is scheduled to release August 2022 and available for digital preorder on Amazon now!

To keep up with all my new releases, you can sign up for my quarterly newsletter or follow my blog at:

Tiffanyshearn.com

ACKNOWLEDGEMENTS

The journey from a story in my head, to a complete novel, to a published book has been long and daunting. I could not have reached this point without the support, help, and advice from many along the way. Any and all errors are mine alone.

To Samantha Millan, who has been through every step of this journey with me, read every iteration, and has never doubted I would reach this point, thank you so much for your support. Guy Parisi, you have helped research aspects of publishing, reached out to strangers for information, and been dragged into an alpha reader position. Thank you for all your help. Éva Rona, your enthusiasm for the story, reader feedback, and support means so much to me.

Jonathan Lebel, thank you for working through the cover art iterations with me from my initial stick figures to the final product. Maxine Meyer, I appreciate all of your quick and responsive editing work. Beta readers provide invaluable feedback. To Laura Thompson, Ashley Cooper, and Melissa McNeice, who helped me learn the beta reader process with an early draft, thank you for your time and education. Thank you also to Ellen Zuckerman and Beba Andric for reading through the final beta draft and providing excellent reader feedback.

I would not be here without all of you. Thank you!

ABOUT THE AUTHOR

Tiffany Shearn is a writer and author of the new novel *Hidden Memory*, her first book in the Hidden Series set in her Realm of Elaria. While working by day in business finance, Tiffany has spent the last two decades bringing her fantasy realm and characters to life. She is already working on *Hidden Sanctuary*, the sequel to her debut novel, to continue their story.

Tiffany is a lifelong reader with a passion for the fantasy genre. She began writing in college when the stories in her head were vivid enough to distract her from lectures, and she has continued to refine her writing style. Tiffany lives just south of Seattle, Washington with her husband, Big Cat, and Little Cat. (tiffanyshearn.com)